Future Winds

Future Winds

Kevin Laymon

Printed in the United States of America

First Printing, 2015

Edited by Danielle Fisher

Published by Ikigai Publishing ™

www.AuthorKevinLaymon.com

www.Twitter.com/Kevin_Laymon

www.Facebook.com/AuthorKevinLaymon

www.Instagram.com/Kevin_Laymon

Table of Contents

Future Winds is dedicated to Sara.
In my darkest hour,
you stood by my side with a sword and a candle.

"Do you think that you will meet God?"
"I'm not so sure God exists."

Dear reader, thank you.
I hope that this piece of work occupies your mind and impacts your outlook on life for years to come. I seek to inspire you to do great things. The power of the mind is extraordinary and you are capable of anything.

Chapter 1
Salvation

Tyler reluctantly peeled his eyelids open for the first time in two years. The light from his newfound planet's primary sun was no different than that of Earth's, but his eyes had to readjust and adapt to him once again being awake and alive. He had been in a cryosleep where his entire body was submerged in a thick goo that consisted of tiny microorganism sized robotics that would slow down his heart rate yet keep him alive, fit, and healthy for his voyage.

Tyler was part of a globalist planetary expansion project. Earth was no longer inhabitable going forward. Her oceans were as toxic as the race of men who dwelled on her surface and called the blue planet home. Humans lived in poverty, struggling with disease, famine, and malnutrition for decades leading up to this point.

The corporate elite lived on space stations orbiting Earth along with the core military establishment that governed the planet. Mining expeditions were under way towards the edge of the solar system where crucial gases and minerals could be harvested to maintain the very existence of life.

Like most technological advances in the past thirty years, galactic travel saw a dramatic jump in overall functionality with the breakthrough of the warp drive system. The research science fiction once dreamed of many generations ago was now a reality. A trip to a cluster of space stations outside Earth from Washington, D.C. would only take about twelve minutes. A ship's warp drive mathematically required more time to cool down than to actually maneuver from one planet to another.

At the turn of the century, humanity mustered up the funds to conduct expeditions deeper into space than ever once previously explored. These series of delicate missions were nicknamed Project Salvation.

Ty chuckled as it dawned on him the irony in the name chosen by his cynical political leaders. Humanity had lived in its sad, disgusting, famine infested world for decades. Only now that the solar system they called home was imploding in on itself, threatening the elitist's *perfect* little lives on their *perfect* little space stations, did they actually decide it necessary to take action.

For generations, scientists believed Earth's sun to be too small in size to ever risk heading into supernova status. But sometimes, that which is unknown can stir up change in that which is known. At this point, humanity knew much about other stars, galaxies, and solar systems, but the small yellow dwarf right in their own back yard had a couple secrets up her sleeve in her dying days. Slowly pulling the solar system in on herself was one of the many ways she cried out in pain. Many didn't believe it to be true, heading in; thinking the official story to be nothing more than an excuse to push some secretive agenda forward but, in the end, being shamed by science, humanity banded together in looking to the stars for expansion.

Project Salvation was fairly simple: six separate single-manned ships each equipped with a warp drive would spend three years traveling out to a cluster of planets and set up a warp gate. This, in a sense, was a glorified magnet that would home in on any incoming vessel and work with a ship's onboard drive to pull it through space and time, thus warping it into the desired planet's atmosphere at a much faster rate. While the six ships made their travel, the globalist assembled massive carriers and filled them with the resources needed to begin terraforming the planets. This was phase one.

"Good morning, Tyler."

Tyler was accompanied in his ship by an artificial intelligence drone named Aries. The bot was a large floating box of circuitry. She had a physical shield positioned in the center of her crown with two thin rectangular antennas protruding underneath. Below her shield resided her weaponry: one rail gun positioned on the left side and two lasers on the right. This powerful and accurate weapons-build was best suited for close combat. At the cost of distance, her guns were superior in their close-quarters destructive right. Her rail gun could penetrate just about anything man-made and her lasers were fast and accurate to a needle within a city block. The drone had its inner chastise shielded from electromagnetic waves, eliminating a potential and untimely death by possibly unstable Sun/Star activity. By means of magnetic suspension, Aries drifted into the room behind Tyler.

His increase in heart rate summoned her up and out of her standby mode. Tyler's organs and nervous system were synced to the drone via wireless communication so that if something were ever to happen to his heart, brain, or lungs, the robot could kick start and maintain his animation until it could physically respond and repair whatever might be wrong with him. Tyler could tap into the robot's inner server database and have anything displayed up on a HUD that was linked deep within his inner eye sockets. The ability for a manual override of a synced drone even existed--though it was difficult and not at all recommended due to the dramatic strain put on the human nervous system.

Aries was as much a part of Tyler as his fingers, toes, and feet, but she still maintained her own unique personality. Artificial Intelligence was so advanced that people debated the existence and connection of souls within robots. A large portion of humans on earth followed in the teachings of Dr. Vince De Luther, founder of Veneration: a sometimes religious extremist group that believed the human soul was a frequency that entered the body upon birth and left it in death. This group preached the idea that a robot's AI was advanced enough that upon spark -or birth- it could capture a soul frequency and use it as its own until death. Tyler never really sided with the theory, but the belief was interesting at least.

The ship began to shake violently and suddenly Tyler felt queasy. After such a long time in cryosleep, it would take his body a bit of time to get readjusted to being awake. The sway of the ship reminded him of his sailing trips with his father when he was but a boy. His early love for naval ships had influenced him in joining the (UIGN) Unified InterGalactic Navy. Instead of crossing the Atlantic sea with his father, he had just crossed an entire solar system with his robot.

"We are within the planet's atmosphere and will be landing in approximately thirty minutes," Aries said, interrupting Tyler's train of thought.

***

The wind violently howled through the vast desert canyons that stretched across the planet's dry, hot crust. Temperatures scorched an average of one hundred and thirty degrees Fahrenheit in the planet's summer solstice months and dropped to a not-much-different ninety-five degrees on average in its winter months. Chaotic fire and shrapnel storms were frequent and about as random as they were deadly.

The plateau was a dark blood-red with pockets of sand dunes and the occasional twisted Lak-Tou: an ancient cactus with no cap to its lifespan. The Lak-Tou was typically purple, but varied in color based on the potency of the hallucinogenic toxins it contained in its thorns. It was lengthy and sprawled across the land in fissures, though generally within valleys where moisture was occasionally found. Rain was extremely rare but not impossible as the water found on the desert planet consisted of a slimy, gooey substance that kept it from evaporating too quickly. The planet's water was a distant cousin to the H_2O found on planet earth.

Kio-Kai's eyes, scanning the horizon with precision, had the appearance of giant rags with scattered ink blots. Kio-Kai was a Vai-Zik. They would eat most anything, but primarily functioned off the fluids found in the spinal cord of living organisms. The Vai-Zik were arthropods with a hive mind. A telepathic based collective conscious group consisting of a four caste system. Twitchers dug tunnels and constructed cities deep beneath the planet's surface, hunters searched for food and defended the colony, grinders processed solids into liquids, and queens laid eggs and controlled the swarm.

This way of life was a dying one. The Vai-Zik species conquered most life on the planet, and in doing so, they exhausted most of their consumable organic resources. This led to weaker queens and, in turn, more freedom of thought within the hive. Ultimately, a consciousness of self-existence had developed and been established.

Kio-Kai was of a young age in terms of a race that could live hundreds of years. Standing upright on his bipedal legs, he was an intimidating seven feet in height. His pincers protruded from his lower jaw about a foot--this length varied for most. Two dark antennae extended out of his spiky head and draped down the side of his eyes. Two massive, sophisticatedly constructed, sharp wings hung down to his lower legs. His body was a sandy brown, jagged with an overall appearance of violence. His arms were lengthy, following the overall theme of being sharp, right down to his ambidextrous six-fingered hands. A long bone-like blade stretched from his elbow joint down to his wrist. The razor was capable of extending out roughly three feet when need be, and both of his arms were equipped with the blades.

In the distance, a large capsule of silver and fire rained from the sky. Fire storms were common on this planet, but this looked to be something different. Kio-Kai abruptly leapt up and took flight forward to investigate the falling object.

***

Tyler called out to Aries, "I'm getting a temperature reading of one twenty-five, the E.S.S. can handle up to what?"

"Your External Skeleton Suit can physically withstand heat up to a level of two hundred degrees and keep your body's heat index at a stable level, preventing hypothermia. In case of any sort of malfunction or puncture I will override the suit and maintain your well-being."

"Yeah, so you got my back, huh, Aries?" Tyler said with a chuckle.

"I got you," Aries volleyed back.

The ship's doors let up with the sound of hydraulics that howled dust and dirt into the quarantine lock. The bot veered outward and up to the left while Tyler started on down the ramp. As soon as he entered the sun's rays, intense radiation began to slow-cook his insides. The swelter was far beyond intense. While his E.S.S. suit had responded to the fluctuation in climate, Tyler's nerves flared out to the layover time he felt in the heat. A few milliseconds felt like a lifetime of being disintegrated by the inferno he just set out upon. Tyler opened his eyes and it was over. The scorching cesspool of a planet now felt like a breezy spring day back home.

Looking up, the sky was skewed red. Dark firestorms churned in the distance. Tyler couldn't help but think that the firestorms that raged up in the clouds ahead sounded like demons being fed through a blender.

"Aries, what's the status on the other incoming ships?" Tyler demanded.

The bot's antennas repositioned to scan the horizon and ping the drones aboard the friendly ships. Usually, she was sharp and to the point with her calculations but, given the overcast, it was difficult for her to utilize her com systems.

"The next ship is entering atmosphere now and will land within two minutes. The other five ships are projected to make landfall within fifteen minutes. They should all be clustering within a half-mile radius of one another," she answered.

"Well, I guess that makes us the first motherfuckers to explore hell," he said with a smirk.

Chapter 2
A Little Sugar and Spice

Kio-Kai abruptly halted his flight to investigate the befallen object when he heard the high-pitched scream of the heavens cry out as a second vessel came raining down. This one would land much closer, and so he shifted his travel south towards the second object.

***

Tyler followed Aries for about an hour in the stinging-hot dessert. While she looked ahead to lead him to the rest of the group, he spent time directing his gaze about the surrounding terrain.

This planet's topography was seemingly similar to that of Mars. Large red mountains cast shadows over the distant landscape, dark canyons bore secrets Tyler aspired to explore, and dust storms howled to the west.

In discovering Flare decades ago, the planet pinged positive for both oxygen and water. Humanity wasted little time rushing forward to lay claim over what appeared to be the holy grail of space exploration.

Little was known about this place. So distant and obscure from clear sky, it was troublesome for scouting drones to analyze much of the data leading up to this point. One thing was for sure though, the oxygen-rich atmosphere granted life to some abnormal, yet extraordinary, creatures.

A small, spiky, eight-legged lizard scurried across the sand, seeking shelter beneath a cluster of big chocolate-colored rocks. Quite large in size, the reptile was quick for having such short, brown little limbs.

Reaching the peak of the plateau where his friends had landed, Tyler stopped and looked around, taking it all in. He could see down into some of the distant canyons. They bore plant life: green, purple, and white colors stretched from within the darkness, sparking his imagination and pleading with his curiosity.

His moment of daydreaming came to a halt when he felt a push along his backside and was overcome with a sudden helpless sensation of vertigo. He free fell, face first, towards the dirt. Trying to save himself from the fall, he jerked his stomach inward, allowing himself to spin just enough so that his shoulder blade absorbed most of the blow to the ground.

He looked around for a culprit and saw no one other than Aries ahead turning back to join him in investigating his fall. His eyes caught the faint shimmering blur of white and orange off to his left, and this confirmed his assumption.

"Ok, you got me, Aisha," he called out.

The blur before him then appeared. Laughing, it was a woman, Aisha Sayegh. She was tall with dark, tan skin and long, choppy hair in a color that accented her skin with its brown hue. White and orange armor covered most of her curvy body and a large, metallic-blue sword rested sheathed on her left side.

She was accompanied by a drone of gold and blue named Pisces. About the only similarity it bore to Tyler's drone, Aries, was its size. Its layout was two large spheres atop a 'Y' shaped body, with a third, larger globe attached to the bottom section. It had one single thin antenna drooping out the back along with hundreds of thin wires of various lengths. The drone had no weapons. Its single purpose was projecting stealth cloaks.

Tyler wasn't sure how exactly Pisces worked, or how stealth technology worked, for that matter. It was quite rare anyone even had such high-tech gear. Aisha was the only one of the squad of six to possess it.

Tyler rose to his feet, brushing himself off of dust and dirt. "Glad to see you landed ok."

"Sorry, I didn't think you would actually fall," she defended with a giggle.

The two walked up the hill, which leveled off to a large plateau that stretched across the barren landscape for miles.

Tyler was greeted by Kaito Shimizu with a smile and a wave, which was far more receiving than Aisha's method of welcoming. Wasn't tough to beat pushing someone down a hill. Tyler would happily take Kaito's simple nod and wave over *that* any day of the week.

Kaito was the youngest of the six, skinny with slick black hair that shined as if he was in a shampoo commercial. The Japanese boy was the most intelligent, on paper, of the crew. His results in exams and testings were close to perfect and the highest ever recorded. His brain was simply genetically wired to be faster than the rest in solving puzzles. His shot placement with a rifle was also the best of the group. He could compete with AI drones in the field of accuracy, and for that he was assigned team sniper and given the best and most powerful rifle of the six, an advanced UIGN sniper rifle.

He wore the rifle draped across his back. The optic scope alone was almost as big as his head. Kaito's drone was a shielding specialty drone named Libra. An incredibly fast, small ball of pure energy, it could intercept incoming attacks, absorb, and vaporize them before they could harm Kaito or his allies. Libra had no weapons.

About fifteen feet behind Kaito was the fourth of the squad of six, Abram Orlav. Abram was tall, thick, and muscular with short, black, buzzed hair. The Russian native had high cheekbones and big, puffy eyes. 'A gentle giant,' Aisha would tease during training, but he was far from gentle when need be.

The giant's weapon was a warhammer that Tyler physically could not even lift. How the Russian-born man could wield such a devastating hunk of metal was beyond him.

Abram's drone, Taurus, was about as rugged as he. Operating on a set of tracks much like an old military tank, it was a landlocked defensive unit. Much bigger than the other drones, Taurus served more as a personal portable shield that had no offensive weapons, let alone data powerhouse.

Abram had excelled through every bit of training thrown his way, even the bits designed to fail him. One test scenario in particular was set up to fail and evaluate how the applicants handled defeat. The challenge was to rescue a comrade encased in bulletproof glass before the timer expired while another two comrades were unconscious beside him. There was a designated blast zone that if anyone was left within would be tagged as dead. This test was intended to resemble the tough choices to be made, where the right answer is to leave the comrade who is stuck behind the glass. There was no way to save this teammate, and the applicant's time was better served escorting the remainder of the unconscious crew to safety.

Abram Orlav, in an immaculate display of brute strength, broke the glass. In doing so, he tore up his arms and required forty-seven stitches, but not before he completed the mission and rescued his comrades. Including the stranded crew member, Abram carried them all to safety on his shoulders with his arm gushing blood.

Tyler remembered being so impressed with the man that day. He had asked him why he didn't stop when he cut his arm down to the bone. The giant man simply concluded that, if this scenario were real, he wouldn't have stopped, so why stop in a test intended to simulate real life?

The man could have been squad leader if politics didn't have their say in every little thing. Though country borders mostly all but disappeared leading up to Project Salvation, the spiteful Americans could never allow a Russian native the power and control of leading the squad whose mission was phase one in saving the human race.

Off to the side, drawing lines in the sand, was Leon Fleisher. He was speaking to his hovering drone as he scribbled into the sand. Tyler, not being able to hear what Leon was saying, thought it looked a little crazy for him to be rambling to a robot as he painted in the dirt.

Rich in German heritage, Leon's parents were immigrants to the United States, and his father actually helped a great deal in the creation of the warp drive back in his mid-twenties.

Leon was a natural-born leader. Thin and clean with blond hair and blue eyes, he was the only member of the crew to have a beard, which was chiseled and upkept to perfection, as was his posture, mannerisms, and leadership. His mind was sharp and, in testing, proved more than capable of thinking outside the box with quick, calm, calculated efficiency.

Leon's drone, Scorpio, was the most similar to Tyler's. If both bots were side by side, one might even misconstrue which was which. The only real differences were the internal workings and color. Scorpio had faster processing power and a larger database of knowledge. He was black and red, while Aries was orange and white.

"Look who I found," Aisha called out to Leon as they approached.

"Nice of you to join us," Leon said, patting Tyler on the shoulder.

The two always did get along in their training sessions.

Leon scratched his beard and continued, "We have been trying to reach the fleet since we landed, but our comm systems won't work. Scorpio said the planet's natural emissions radiate an interference that our tech just can't penetrate, so there is that."

The five of them stood around in silence for a minute as Leon pondered their next move. Without communication to the fleet, they were on their own.

"It's hot as hell on this planet," Abram chimed in, cutting into the quietness of the group.

Together, they all laughed, forgetting for a moment that they carried the weight of humanity's salvation on their shoulders.

***

Valerie Fournier awoke to the smell of burning hair and sulfur; a smell that couldn't be any more unique to the human senses. She began to vomit in both pain and disgust. Her body shrieked out in punishment from her foolish attempt to rise up and get to her feet. She did it anyway.

Calling out to her drone, Virgo, with no response, she limped towards a mirror and froze in horror. Her face was burnt and her hair gone. All that was left where dark scabs of grotesque mutilation upon her face. Her heart-rate elevated as she began to panic. She looked around and called out again to

Virgo. No response.

Small fires burned sporadically throughout the vessel, most of which were coupled with torn holes through the craft's exterior. Warped, jagged steel lay uselessly scattered about like a car's blown-out tire strewn across a highway.

Valerie sank to the floor crying as she held her once-beautiful face. For her whole life she was told that she looked like her mother: the most beautiful woman Valerie had ever known. Today, that comparison would be an insult. Today she looked as beaten and ugly as her father, long since dead, consumed by the sickness of hatred and alcohol addiction.

"I will not die weak and afraid like him," she sniffled out.

Again she forced herself to rise to her feet. She stumbled towards the exit of the craft, but it was twisted and torn into pieces. Rock and fire blocked the path. She faltered over to the other side of the ship and punched the release for the emergency hydraulic escape hatch. It blew out with a boom and she fell to her knees in agony to crawl out.

She sniffled back tears and rolled over onto her back.

Dusty clouds obscured the skies all around her, with the exception of what sat directly above. She was granted her own little cut-out view of clear space. Trails of purple and blue gasses mingled with nebulas that encased planets and stars light years away.

What a view, she thought. In that brief moment of awe, she felt no pain.

***

"What about the French girl?" Abram suggested.

"Her name is Valerie, you big dumb ogre," Aisha corrected whilst poking fun.

"Alright, ladies, let's get to work," Leon demanded. "Kaito, you and I will go scout out what's going on with Valerie. Most likely, she has some sort of a communication error and has lost her bearings. Scorpio confirmed earlier that she landed and her vessel was intact, so hopefully she stayed put. We will go grab her and meet back here. How long is a day on this shit hole?" he added, looking up to his drone.

"A daily cycle on planet Flare is approximately forty-six hours. At this particular latitude, longitude, and time of year, twenty-five of those hours are daylight and the other twenty-one hours are spent in darkness. The next night cycle begins in approximately nineteen hours," the bot was quick to respond.

"We have four intact warp drives at our disposal. Luckily, we only need to utilize four to construct the warp gate. So that spares us the time needed to go grab Tyler and Valerie's ships. We can salvage the other two at a later date and use them for spare parts. Should be done with construction by sundown," Leon commanded.

***

Firestorms raged to the south. This meant that the first crucial order of business was to set up the magnetic shield. The warp gate had to be fully powered and functional to activate its defensive shielding; putting pressure on the crew to get things up and running as soon as possible.

Abram, Tyler, Aisha, and their three bots worked on constructing the warp gate all afternoon. Abram stripped the three ships of parts needed and positioned the pieces to where they must correctly reside with Taurus as his ferry for bulk transport. Aisha ran color coded wire down through steel conduits. Tyler welded parts together while Aries educated him on how to build such an intricate piece of technology.

The crew was lucky that the UIGN constructed their ships to be easily stripped apart and put back together to form the warp gate. For the most part, it was a matter of reading and executing fairly simple instructions.

Tyler noticed the flame of his welding torch jump. Eight seconds later, it did it again. He looked to his hands and made sure he wasn't shaking. Another eight seconds passed and he felt the tremor once more.

"You guys feel that?" Aisha asked, climbing out of a steel shaft.

"Earthquake?" Abram guessed.

Another eight seconds passed in between the light tremor. Each one that erupted felt more intense than the last.

"It is too consistent to be an earthquake," Tyler said.

Aisha scurried to the edge of the plateau and scanned the distant skyline of mountains, hills, and valleys. That was when she saw it. A large creature emerged from behind one of the mountains, advancing across the desert on four legs.

Abram dropped the heavy piece of equipment he was holding to the ground and stood to his feet. "Holy shit," he paused. "Is that mountain moving?" He rubbed his eyes in disbelief. This insignificant gesture did more harm than good as he unnoticeably spread black axle grease all over his face.

"I don't know, it almost reminds me of the long-since-extinct wooly mammoth, only bigger" Aisha let out with a gasp.

"Yeah, way bigger," Abram confirmed.

No doubt was the creature enormous. If it were walking about in downtown Manhattan, it would easily take up a city block or two.

"Actually, I'd guess more of a mythical centaur. It has the four legged body of a giant mammoth but an upper torso and arms similar to a man!" Aisha added.

Tyler finally jumped down off the platform and walked over to the ledge of the canyon that separated them from the colossus. He gazed up at the marvelous creature, astounded by just how intricate of a being it truly was. Its noseless face was long and narrow. It had great tusks of stone that hung from its mouth. Massive leaves grew from its monstrous shoulders and draped down its chest as ivy scaled up its torso. Moss covered the north-most side of its four legs. Red, orange, and yellow flowers bloomed off of its back, creating a great exoskeleton of color.

"So, what happens if that thing rips apart the warp gate?" Abram asked.

"What happens if that thing rips apart us?" Aisha added.

"I don't know," Tyler confessed, snapping out of his momentary mesmerization over the giant. "We are on a pretty large plateau, mostly surrounded by canyons. So it seems unlikely it would run up here to do that."

Abram was sharp to confront Tyler's uncertainty. "Unlikely? We know nothing about this thing, let alone how it behaves."

"Well, we cannot just go out massacring anything we do not understand," Tyler defended.

"Psh, why not? That is, after all, human nature, no?" Aisha sarcastically inserted. "To fear the things we cannot fully comprehend, deem them evil, and eradicate them?"

Tyler ignored her sass and continued watching the giant as it steadily made its way up over the horizon. Its massive biceps and face were free of greenery and on further observation it was concluded to be a creature of mostly stone. If the three of them had to take it down, the task would be hard-pressed, even with their advanced weaponry. The giant walked on, disappearing off over the horizon.

Tyler hated leadership, but obedience and intelligence granted him the position of second in command to Leon on these series of delicate missions. With Leon away, Tyler had to play. So he picked up his bat and swung at the pitch.

"We are equipped with the technology and weaponry to defend ourselves and the warp gate if necessary. The UIGN knew there was life on this planet-- just unsure of what kind of life that might be. In our training, it was made perfectly clear we are not to disturb any native organism or start any type of unnecessary conflict. Now, let's get back to work."

***

Sublimation: the process of a solid becoming a gas, skipping the usual in-between liquid phase. The occurrence is rare on earth. It happens more often in scientific studies performed in manmade laboratories and teachings than in nature.

Somehow, whatever was the primary composition of this planet's outer crust, was capable of performing this procedure. Thin layers of rock and dust evaporated into a gas substance, which then was triggered to ignite and reform chunks of jagged rock, hailing balls of fire from the sky.

"It's an incredible thing, the likes of which we have never seen on earth," Kaito claimed, watching the storms churning about in the distance.

"What's that?" Leon asked.

"The fire."

"It's some twilight zone shit, that's for sure," Leon panted out.

The two reached the summit of the small mountain that they had to scale in order to reach Val's ship. From its peak, they had a view of the craft resting in the valley below. Torn into pieces, ash and soot scattered the land around it.

"I am not so sure our companion would be so intrigued by the natural phenomenon," Leon added.

Kaito reached the peak and joined Leon in looking upon the ship. "Oh, fuck."

"Scorpio, get down there and see if you can find her. Let's hope she is still alive," Leon commanded his bot. His drone gently scaled down the mountain ahead of him as he began to slowly descend behind it. Stopping, he ripped a bag from his belt and tossed it up to Kaito. "You stay up here and keep lookout. Also, tie some rope around your bot. If Val is mangled and alive we will have to lift her up over this mountain to get her back."

Kaito pulled the steel cable from the satchel and draped it around Libra, then kneeled down and set up his rifle. If such a formal title existed as 'sniper' within their squad, it would belong to him. Kaito's rifle was superior in range and his personal skill level of accuracy was well above the other five--at least in training sessions leading up to this point.

He scanned the craft with his scope; smoke still billowed out from the ship's many wounds.

"What are the odds she is alive, Libra?"

"If she awoke from her cryosleep in time, it is possible she escaped. But I am not pinging her drone, so one can only assume it got destroyed, caught up in the storm."
Kaito cut the drone off, "I didn't ask for a bedtime story. What are the odds, tin can?"

He didn't dislike technology by any means, but the drone he was assigned was, by far, the weakest of the team. Libra did not even have weapons. It was a shield bot; meaning it projected a magnetic shield around its small, spherical body. That was about all it was used for. No destructive purpose, no healing abilities, no limitless database of wisdom, nothing but a hovering, metallic ball of energy. Leon and Tyler had the best of the drones by far.

"My analytic guess of survivability is below thirty percent," the drone responded.

***

"Hey Tyler, you think that giant was an intelligent alien?" asked Aisha, half buried in a large conduit as she ripped wire through and soldered color-coded ends together.

Tyler thought about the question for a minute. It was one that was on his mind all afternoon. "Well for one, an alien--no.

We are the aliens in this world. As for intelligent, sure, I would think so. You must be smart to survive on this rock of fire and shit, no?"

"Or really stupid to be here in the first place," Aisha added with a laugh. "I guess that makes us unintelligent aliens."

He smirked. Her sarcasm was unyielding. "Yes and no. We are saving our species. We cannot sustain on Earth, so here we are."

"Yea, like I didn't hear that pick-up line enough times in training. In all honesty though, there are plenty of planets between this one and Earth. Hell, a few even have repair stations, small outposts, and even mining operations already established on them. So why this one?"

"Well, there is life on this planet, so that shows it is doable, for one. There is plenty of oxygen within the atmosphere, the size of the planet triumphs greatly over our Earth, and it serves a good location to establish a warp gate."

She laughed "Is that what they spoon-fed you in officer training?"

He chuckled "Na, When I asked that question, all I ever got was a lengthy political response that I will spare you. This is just my own conclusion. Besides, the warp gate serves dual purpose: not only to pull vessels in at a faster rate, but also to slingshot them out further. Who knows what's even further out there?"

"More shit for our species to conquer over, I am sure." Her voice echoed from the metal tubing as she submerged herself further in.

Tyler wondered what would happen when the carriers arrived, and what the hierarchy would do about any native organism to this planet. Most of the carriers' population consisted of civilians who pledged an allegiance to Earth's empire. In exchange for free transportation to the new world, they sold themselves into a caste system. Either you were rich and held political influence, buying your way through life, or you were poor and did the job society told you to do. If you did not fall into these two categories or disliked your present job, you joined the military--a lifelong commitment.

Tyler's parents were wise to urge him into the military at a very young age. Thirteen was the earliest kids could sign up with parental consent. That would put them through years of military education and give them a better shot at climbing the ranks well before the real training even began.

At the age of twenty-seven, his being a little over a decade within the military paid off. He was one of the first six human beings to set foot on this new world, and he could only thank his parents' guidance and wisdom for helping him get there. If only they were still alive to see him get this far today.

***

The entrance to Valerie's ship was caved in with smoldering rock--still smoking, it would be way too hot to touch. Leon walked to the other side to where the escape hatch was blown out.

"Scorpio, go through and see if she is in there."

The drone drifted into the vessel and poked around. If the escape hatch was blown out, it was most likely Valerie's doing so. She must have made it out, but no reason not to be thorough in a manhunt.

Leon twirled around, observing the ground.

Blood trails and marks in the soil. She was here, struggled perhaps? Or possibly crawled away injured, Leon thought.

He looked up to Kaito, who rested atop the small mountain behind him, and signaled him to climb down.

"You had to wander off in the opposite direction, didn't you," Leon sighed, looking ahead, his gaze directed by a faint trickling trail of blood and scuff marks in the ground.

***

Kio-Kai entered through a large opening in the side of the valley's red rock, carrying the corpse of his catch. Quite a strange creature it was. He couldn't shake the thought of catching it. He remembered the screams and cries it made when he stuck it through the belly. It flailing about and sobbing moments before death. It clearly belonged to a race of weak organisms, the likes of which he had never seen before. When it bled out before his eyes, he couldn't help but feel remorse and guilt. Injured far before the kill, it was caught up in a firestorm. So maybe he did the animal a favor in killing the primate-like being, ending its suffering before ultimately carrying it here to be processed.

He heaved the sack of flesh and meat towards one of the creatures that dwelled in the cave. The carcass landed with a thud and some of its entrails leaked out of its abdomen onto the cold, hard ground.

A creature instantly approached. It had a twisted and warped lipless face. Thousands of jagged teeth filled its mouth of black rot, and the lack of lips bore no wonder at the wretched horror that lay within the beast's mouth. Its movement was sporadic, but it did not seem to show interest in any other actions that may dwell within the cave, rather, it had a purpose. One of the lower ranks within the Vai-Zik, this was one of the clan's worker drones. Worker drones came in two varieties: this one was a grinder, its only purpose within the hive was grinding up corpses and regurgitating them into canals that lead to queens, deep underground. Essentially, these workers were master chefs: a super blender of any ingredient the hunters threw their way to grind up into the life blood that served their queen, her eggs, and the clan.

The grinder looked up at Kio-Kai and back down to the body before digging its small precision claws in the flesh. It stuffed its mouth with bones, organs, and muscle, then reached its head over to a small canal and extracted the liquefied mush through its teeth before going back for more.

Kio-Kai stood over the grinder, watching it execute its single purpose. Like its ancestors before him, day in and day out, for the good of the hive, the beast chewed whatever the hunters brought it and slew the mixture of acid and vomit into the canals that slowly oozed down to the lower levels of the cavern. It passed through a series of networks until reaching a great red sea surrounded by eggs. In a matter of minutes, nothing remained of the fallen corpse and so the grinder looked up at Kio-Kai to confirm there was no more work to be processed. Kio gave the beast a nod, and it crept back into the shadows to rest until it was once again needed.

It was not that long ago that grinders were worked day and night with very little sleep. But the glory days of the hive were behind. A teenager now, Kio-Kai remembered the stories told by his now-dead ancestors of a time long ago. A time when his family was strong and proud. This planet was not always such a barren desert of wasteland. Once, it was luscious and full of life. The hive thrived with an unbroken will backed by powerful queens, but today a sickness lay deep within the planet, one that had single handedly befallen the Vai-Zik.

This sickness was a race of pale, wretched creatures. Though Kio-Kai had never laid his eyes upon them, it was known that they were little sacks of flesh and meat who declared themselves to be Gods. Blackness, greed, and envy filled their hearts. They overtook the most powerful of queens deep within the hive and, in doing so, earned control of the Vai-Zik.

In the beginning, there was a rebellion within the hive. Clans broke free, gaining their own will and freedom of thought. They unified against the virus and fought it off, liberating queens from the maleficent grasp of their newfound overlords, but these lords were smart. They chose the most powerful of clans to control and used them as a defensive strategy to win the long, bloody war. After doing this, they used the Vai-Zik to bleed the planet dry of near all life--for gluttony was one of the many defining desires of the small, pale lords that now enslaved the Vai-Zik and, in turn, this planet.

Chapter 3
It's No Joke, It's a Rope

"Should we wait for Leon to get back to activate the warp gate?" Abram asked without looking directly at Tyler.

He knew the answer, but was obedient to the navy's chain of command, even if he thought Tyler a weak leader.

Tyler marveled for a moment over what the three of them had accomplished in just a single afternoon. "Na, we have to get this bad turkey going. Aries, start it up," Tyler commanded.

The drone hovered above the three massive turbines, calling out in robotic frequencies. The giant gate sparked to life and listened to her commands. Its defensive shielding kicked in; a clear ball of magnetic-based energy encompassed the large gate.

Three massive turbines began to twirl around the center

tower, which gave off an eerie wobble sound. The amount of power the device generated was enough to vaporize an entire country.

And once, not too long ago, one of these devices was used for just that. It is what fueled the research for true, reliable artificial intelligence. Mankind could not be trusted with such a tool on its own anymore, so expert systems of limitless knowledge controlled the operation of these types of gadgets.

Abram despised the fact that the team had to be accompanied by AI drones. It was like forcing an adult to hold hands with an elder, as a child would. Way he saw it, these glorified calculators were good for two things: cleaning and gambling.

This was supposed to be humanity's last stand at existence--the will of billions united for one purpose: survival.

God knows we don't need robots to survive. Lived without them for eons. Their very creation in the late twenty second century has always been the defining moment of society's undoing. The transition into dependence on technology, he thought.

His assigned robot was the ground-based unit, Taurus, which had four large, metal plated shields sticking out from a torso of tan and brown that rested atop a caterpillar track. A type of tank tread made popular in twentieth century warfare.

Taurus's specialty was to take a beating and still pull through in just about any scenario. Despite Abram's distrust in artificial intelligence, he had a certain admiration for Taurus. It resembled a piece of machinery from a better time. One where a machine was man's tool and not man's friend.

***

Kio-Kai heard something lingering in the dark. It was a familiar sounding voice. Someone was there, conversing with one of the drones.

"Lai-Kai?" he called out.

From the shadows emerged a female huntress. Her appearance was much like Kio-Kai's, though being effeminate granted her a much thinner and more attractive frame. Her wings were a bit longer and more narrow. Her antennae were much larger than his and, when standing upright, she was a little shorter.

Lai-Kai bore the same surname as Kio-Kai; this meant they were of the same clan. A clan was defined by its queen. In the case of these two, it meant that Kai-Zul was their queen. All of the children a queen bore inherited her first name as their last. This was tradition. One day Lai-Kai might be a queen and that would spawn a clan of Lai.

"Haven't seen you in a while," she pointed out. "What are you doing here?"

"I just delivered a catch," he explained. "Was something strange I have never seen before."

"Where is it?" she asked.

"Ground up, now."

"Hmm. Well, I am about to go down to the amphitheater and watch a fight. Want to come with?" she asked.

Hunters rarely partook in watching arena fights. It was mostly drones who fell for such theatrics.

"Why would I want to go watch Vai-Zik clans kill each other?"

Lai-Kai ignored him. She had a habit of tuning out the things she did not want to hear.

Kio-Kai reminisced of a time when his elders would convey their wisdoms. Not to fall prey to this new society's interest in self-pleasure was one of many great teachings. After all, they did not build such a large and powerful empire by taking part in the ways of the overlords.

"Stay unvarnished to your queen and your clan, self-preservation not of yourself, but your clan, is the only fidelity you need. Obey your queen and fulfill her will as she has fulfilled her queen's and the queen before her," Kio-Kai recited. An elder hunter, now since passed, had once shared with him these wisdoms. It was presently a contradictory rule, as the current queens in power mostly obeyed the overlords.

The colosseum did not exist before the great rulers that plagued the Vai-Zik came about, because entertaining the masses was never really needed. The one true will to simply survive and provide for the hive and all of the clans that comprised it was life's great priority.

"Come on, you haven't much else to do. You just said that you caught food for the day," she pointed out.

"Yeah, suppose you're right."

"Bending one's will to my own, maybe I will make a good queen someday after all," she giggled, taking flight down the tunnel.

"Maybe, but not my queen, Lady Lai," He smirked, following her.

***

Kaito watched through the scope of his railgun as Leon emerged from the wreckage of Valerie's ship. Empty handed, he shook his head up at Kaito. Leon spun in a circle, observing the ground around him, and looked back up to Kaito, signaling him down off the mountain.

Kaito rose to his feet, slung his rifle behind his back and slid down the summit. Libra silently drifted behind him. Towards the bottom, he lost his footing and face-planted into the dirt before rolling the rest of the way down. He stood back up to his feet. Now covered in dust and coughing, he patted himself off and spit out a mouthful of blood before limping over to Leon.

"Take lead and scan for life," Leon instructed Scorpio before turning to face Kaito. "You alright?" he asked, noticing the dirt caking Kaito's face.

Kaito nodded despite his body aching from his clumsy and embarrassing tumble.

"She isn't here, but she was. There is blood on the soil about ten yards out and some marks in the ground, as if she crawled or limped away."

"But why would she go in the opposite direction of where we landed?" Kaito questioned.

"Her electronics are fried...must have not seen us land," concluded Leon.

The two walked for some time, following the small trickles of blood until reaching a cave. They looked at each other and nodded. Leon drew his two energy pistols, activating the flashlights on them, while Kaito unslung his rifle and activated his own light.

The cave's air was cool, and a breeze suggested it had more than one entrance. Stalactites dripped from above, and chatter from some type of bat native to this planet echoed through the darkness. Kaito's eyes scanned through the stillness of his surroundings until he spotted one. Sure enough, it was a bat the size of a small child drifting by silently ahead. *Fuck that,* he thought, observing above with his flashlight. His eyes locked onto one of the bats, who was upside-down, sleeping. *No fucking way*, he thought as his spine went cold in looking over the giant bat. This one was the size of a full grown man. It slept suspended fifteen feet up in the air, attached to a crack in the cavern's ceiling.

"Valerie," Leon yelled, his voice echoing into the cave for miles.

Kaito's stomach dropped in fear. "What are you doing?" he hoarsely whispered.

"Not wasting any more time looking for this girl," Leon fired back. "Either she is alive in this cave, or dead. The trail goes cold here with this puddle of blood," he added, pointing to a large red blotch on the ground.

"Yeah, but you are going to piss off whatever could live in here," Kaito choked out.

Leon ignored him, and Kaito was grateful for that. Something about poking around in the darkness of a foreign planet made him uneasy, but he should have never shown his fear or lack of faith in an officer's decision.

"Valerie!" Again Leon shouted.

His voice seemed to echo for miles off into the unknown darkness.

Then, out of nowhere emerged a tall, deformed creature that looked like the dead corpse of a giant, rotting, hairless, cross between a rodent and a maggot. Holes in the face exposed dark mucus and membrane. Sharp teeth lined its mouth, which overtook most of its face. Six tiny arms resided curled-up on its sides. Its many legs looked mangled and broken, forcing it to almost limp its way towards them.

It stopped dead in its tracks when the men and their drones' flashlights lit up the creature's face. Kaito did not know what to feel. While he was slightly curious, the level to which he was sickened by the distorted appearance of the unknown alien prevailed as the dominant emotion in his current spectrum of being. Fear overtook him, and he began to slowly backpedal out towards the entrance of the cave.

Leon's eyes and pistols were fearlessly locked onto the creature until Kaito began to backpedal. Glancing over without actually moving his head, he too began to slowly back away.

The beast raised its face up into the air at the sight of the two men retreating. It then bellowed a loud, nasally snort from its mouth.

It is calling for something. No, maybe it's just trying to communicate, Kaito thought, trying to comfort his worry.

The creature got louder, flailing its face up in the air and snorting about.

Definitely pissed off. Come on Leon, let's get out of here, he pleaded in his mind, wishing in that moment that his leader was a mind reader.

The creature slowly approached, and Leon stopped his backwards motion and stood his ground. His thumbs activated the laser sights on his energy pistols, and he did not hesitate a moment longer to double tap both weapons.

Four shots total sprayed the creature's bones and brain all over the wall of the cave, and what seemed more intense than the disintegration of the creature was the echo of gunfire down the cave's tunnels.

Everything and anything alive in this cave had heard it, too. The bats above began to flee by the hundreds and, before the lower half of the creature's now headless torso could fall to the ground and twitch out what was left of its existence, the two men and their drones turned, making a dash for the cave's entrance and back out into the seemingly safe sunlight.

***

The warp gate rattled the soil in all directions as it homed in on a carrier ship that was well over half the distance away between Earth and Flare.

Aisha's lips moved but no words came out. General physics would never allow the human vocal chords to be louder than the noise that erupted from the gate.

In an instant, the three of them could be vaporized into oblivion.

"Here is hoping," Tyler mouthed out loud, wordlessly.

The warp gate carried on flailing about, screaming up into the heavens for about five minutes, then it just stopped. It let out heat and cooled down, but was seemingly inactive. Then, superficially out of nowhere, a massive carrier ship appeared high up in the atmosphere of planet Flare. It floated up there for a few minutes before engaging its thrusters and making its descension to the planet's surface.

Astonished, the three watched the event play out over the course of ten minutes. Upon making landfall, the hydraulics kicked in on the giant quarter mile ship, spraying dust and dirt in every direction. Taurus anticipated the dust spray and stepped up to shield Abram's face.

Tyler and Aisha were not so lucky to be protected from the dirt and debris. Looking at Abram with their faces caked in dust, ears still ringing, the trio began to laugh.

A few minutes of camaraderie and cheering passed.

"Well, shall we go welcome these aliens?" Tyler said, wiping his eyes, and before he could finish his sentence, Aisha was off and sprinting towards the carrier.

***

Kio-Kai and Lai-Kai reached the end of the tunnel. It opened up to unveil the city of Val-Muel. Named after the queen of the clan who had her spawn construct it, Val-Muel was not the largest of Vai-Zik cities by any means, but it was the largest major city to lay so closely to the land's surface. Due to this, it served as the commoners' metropolitan.

Now walking instead of flying, the two passed a grinder drone arguing with two hunters. As things escalated, he spat acid in one of the hunter's faces as the other hunter stuck him through the face with his blade.

The drone fell to the floor and convulsed out the rest of his existence alone on the ground. The hunter that stuck him payed no attention to the dying drone as he went on to help his friend, who was screaming and holding his face as it melted away in his hands.

"It never used to be this way," Lai-Kai claimed while walking on ahead. She payed no more mind to the rowdy outburst than a meager glance.

All of his life, Kio-Kai knew nothing but violence, but Lai-Kai was right. The elders spoke of peace amongst the clans for many generations before the overlords split them apart.

The city was impressive and diverse in its intricate, sharp architecture. Large holes resided on all sides of the greater edges, highways interconnected other cities and stretched to cover over an eighth of planet Flare's entirety.

The Vai-Zik empire stretched as far as it could build its cities within the earth. Spanning from the farthest reaches of the western border of the empire lay underground lava streams that flowed to the southernmost section. To the north: worms, golems, and rebel outcast clans claimed barren wasteland. This left expansion to the east as the only option for growth. Though, since falling into the malfeasance grasp of the overlords, queens had halted all expansion. More land wasn't needed with a declining populous. Nonetheless, the Vai-Zik empire was vast, and what they owned they owned in plenty.

Ahead stood the great colosseum. It towered over all other buildings within the city. Lai-Kai and Kio-Kai took flight to enter the arena from above to avoid the massive lines that spilled out the structure's many entrances, where gamblers placed bids on fights to come.

The two found some seats high up in the stands of the east-most side. The lower level was filling up quickly, as the fights were to begin shortly.

Kio-Kai surveyed the ground floor of the arena. Two main gates on both ends served as the entrance points for combatants.

"So, who is fighting that makes this so special?" Kio-Kai asked.

"Well, remember when Brutalius got injured winning that fight against the hydra worm?" Lai-Kai reminisced.

"Yeah, both were undefeated crowd favorites," Kio-Kai answered.

"Sure were. Brutalius ripped off each of the worm's five relentless heads one by one. It was the craziest, longest fight I have ever seen, and not once did the level of excitement drop. Anyway, this is Brutalius's debut return to the arena," she excitedly explained.

Brutalius once belonged to a civilization of stone golems called Anolems. Not to be confused with a Rock Giant: a nomadic, four-legged behemoth of stone who grew plant life along its enormous body and actually *fed upon* the Anolems. The Anolems were a much smaller, two-legged race of purely jagged, molten rock. Despite being bulky, mighty, and boulderous warriors, they were mostly considered to be a neutral faction when left alone. It was rumored that these stone lava golems were born from volcanoes and built up their thick outer coat shells from the consumption of nutrient-rich rocks.

Brutalius was captured by the Vai-Zik, as per demand, for the overlords. A champion within the arena, his wins were countless and it had reached a point where the overlords deemed it unfair for him to fight any outlaw or slave sentenced to the arena alone one-on-one. Teams were formed, some even given weapons or tools if they behaved well in captivity.

Today's match-up was a squad of four rebels to the Vai-Zik empire versus Brutalius. The four rebels belonged to a small clan that broke away in a resistance movement many years ago in response to the overlords that enslaved and killed their respective queen. Their will was entirely their own, and today they would pay the price for such ownership.

Vai-Zik entering the arena always had their wings smashed and broken, eliminating the risk of their escape, but done in such a way that they could still flutter--a tactical necessity.

The crowd of roughly sixty-five thousand Vai-Zik, erupted into cheers as the four rebels entered the arena. It was not so much that anyone really wanted outlaws to win, but rather it was a custom to honor their distant brothers and sisters, especially when they were facing their imminent death.

"Who doesn't love an underdog in a battle to the death?" Lai-Kai laughed.

All four were hunters and, despite their broken wings, all but one appeared pretty healthy and strong. Certainly any other than the single, sickly-looking runt could serve as a formidable matchup against Kio-Kai.

The sickly-looking hunter was thinner and stood behind the other three. He was hunched over as he walked out at a slower pace than the others. Even facing their demise, the four radiated a sense of integrity and conviviality. Today, the overlords were going to break that honor and spit in the face of the camaraderie the four held for one another.

"We gather in the great coliseum to watch a sacred blood tribute of four insurgents for their crimes against the hive. Because our lord beith so graceful and merciful, these four radicals will be given the opportunity to earn a life of servitude if they can be victorious in three matches in the arena!" A cold voice echoed through a sea of Vai-Zik. Only this voice was not one of a drone, nor one of a hunter, and certainly not the voice of a queen. This was a voice of an overlord. It spoke the language of the Vai-Zik fluently, but he was not born of the hive nor did he belong to any clan.

"If anyone could manage to defeat Brutalius in combat, they should be granted freedom and awarded eternal prominence," Lai-Kai snickered. "But no, if they manage to beat the champion, they still would then have to win twice more against other opponents."

She was amused, and why shouldn't she be? This was, after all, a spectacle of amusement for Vai-Zik. Tear the clans apart and run down and belittle the ones that oppose the overlords.

Kio-Kai squinted his eyes as he tried to find the speaker in the crowd across the arena.

"Who is that?" he asked Lai-Kai as he searched for the announcer.

"It's an overlord. I do not remember his name, but he is in charge of overseeing the colosseum," she answered.

Kio-Kai had heard stories as a child of the overlords. They were rumored to be a plague that had hold of the queens of the empire. For far too long, the overlords leached from the Vai-Zik. This was the driving factor to many clans rebelling, and being executed, when Kio-Kai was just a larva.

Kio Kai found him in the crowd and quickly became uneasy. He couldn't believe it. He thought this was his first time ever laying eyes on an overlord, but it was not. There was another time he had witnessed one of these soft sacks of meat and flesh. It was only a few hours ago, when he had found one in the wreckage of the silver craft that fell from the sky. Not only had he captured and killed it, but he also fed it to a grinder for processing.

Chapter 4
Dance Bitches

The alarms of New Horizon sounded off a high pitch squeal and Ness jumped up, smashing his face on the bunk above. Blue lights flashed, filling the corridors.

"Blue lights. Red means fire, white means lockdown, green is a breach in the haul, and blue is buckle your damn seat belts we are about to enter accelerated warp," a much younger voice from below recited.

Ness lay back in his bunk, clutching his face in pain as blood dripped from his nose. He reached for his seat belt and strapped himself in.

The pioneers were expected to make landfall this week. If they had reached a hospitable planet, could they have constructed a warp gate already? Ness knew for weeks aboard the carrier named New Horizon that he would soon be on a desolate new planet called Flare. He knew for months that most all of humanity were going to board these carriers and set sail off into the future, but it was only now that it all seemed to sink in.

"I thought they were going to announce when the pioneer squad landed?" Ness called out.

Now buckled in, he again attended to his bleeding nose.

"Were going to do a lot of things," Lucas complained from below. "We were supposed to have chicken and biscuits for dinner last night, but had slop like the day before and the day before that. We were supposed to be on the same ship as mom, but we are going ahead because we are 'young and fit'. We are supposed to be on a 'carrier fit to transport over a million people comfortably,' but we have been living in three by ten bunks stacked five-high for weeks!"

Lucas was a talker, skinny and awkward in his demeanor. The messy brown-haired, brown-eyed boy of fourteen had gotten through life on his words over his looks or ability to do much manual work.

Ness, eighteen, was a little taller than his younger brother. His hair, also brown, was much shorter and his eyes mostly observed rather than wondered. He had more muscle about him--broader shoulders and a face not quite as long and slender as his younger brother's.

After a few minutes of verbal silence amidst the blue, eerie lights that flashed brightly in all directions, Lucas called up to his older sibling, "Hey, Ness?"

"Yeah, Buddy?"

"Do you think that we are slaves?" The younger boy questioned in a prepubescent squeak.

It was probably the most debated subject since the creation of artificial intelligence. The fear was that anyone who could not afford a ticket off of Earth had to meet the requirements to sign up for a worker placement program, thus; essentially selling themselves into a life of slavery.

Ness wasn't sure of the correct answer, so he lied. Way he saw it, he had a fifty/fifty shot of getting it right, anyway. "Na, we aren't slaves, Lucas. You think Ma would have let us get on this ship if that were the case?"

The younger boy began to quietly weep. "I miss Mom," he reminded his older brother, just as he had the day before and the day before that.

"Yeah me too, Buddy, but we will see her soon," Ness lied once more.

The last time Ness saw his mother, she hugged them; squeezing them ever so tight as she cried just moments before they left for the carrier ship. She promised she would be on a flight down the line, but she did not meet the requirements of worker placement and living in poverty meant she would never in a million years be able to afford a ticket.

Either you paid for your ticket, you were in the military, you were a political leader, or you fit the requirements of the current controversial worker placement ticket program. One of the baseline requirements was being under the age forty-five. Their mother had celebrated her forty sixth birthday just three weeks prior to phase one ships launching off into orbit, and thus she was left behind.

The government promised that the next wave of flights to leave earth would have less strict requirements for worker placement: being that jobs will have, by then, been established in the new world.

Recent grumblings amongst civilians planted the idea in Ness' head that there was no phase two planned. He refused to believe it, but the point was raised-- if all the rich, the political elite, the members of the military, and the young, fit civilians capable of doing immense strenuous labor-- if all the AI drones, warp drives, and advanced tech had been rushed off of Earth, then who was left behind to build more transport ships?

The flaw in that cynical assumption is that not all members of military, AI tech, and warp drive tech were within the fleet. Some did indeed stay behind, but comparatively, the numbers were minimal.

The two boys shared their small living quarters with a couple hundred other people. Labeled block sixty-five, it was one of a couple hundred thousand that resided within the ship. Block sixty-five was assigned to construction labor like most other blocks aboard New Horizon. Their first task when they arrived would be to lay the foundation for the first future city, Liberty.

Four navy security guards, wearing white and green armor, were assigned to their block. They strapped themselves into the walls near the exit. A sharp squeal overtook the living quarters the two boys shared with all the other civilians as space began to bend, hiss, and cry around them.

This is no drill, we are actually warping, Ness thought. *I mean, technically, we have been warping since shortly after departing earth, but the gate on the other end is active and pulling us at a much faster rate now.*

Lucas began to vomit and cry below, but the noise the small boy emitted was seemingly silent, overshadowed by the squeal the ship made as it accelerated at unimaginable speeds through the galaxy.

***

Aisha sprinted ahead of the two men, partly from excitement and partly from a desire to beat them to reach the large carrier that had landed ahead. Her drone, Pisces, orbited around her as she ran, and this forced a smile on her face.

If this were indeed a race, Tyler and Aries would be in second place at a steady but light jog, and the large brute Abram would come in last, panting, as he struggled to keep up.

She stopped short at one of the carrier's main doors. The thing was massive, one of the biggest structures Aisha had ever seen in her life. Behind multiple feet of solid steel were a little over two million lives packed into a vessel manufactured originally to transport half that amount.

"Hey, open up," Aisha yelled with no response.

She picked up a rock and tossed it. The rock slammed against the hull of the ship, but the sound it made was mostly insignificant. Like a pebble being thrown at a passing train. It would be impossible for anyone inside to hear her. What she did was mostly out of amusement for herself.

"Don't go scaring them off, now," Tyler said with a chuckle, joining her from behind.

"Maybe they realize this hot desert is no place to call home," Abram panted out as he approached, sweat beading down his face.

As if on cue, the large, broad blast door began to open: hydraulics sprayed air and dust in all directions. This time the three of them were wise enough to cover their faces. The dust settled and down the platform walked a woman. Her armor was colored blue, which meant she was a high-ranking commander of some sort. Her stripes and the badge coated along her chest confirmed as such. She was of grave importance. Two men escorted her down the platform. Equipped with high powered energy rifles, their armor was colored blue and white, meaning they were only a single rank below Aisha, Abram, and Tyler.

Aisha dropped her smile and joined the other two with a clean, emotionless face that reflected obedience. Together they formed a horizontal line, straightening their backs, and saluted. All three drones dropped to the ground to the rightmost side of the soldiers they were assigned to, for this was a custom.

"At ease, soldiers," the woman consoled in a thick British accent.

She took a long, heavy breath of the fresh air and exhaled as her eyes thoroughly scanned the distant horizon. Something about the skew of reddish color this planet gave off awarded the barren desert of rock and dust a certain sense of beauty.

The woman then squatted down to the ground to grasp some of the soil in her hands. She watched it spread between her fingers and fall to the ground.

She began to smirk. "So here we are, the edge of the galaxy on a prayer, to grow beans in the desert."

"I am no farmer, Ma'am, but I am willing to bet you got all kinds of advanced gadgets on that ship that could grow fish in a tube," Abram conveyed.

This turned her smirk into a full smile on her awkwardly thin face. "That we do. Though, I admit, I too know very little of farming. We have some great scientists aboard eager to come out and play, but first we must rendezvous on what we know of our newfound world."

She rose to her feet and brushed her hands free of the dirt she held just a moment ago.

"My name is Vice Admiral Natalia Fox. Until Admiral Vetrov arrives on his carrier, I will be leading commander of the Project Salvation's naval defense fleet. Now please, tell me everything you have gathered thus far."

That's right, we shook hands with this woman once during our training, Aisha thought. *Figures she wouldn't actually remember any of us by name.*

"Not much-" Abram began to answer, but was cut off.

"In absence of officer Leon Fleisher, I am Commanding Officer Tyler Flynn. This is Specialist Aisha Sayegh and Specialist Abram Orlav," Tyler trumpeted out, interrupting Abram.

Wow, Aisha thought, *that came off rude as hell. That was very much unlike Tyler, but in the presence of such a high-ranking commander, it's important to follow the edict in chain of command.*

"And what happened to officer Fleisher?" asked the admiral.

Her eyes darted about the three of them, looking for any sort of discontent.

The friendly welcoming party Aisha had hoped for-- perhaps with balloons and cake-- had been squashed before it had even started.

"As I am sure you are aware, there were six pioneers total. Everyone made landfall, clustered relatively close to one another, but one ship--containing Valerie Fournier--went astray, landing a little further from the rest, off to the east. Failed attempts in communication resulted in Fleisher and Kaito Shimizu venturing off to bring her back to the group."

"I see. And you have yet to hear back from the other half of your squad?" she continued with her interrogation. "How long have they been gone?"

"Well, they left soon after we landed this morning."

"Wait," she frowned, "you guys made landfall this morning and constructed the warp gate in a single afternoon? Then continued to pull in a vessel packed full of civilians to your location? Did you even follow through with inspections to be sure the gate was constructed correctly?" her tone now elevated to a level reflecting her annoyance in the three.

"Well-" Tyler tried to defend.

She was quick to cut him off, snapping her fingers to one of her escorts. "Bring me two chief mechanics. Abram will escort them to the warp gate to thoroughly inspect it for malfunction before we even consider pulling in another carrier." Her eyes jumped back over to Tyler. "Pardon my lack of compassion, but when there is zero communication from you and your squad up until my ship and I, with millions of lives aboard--lives I am directly responsible for--were ripped from one end of the galaxy to the other using super advanced technology that you three, half the number of your actual squad, hastily constructed in one afternoon," she paused, "I just cannot help but feel a little uneasy with that."

"That was the plan though, no?" Tyler faltered.

"If your mission is to escort a lady to the prom, do you go to her bedroom early in the wee hours of the a.m. unannounced and drag her out by her hair like some caveman with a club?" she questioned with intimidation.

Tyler rallied a dash of courage. "Ma'am, our mission was not to escort a lady to the prom, it was to land on a scorching hot planet, establish a warp gate, and begin pulling in ships to establish a new world to call home. Now, we tried to send outbound communications, but the anomalies that be would not allow it to be done with success."

Her frown turned to a very awkward smile, "Well, as long as you gave it the ole college try." Then her smile returned back to a serious scowl, "Go find the other half of your squad, Tyler Flynn."

Are all the captains of these space carriers bipolar sociopaths? Aisha wondered.

***

Leon and Kaito walked back towards the original landing site at a much slower pace than the one from when they left. Not only had they engaged in conflict that was debatably avoidable, but they also had not found or retrieved their comrade.

"So, you wanna talk about that cave?" Kaito suggested.

"What's there to talk about?" Leon responded coldly.

I was afraid he would say that, Kaito thought. "Well, what was that bug thing?"

Leon stopped, turning to face Kaito as Scorpio continued ahead, not noticing. "It was just that: a big, nasty bug that I squished. I had a moment of fear for both my life and yours and acted on my instinct to survive. Was it the right thing to do? I have no idea, but given the scenario again, I would have shot it in the fucking face ten out of ten times. Any more questions?"

"Woah, Man, just asking," Kaito said, raising his hands. "I would have done the same, and I am not second guessing what you did at all...just," he paused. "What was it? Do you think it killed Valerie?"

Leon faced forward again, continuing on. "The girl entered that cave--by her own accord or someone else's, I do not know--but I am sure she entered that cave. My faith that she exited alive simply does not exist. Hell, I don't think anything gets out of there alive often for that matter, and we should be grateful that the walking maggot corpse died in there instead of us."

He isn't wrong. Fuck everything about that cave: its enormous, creepy bats, its wretched stench, and whatever the fuck that maggot bug thing was, Kaito thought.

"Well, look at that," Leon pointed out, "Looks like our friends have been quite busy in our absence."

Kaito looked ahead to see not only a fully constructed warp gate off in the distance, but also the citadel of a carrier ship that had been warped in while they were gone.

"Those things are way bigger in person than they appear on television," Kaito said in amazement.

"Yeah, and just think, we are about two miles out from it. Let's go," he said as the two picked up their pace forward.

***

The gate further from where Kio-Kai sat in the great colosseum of glory slowly raised and, if the crowd cheered before for the rebels of Ikan clan, they now bellowed a thunderous roar of appreciation for the beast that lay behind the lifting gate. He was their champion and a gift of gratitude from the overlords for their loyalty and hard work.

The rock golem Brutalius emerged. A body of irregular, uneven stone from head to toe radiated red as if fire burned within its very soul. He wasted no time thumping his chest, hyping not only himself up to kill, but the crowd to equally feel a part of what it was he was about to do. The arena was his world and his fans were his family.

The three Vai-Zik hunters that guarded the smaller, weaker one began to advance towards the Anolem. No sense in delaying the inevitable conflict, they aimed to strike first before the golem could get himself psyched up.

"It's a smart move," Lai-Kai chimed in, glued to the sport below.

The golem caught on to their ploy for a quick attack and began to advance towards them to cut off their momentum.

As the two parties gained speed, heading straight for each other, the three hunters branched out, one fluttering ahead on the right, another to the left, as the third stayed centered at ground level and advanced straight for Brutalius.

Like a bull seeing red, the brute continued its charge for the ground level hunter--passing the two that fluttered by his sides.

The two in the air doubled back and dive-bombed towards the hunter still advancing at ground level. It was a trap, and at the very last second, the hunter that played the role of bait rolled safely off and to the side.

Brutalius continued on, gaining momentum, not bothering to stop and re-engage them. The two hunters that dive-bombed from above hit the ground empty handed.

"He could care less about the three of them," Lai-Kai commentated dispassionately, as if she had solved some great secret.

The three hunters took but a couple of seconds to realize what was happening. They jumped up and dashed back towards the fourth half-pint, defenseless hunter they had left behind. Clearly, they went on the offense early in an attempt to defend it, but they did not expect the golem to completely disregard their assault and not engage at all.

The runt backpedaled, tripping on its own awkward feet, and began to squeal in fear as Brutalius showed no ambition of yielding his charge. The other three hunters tried to catch him, but he was too far gone and before any of them could even come close, he ran through the runt's small, fragile body. The shattering of its bones could be heard cracking apart throughout the great colosseum.

Brutalius doubled back and made it to the broken grunt just as the other three hunters arrived. Fragmented into multiple pieces, it lay on the ground twitching and convulsing. They could do nothing for him, and one even fell to its knees out of heartache for its brethren.

Brutalius cackled maniacally and picked up the torso of the twitching child. Not hesitating for a second, he began to pick apart its legs from their sockets and toss them down into the dirt before the hunter that lay on his knees in dismay. He then popped off the still-living head that was going through spasms as it died in complete fear, horror, and pain. Cupping the face of their comrade, he smashed it into his stone chest, spewing chunks of shell, blood, and viscera in all directions.

One of the hunters on his feet zoomed forward in a fit of rage. The second joined in on the charge and, as soon as he had, the big brute of a golem countered the attack. He caught the thrusting arm of the first hunter in the air and added to his momentum--spinning him around much faster than he had taken off. Using him as a bat, he swung the helpless insect around and smashed him into the other that still charged forward behind him.

The collision crushed their bones and, once again, the sound of cracking cartilage echoed through the arena. The final hunter perched, still on his knees, blood caking his face as he watched in speechless horror. Brutalius approached the lonely hunter. He stepped on and crushed a pile of mangled body parts as he came closer. The single hunter sat watching a leg on the ground before him twitching as if attached to a body that was still alive. Much like their bodies, his spirit was broken. He no longer needed to die to be defeated.

Brutalius palmed the face of the hunter on his knees and detached the head. Making it look easy, he plucked off the antennae, discarded them to the ground of blood and gore, and raised the head to his face to look within the eyes of his fallen enemy. He smiled, then raised it higher above his own head to show the crowd, whose silence in awe erupted into cheers of admiration.

I require the presence of you before me, my child. A voice as clear as the dead bits of hunter down in the arena below spoke directly inside Kio-Kai's head.

His antennae twitched a bit, as they always did when receiving commands from his queen, Lady Kai-Zul, and he looked over to Lai-Kai, who appeared to have gotten the same message. It was rare for a queen to summon an individual. She would spread her will amongst the clan daily, but as far as personal commands went, she had workers that spent their lives catering to her direct needs who almost never left her side.

"What do you think this is about?" Lai-Kai asked him.

Kio-Kai shrugged and the two took flight from the arena, working their way into one of the many thruway transit systems that led deeper into the hive. The crowds behind could still be heard roaring in praise of Brutalius.

***

Two mechanics exited the carrier ship and Abram, as instructed, lead the two over towards the warp gate while the vice admiral and her escorts retreated back into the vessel.

"Alright, Aries, see if you can get a fix on Leon," Tyler instructed his drone.

Aisha perched against a rock, "So what the hell was that about?"

Tyler ignored her. He wasn't expecting to be ripped apart like that and did not feel as though he had done anything wrong to deserve it. When dealing with that level of authority, he figured it was best to just simply comply.

After pinging Leon's drone, Scorpio, Aries computed her results out loud, "The distance between our current location and Scorpio is approximately four hundred and thirty-five yards due east."

"Wait, what?" Tyler questioned, spinning around to look.

Just below the warp gate, within the shadow it casted across the ground approached Leon and his drone. Kaito and his bot were right behind him.

Tyler began to jog over to meet the other two, and Aisha jumped to her feet to follow suit.

"Well, that was easy," she sarcastically spat out.

Tyler was stoked to see Leon; aside from considering him a friend, this also meant he wouldn't have to directly deal with the vice admiral.

"Long time no see," he called out as they met.

"You guys have been busy, I see. What did we miss?" Leon responded.

"Well, it looks like we report to a humbling women by the name of Vice Admiral Natalia Fox," Tyler said.

Leon's face looked as though his brain was trying to recall the familiar sounding name, "Yeah, I remember meeting her once in our training," he said. "Eyes that can cut through steel."

"Yeah, she is a real peach. Anyway, she has Abram and a few tech guys going over the gate, making sure it is a hundred percent, while the two of us were supposed to head out and find you three." He paused, noticing there were only two: Leon and Kaito. "Where is Valerie?"

"We found her ship. It got torn to pieces in that fire storm that flailed about all day."

"Holy shit, did you find her body?"

"That's the thing, she didn't die in the wreckage. We followed a trail of blood to a cavern where we made contact with hostile alien life."

"What do you mean hostile? Did it attack you? What was it?"

"I don't know what it was. A sizeable humanoid-like creature, though. I wouldn't say it's cause for concern, but it's definitely a matter of interest we should look into."

"Aries, get a message to Fox. Tell her we found the team and we have new intel on a potential threat."

"Transmission sent," Aries confirmed. Almost instantly after her statement was made, Aries alerted, "Incoming live comm."

"Patch it through," Tyler complied. Before them, Aries spat out an array of color that created a high resolution holographic image of the vice admiral.

"That didn't seem to take long. Were they hiding off in the bushes?" The vice admiral spat.

***

Kio-Kai and Lai-Kai approached their queen's lair. A small opening led into a hollowed-out room with stagnant ponds and streams of blood that once flowed from the upper levels of the hive. Thick, gooey eggs, varying in size, were attached to the streams via heavy umbilical cords. When a queen lay an egg, a twitch drone would puncture the egg and grab the umbilical cord so that he could run it over and submerge the tubing into a body of lifeblood.

Twitch drones were another type of worker unit within the Vai-Zik empire. They rarely slept and were considered the working ground force, as they constructed cities and catered directly to the queen's needs.

Kio-Kai passed one of the eggs--pulsing with life from within. Somewhat transparent, he could make out a small fetus suspended in a clear, red gel. He had a cloudy memory, decades old, of being in the hatchery. He hadn't been here since birth. It intrigued him to actually see the inner workings firsthand and with much older, more mature eyes.

From around a corridor emerged a twitcher: bipedal with three sets of arms and much smaller wings than that of a hunter, he approached. He had a smaller frame and smaller antennae. In general, twitch drones never ventured too far from their queen and never engaged in combat, just manual labor day in and day out.

"Are you the two Lady Kai has summoned?" he hissed.

"No, we are just tourists looking for a view," Lai-Kai joked.

The twitcher's ugly face looked perplexed. It did not comprehend humor, for it lived its life stuck in the old ways of the swarm--forever loyal and bound to the queen's will. Humor was an emotion that manifested with freedom of thought. Freedom of thought was still a new and cloudy idea to most. Some accepted it and some did not--staying loyal to the past.

"We are the two she called for," Kio-Kai said in a serious manner.

The twitcher looked at Kio-Kai and nodded, then beckoned them to follow him as he led them through a swamp of blood and eggs to their queen's domain.

Dark green and red veins pulsated along the walls. An organic plant-like substance fed on minimal amounts of the lifeblood. The Vai-Zik never cleansed their layers of the leaching plants since they acted as a free, interconnected system of pipes and tubes. If a twitcher needed to access a pool of blood from a distance, it only need puncture one of the vein plants and it would gush the liquid out like a fountain for hours before the wound would eventually coagulate and seal.

The three entered through a large opening that was surrounded by hundreds of thousands of hieroglyphics, most dating back to a time history had long since forgotten. Languages, dead and gone, left only mystery and speculation as to their curators and meanings.

In the next room, lit by the light of a thousand candles, was Lady Kai, queen of her clan. She was beautiful. A queen could evolve from any species of Vai-Zik, be it grinder, twitcher, or hunter, and might maintain some of the traits from being such. When a female embraced the destiny of queen, a large abdomen would rupture from her spine and grow in enormous size along with four to eight very small additional legs that could help carry the added weight.

Lady Kai's antennae were tremendous and hung down to her belly. She had three sets of arms, which led Kio-Kai to the conclusion that she once was a twitcher herself, very long ago.

Kio-Kai and Lai-Kai dropped to one knee and bowed before their queen. Hunters rarely got to meet a queen, after all.

"Rise, my children," her speechless voice spoke directly into their minds.

Behind their queen, in the shadows, stood a creature Kio-Kai had never seen. It was much like the overlord at the arena today, only it had skin that was mangled and broken. Fragments of broken bone protruded from its skin as blood and puss slowly oozed from its many wounds.

"I called you down here to meet someone of grave importance," Lady Kai continued, *"He is a very old friend and trusted advisor to the hive."*

"Why, hello," the creature said in a sharp tone as he approached Lai-Kai and kissed her on the hand with his grotesque lips, "My name is Naberius and I am quite excited to have made your acquaintance, little huntress. I have heard much of you. Word is you will be a fitting queen someday soon and spawn a clan of your own, Lai-Kai."

Seemingly overwhelmed with the overall experience before her, she simply responded with a wide-eyed nod.

The pale beast's eyes imprisoned a look of a million years of pain as they slowly drifted over to meet Kio-Kai.

"And you, young hunter. I admit, I did not know much about you up until today, when it seems you brought in quite the catch."

For the first time in a long time, Kio-Kai felt tremendous amounts of fear. *How does he know what I brought in?* he thought. *Ah cave whiskers.*

All of the major entrances to the interconnected colonies within the Vai-Zik empire, mostly empty caverns, were lined with whiskers: a highly sensitive plant-like fungi that detected, observed, and reported on all activity amongst the clans. Though Kio-Kai never fully understood to whom they might report and of what language they even spoke, he realized that one of many talents and languages the overlords spoke was that of a cave whisker.

How was I supposed to know that thing was an overlord? he thought, *I have never seen one before.* He tried to justify it in his own head before it could be brought up in the conversation.

"Do you know what it is you caught today, young hunter?" the overlord questioned.

"*It is ok, my child. You did not do anything wrong,*" Lady Kai comforted, sensing his sudden overwhelming emotion of fear.

"I did not know until after it was processed," Kio-Kai admitted.

The creature painfully raised its head up and down in understanding.

Kio-Kai just went ahead and said it, "It was an overlord."

"No, it was a woman," Naberius corrected, "From the species of man or, more commonly, they refer to themselves as human beings,"

Naberius's demeanor coupled with his voice was hypnotizing, thoroughly capturing the attention of Kio-Kai and Lai-Kai in an unbroken level of obedient attention.

"But today at the arena, the man we saw?" Kio-Kai disputed.

"Was a daemon, one of my many followers. They hold various seats of power within your empire to ensure stability and peace within. They look similar to the humans, but are very different. They are loyal to our collective cause and prideful natives to our land."

"Are you an overlord?" Lai-Kai questioned.

The beast's face twisted and turned. "I have been called that before, among various other things, but I very much prefer Naberius-- that is, after all, what my father calls me. Now, boy, the reason I summoned you two down here is that there are more of the humans, like the one you saw today. Many more. They landed only a short distance off from where you discovered the girl. These aliens that landed on our sacred planet are a very dangerous and a very real threat. Did you know they killed the grinder that processed that girl for you?"

Kio-Kai was quickly overwhelmed with guilt. *They must have followed me to the cave*, he concluded.

"I thought it appropriate to ask that you two be the blades of vengeance for your slain brethren in this matter. The humans made landfall on the outskirts of an entrapment field, so taking them by surprise should be easy. Take two hundred hunters and four dozen grinders, catch the humans off guard, shake them up a bit, and bring me their finest warrior."

Kio-Kai looked over to his queen as if silently asking her if this was what she wanted. She gave him a nod of approval.

"If my queen desires as such, then I submit myself to you," Kio-Kai said as he kneeled to Naberius. "It will be done,"

Lai-Kai silently followed in the symbolic gesture.

Kio-Kai and Lai-Kai rose to their feet and took leave to carry out the overlord's commands.

Chapter 5
Play Date

A short, round man waddled into the entrance of block sixty-five, calling attention to its inhabitants. "Alright people, we have spent weeks learning our roles and so, by now, you should all have a pretty good grasp on what that is and how to do it. If anyone has questions, they can ask me at any time. Please line up in an orderly fashion and follow me. We will be getting right to work."

The room filled quickly with conversation, speculation, and excitement for the tasks ahead as the workers, mostly young men and women, lined up to the door.

"Looks like we are jumping right in," Ness pointed out to his little brother. "We just landed less than an hour ago."

"That's ok. I have been dying to get out of this stuffy, stinky room anyway," the smaller boy replied. He put on his backpack as if preparing for the first day of school in a new town.

Everyone in the unit was assigned a 'day one' backpack, which was a small black sack that contained a shovel, a wash cloth, a canteen of water, and three stimpacks.

Stimpacks were injections that substituted the need to eat. A small, yet highly concentrated liquid of vitamins, minerals, and energy that could not only sustain a human being in regular functions, but also increase his or her mental and physical output. A human being could survive off of stimpacks alone for almost a full year, at least that was the record set in a scientific study a few years prior. After three hundred and forty-nine days of stimpacks alone, the test subject died of a brain aneurysm. It was concluded that lack of food and nutrients was not the cause of death, but rather the strenuous output on the cerebrum caused by the concentrated potency of a pure stimpack diet.

The team would be required to work through the first twenty-four hours straight with only a single one-hour break at the eighteen-hour mark.

The crew shuffled out behind the round man, who waddled ahead like a duck. They walked through long corridors within the ship, passing other blocks where teams assembled to begin work on whatever tasks and missions they may have been assigned to.

Finally reaching a large blast door, the fat man turned to face his crew. "You guys ready?" he asked with his cheeks rolling up like a soft, squishy dough.

The crowd cheered in excitement. Ness had butterflies in his stomach. This was it--halfway across the galaxy to establish a new world, a new home.

He glanced down towards his younger brother, who had his eyes clenched shut. He was gripping the cross he wore around his neck as if someone were about to snatch it away. It was a gift from their mother just before they left. She always was quite religious, though Ness never was. He figured it best not to discredit the symbol that his younger brother wore in comfort--better to just leave him be in peace.

No loving god would ever allow the series of events that plagued the earth to ever happen in the first place, he thought.

The doors slowly raised, allowing light to shine through into the ship. The crowd covered their eyes in blindness. They had not directly seen a sun in quite some time.

A comforting, warm draft of heat blew in with dust and dirt. They had been in space for a long time and not only was it dark in space, but it was also tremendously cold. The extreme heat felt incredible to Ness as he regained sight and stepped out into the world. Red mountains in the distance cut into the sky of scattered clouds, crafting a landscape of bright, vibrant colors.

"You smell that?" Ness asked, taking in a deep breath.

"Dirt?" his little brother joked.

"No, man, fresh air. Not that recycled crap we breathed on the ship, but clean, natural air!"

The sun was setting in the desert valley. A sky of pink light grew increasingly darker with every minute that passed by.

"How are we going to work through the night in the dark?" A woman ahead of the two boys asked her friend in a tone of concern.

"The carrier has spotlights all along the side of it," her friend answered, pointing back to the ship.

A Humvee ran yellow tape ahead, laying out their designated dig site before moving on to taper off another crew's assigned work zone nearby.

A large, two-legged mech, clunky in motion, maneuvered towards them, stopping just shy of the dig site. Twenty feet high, this was no militarized mech. It was equipped with drills used to soften the soil and make it easier for civilians to dig. A wobbly vehicle such as this, looking like it could fall apart at any minute, would never meet the high standards of military use. But civilian-based construction was a fitting purpose for the old hunk of outdated manmade technology.

***

Leon sat perched against a boulder as he filed his report on the events from the day. As he typed away on the thin, transparent piece of glass, he watched an abundance of entryways open, releasing thousands of civilians from New Horizon. Like water from a levy system, they poured out and spread in front of the massive vessel.

"Looks like they are wasting little time in getting right to work," Leon said to his drone, Scorpio. "Is Kaito still in the debriefing with the vice admiral?"

The drone pinged Kaito's. "He appears to currently be engaged in communication with Vice Admiral Natalia Fox."

Leon repositioned himself against the uncomfortable rock. Debriefing with this vice admiral was perhaps the most tedious thirty minutes of his life, and being back outside under the brutality of Flare's sun was pleasant and refreshing in comparison.

Watching the construction crews get to work felt like a milestone reached in preserving the fate of the human race. Here they were on a planet they knew very little about, other than its mediocre potential to sustain life. Here they were quite literally laying the foundation for future generations to come and ensuring the safety of those generations via escaping Earth and her volatile sun.

The moon was beginning to rise and take its place in the sky on one end of the horizon as the sun set on another. It was an eerie transition on the alien world, for the moon was much bigger. Brighter than Earth's, the sky above exposed much detail of a bustling array of activity in this end of the galaxy.

Watching the sky above, Leon abruptly jumped upright as the ground beneath his feet progressively shook to life. It changed from a minute, subtle rattle of rocks and pebbles to a much more violent vibration. He watched as what appeared to be a sinkhole wobbled to life. He jumped back and suddenly spotted what looked like a large ant on two legs. With claws and long, sharp blade-like bones running from the arms, the creature leapt up from the ditch with a flutter of its wings. It latched on to Scorpio and dragged the drone back down into the crater.

It all happened so fast, much like how a trapdoor spider of his home world would catch its prey. Scorpio was gone, down into the earth.

In disbelief over what he had just witnessed, he turned to confirm if anyone else had seen what he had, but no one seemed to have noticed the event occur.

It was like some giant humanoid locust, Leon contemplated.

Leon's eyes fixated on the dirt that was shaking out by a cluster of civilians. His heart sank and he found it difficult to form words in his dry mouth.

"Everyone get back to the carrier!" he yelled, unholstering his two high energy pistols. He activated the laser's optics on the weapons and silently scanned the ground, waiting for the next attack.

A few people looked at him as if he had gone mental.

The earth began to rattle beneath a young girl with long, blond hair who had triggered one of the traps. Leon's lasers drifted over to the girl as one of the locusts manifested from below. He sprayed the creature in the backside, tearing a hole clean through it. The girl fell to the ground and got showered in the insect's entrails. Wasting no time, she crawled back to her feet and began to scream as she fled.

Looks like they saw that one, Leon thought as the crowd began to panic and run.

The horrific sound of screaming echoed through the air as civilians got caught in the creatures' traps. Their blades and claws impaled construction workers before they dragged the helpless human beings off into the ground.

Leon was the first to fire a weapon, let alone kill one of the large humanoid insects, but he would not be the last.

Aisha ran towards him as another insect leapt up to pull her under. She sprang forward and barrel-rolled off to the side to safety. Pisces activated their stealth tech and, quickly, the two of them became invisible.

A faint blur could be seen as the locust that had attempted to snatch the girl was cut, severed from the waist down.

The insects were coming from the ground now and engaging in full-fledged combat. Their trickery was done after claiming roughly thirty to forty civilians and military escort alike, down into the red dirt.

Gunfire volleyed fourth from a half a dozen military personnel who were getting cornered by a handful of the insects. Two men were impaled and bled out on the ground while their comrades dismantled the culprits with hailing energy beams, lasers, and railguns.

Behind one of the fallen insects was one of the creatures Leon and Kaito had engaged in the cave just earlier in the day. It sprayed liquid all over three men as they ripped it to pieces with gunfire. The men were quick to clench their faces and fall to the ground, screaming in agony as their skin bubbled and burned away.

Abram bellowed out in the distance, a cry of bloodlust, as he swung his warhammer, collecting piles of dead insects. Despite his success, he was getting swarmed and overrun. Four of the locusts jumped on him, wrestling him to the ground. He dropped his weapon and fought back with his massive fists, breaking them apart with his bare hands until three more joined in to help plunge the giant down under the ground.

Leon killed dozens of the insects trying to make his way to any nearby comrade. A rookie soldier-- a young boy no older than twenty-- was his closest fighting ally just a few yards away. Leon made his way to him, dropping enemies with accurate shots to their faces, one after another. He reached the ally just as a locust poked the boy straight through the neck with a long, sharp blade. Leon dropped the bug, tearing its face, neck, and shoulders off in a hail of fire, then looked down to the boy, who clenched his neck as if he could stop the bleeding that gushed freely as a fountain and drowned him where he lay.

While maintaining direct eye contact with the boy, Leon quickly raised one of his pistols over the kid's face and fired twice. He figured the least he could do was give him a quick, painless death before he moved forward in the slaughter for survival.

Tyler and Aries advanced the side flank, gunning down one after another in a perfectly executed sequence, but they would never reach Leon in time.

The bugs simply would not stop coming. As soon as one died, two more would emerge from the ground to take its place.

Leon's pistols were dangerously close to overheating. It wasn't a matter of *if* it happened, but rather *when*. He glanced down to the heat index indicator on the side of his weapons. The meters had reached fully into the red hazard zone. He had no choice but to keep firing. Gambling the risk of his firearms exploding in his hand over the other option of allowing himself to get overwhelmed by the giant insects, there was only one true choice.

He could feel the heat radiating off the weapons. His instincts begged him to call out to Scorpio, but the bot was gone and presumably dead. The pistols stung his fingers and began melting his gloves away as he continued to drop more of the locusts.

Just as all seemed lost, surrounded by over a dozen of the things with his death inevitably drawing ever so near, a shot rang out, crackling across the sky like lightning. In the smallest of nanoseconds, a path was fully cleared ahead of him. Nothing but smoldering mush lay on the ground; there was now a clear and present runway for escape.

The aftershock boom felt as though it blew Leon's eardrums from his head. His entire face was ringing and, in a slight daze, Leon saw Kaito off in the distance, peeking his face up above the scope of his sniper rifle, barrel still smoking. He seemed to mouth the word 'run'.

***

Aisha slashed down one after another. She was mostly invisible to them, thus she held an immeasurable tactical advantage. Her killing spree was cut short by a large sack of a rotting larva, seemingly confused as it witnessed its comrades falling to the ground, getting their ligaments ripped apart by some incomprehensible, invisible force. In panic, it spewed acid in all directions before it.

Pisces got engulfed in most of the spray and Aisha raised her hand to shield her face from what was left incoming through the air.

The liquid covered her left hand and forearm. Very quickly, her armor, her clothing, her skin and bone was eaten alive by this acid. She shrieked in pain as Pisces fell to the ground, dissolving in the acid and causing her stealth cloak to vanish.

She fell to her knees in shock, not knowing what to do as she watched her arm quickly become a gooey string of useless muscle. The tendons and fibers liquefied before her very eyes and dripped right off the bone.

She acted quickly, using her blade, she ran it up against the backside of her shoulder and sliced her arm clean off. Hacking off what was melting away, she began to lose a lot of blood. She felt dizzy and sick. Succumbing into a state of shock, she fell backwards and passed out.

***

Aries was forced to halt her assault as her laser weaponry overheated from such rapid fire. Her guns radiated a bright red glow, excreting tremendous heat and forcing her to retreat back with Tyler.

Aisha lay on the ground ahead, missing her left arm entirely. She was turning pale and beginning to flail on the ground intensely. Vomiting on herself, she was covered in her own blood, sweat, and puke.

"Aries! Save her!" Tyler shouted out as he tossed an energy grenade up over the rock he sought shelter behind.

Four large locusts were ripping Abram's drone, Taurus, to pieces, dissecting the bot's internal wiring as if it were a man and his intestines. In their frenzy, the insects paid no mind to the grenade drifting towards them. It had an LED indicator that was pulsing a bright green color as it landed and slid to a stop just below their feet. Its green blinking halted and it pulsed a redness three times before detonating.

Time and space bent inwards. Within seconds the energy explosive rapidly pulled in all matter around them, ripping apart the atoms that made up objects. It mixed the ingredients and combusted them.

Within a six-yard radius, bits and pieces of matter-- unrecognizable to the naked eye without a microscope-- fell. All fibers of being that once existed in that location were now apart on the ground--collectively a mesh of dark, red mush.

Aries zoomed over to Aisha and homed her overheated lasers in on the shoulder blade that was quickly draining the girl of all the blood she held inside. The bot overrode the overheat failsafe and set the lasers to a short, immensely hot burst that quickly cauterized the wound-- turning it to a large, stinking, black scab that ultimately sealed it off. Aries then levitated the girl up into the air and, zig-zagging between gunfire, escorted her back towards the carrier ship.

Leon was off ahead, getting swamped. Tyler advanced forward behind his cover and began laying down some of the bugs ahead, but he knew he would never reach Leon in time. A shot then pierced through the air that bellowed a war cry of death and decay.

Tyler knew just what this was. This was an ultra-high-powered UIGN issued sniper rifle. Before him, ten of the bugs disintegrated into body parts and blood. Leon had a full path to retreat back and, in doing so, the chaos seemed to settle ahead. The assault was ceasing.

***

White lights subtlety blinked through the corridors, casting eerie shadows within the blocks nestled away in New Horizon. All civilian personnel were in a state of lockdown that night following the events of the evening prior. People were calling it 'the day one massacre'. With no official word given, everyone was left to speculate in fear over the survivor's' recollection of events.

Ness remembered all too vividly watching helplessly as those creatures stole hundreds of lives just hours before, dragging them off into the ground. Those people were gone forever.

It all happened so fast: thousands of people running back towards the ship, most of which didn't even know what it was they were actually even running from. They merely followed the rest of the frenzied flock to safety.

At one point, his younger brother got caught in the stampede, fell to the ground, and was trampled. Ness had to double back and fight through the scared horde, pushing and getting tossed around like a rag doll, until ultimately reaching his bloody sibling so that he might carry him the rest of the way to safety.

Ness stayed up all night because he couldn't help but indulge in the mass conjectured chatter. Even the guards assigned to their block had no answers, no insight, nothing but looks of concern about their own faces as they talked amongst themselves.

Lucas, doped up on high-grade painkillers, slept soundly despite his broken face. A puffy, purple eye, a broken nose, two missing teeth, and a wound requiring fourteen stitches across the back of his skull were the injuries he had accumulated. A doctor had to shave his head in order to stitch him up adequately.

Ness felt incredibly bad for his brother, but Lucas, through it all, was strangely positive. He had joked earlier that he had never had pain killers before and he wasn't sure if he was drooling all down his own face or not. Clearly Lucas had not actually witnessed the massacre with his own eyes, something Ness was truly grateful for.

***

Tyler sat on the austral ledge of the canyon. The area was lit up by the large moon to the west in the welkin. It casted an eerie color to the fires that fell from the sky to the south. The moon vastly trumped Earth's own. It was so big, bright, and visible, Tyler almost felt as though he could reach out and touch it. Aires perched by his side like an obedient dog, looking with him up to the clear night sky.

That evening, the crew was instructed to keep watch and guard the warp gate, whose magnetic field of defense would be useless if the creatures attacked again from the ground.

For the first time since their arrival, the sky was mostly clear. There were no dust storms, no lightning, and no fire. All the chaos was far off to the southwest. Above was simply a calm galaxy of stars with very few clouds to obscure the view. The night sky revealed the most amazing view of space Tyler had ever seen. He could see large clusters of stars, trails of space gasses-- some purple, some green-- and dark collections of matter only a few light years away.

Two hellcats, small, single manned aircrafts, screeched through the sky as they left New Horizon--most likely on a recon mission. Tyler couldn't help but think he had climbed the wrong ranks within the military.

"Guess I should have been a pilot, huh, Aries?" he said out loud to the bot.

"You would have never gotten in with your less-than-perfect eyesight," she logically fired back.

She was heartlessly correct but, nonetheless, he wanted to be one of the first to lead humanity into a better future. He wanted to explore distant lands and discover the marvelous wonders this planet potentially harbored. He wanted to be the leader he always thought he was born to be; but he was none of these. He was just some midnight security guard standing watch over a hunk of expensive tech.

He felt directly responsible for the lives lost that night. It was his ignorance that murdered hundreds of people-- massacred in a single afternoon. The team should have scouted the planet better before warping in a carrier with innocent lives aboard.

Leon appeared behind him. He was wrapping his burnt hands in a fresh set of gauze as he approached, back from a meeting aboard New Horizon.

"So, how is Aisha?" Tyler questioned.

"She will be alright. They stabilized her and put her under. They are going to open that wound up and fit her with some advanced prosthetics."

"Girl could have dropped every last one of them if her cloak didn't drop," Tyler pointed out.

"I know. Only piece of stealth tech we had and it's gone until more carriers arrive with whatever they have. But maybe those crazy tech guys can salvage something from the portion of Pisces you found," Leon suggested.

"What do you think happened to Abram?" Tyler continued.

Leon looked off into the distance with a pause. "I don't know. If they were going to kill him, they would have done it before dragging him off, kicking and flailing about."

"So, you think he is alive?" Tyler guessed.

"If he isn't, I have no doubt that that big ogre snapped thirty of their necks going down."

This forced a faint smile on Tyler's face. "The cave you and Kaito found, think that's where they went?"

"That would be my best guess."

"Think they followed you guys back?"

Leon didn't respond and Tyler quickly felt bad for asking, realizing that the thought must have plagued Leon all through the night.

"Fox has some scientist dissecting a few of the dead bugs. She said the president will make an announcement soon to comfort the civilians and get them back to work, and in the morning the three of us are to make way for the cave, see what we can find," Leon said coldly.

Perhaps this was punishment. It sounded like suicide.

"When do we leave?" Tyler asked.

"Two hours before sunrise, about three hours from now. I told Kaito to rest his eyes for a bit before we head out. You should prolly do the same."

Leon pulled a stimpack from a satchel strapped to his arm and bit off the plastic shielding around the tip of the needle. Spitting the unwanted piece away, he stuck the needle into his arm and plunged the syringe, injecting the collection of biofuel into his bloodstream.

Tyler cringed in watching. He didn't so much dislike needles, but to watch Leon go through with the act of self-injections so easily, as if living off of stimpacks were somehow the norm, seemed strange.

Leon stood up to walk away and Tyler laid himself down against a rock, staring straight up into the estranged alien night sky before closing his eyes. He wouldn't sleep that night, but he would be lying if he didn't admit that closing his eyes felt incredible.

***

Ness awoke from his faint nap in the middle of the night to the sound of people crowding around the forty-foot screen perched above the entrance of their block. The time had come for the promised statement and people were eager for answers. Even the guards looked up to the glass, eyes glued for what the announcement might entail.

The president of the United Intergalactic Movement appeared on the transparent glass dressed in military gear and holstering a rifle.

"Look at this pompous ass-hat, dressed from head to toe in propaganda as if he is going to personally defend us from the safety of his carrier light years away," a man in his thirties yelled up to the glass.

People in the crowd grumbled for the man to be quiet so they could listen as the speech began.

"Almost two decades ago the people of Earth were forced to begin facing the greatest series of ultimate truths and challenges man had ever encountered. Yesterday, the squad we sent out into space two years ago to construct a device that would pull us through time and space, saving us from our ultimate demise, successfully made landfall and constructed the device we refer to today as the warp gate. They triumphantly pulled in New Horizon, the first of many carrier ships planned for phase one evacuation. The civilian inhabitants of New Horizon are tasked with breaking ground on planet Flare and laying the foundation for our future city, Liberty. Soon after beginning their jobs, the civilians were attacked by a species of vile bugs native to the land.

Now while we all share in mourning the loss of our family and friends and wish to spend time in grief, we must also stay focused at the very real and very serious task at hand. The sooner we continue and finalize the construction phase, the safer a future we provide for all. Now we have a very skilled collection of scientists aboard New Horizon, who dissected those bugs and feel as though we have learned a lot. We have a series of recon missions in the final phase of fruition and I am certain we are more than capable of squashing these cockroaches and eradicating them from our new home world in a timely manner.

So please, I beg you, sleep easy this night. No boogeyman is coming to get you. I cannot drive home just how crucial it is that we construct our great city to ensure the safety of all future generations. Now I know what society asks of you is not easy, but I assure you, we all bear this burden and share in this troubling time. In the coming weeks more carriers with supplies, food, and workforce will be warped into Flare as humanity shifts its existence from one galaxy to another. Turning back is not an option; our homeworld draws closer to its inevitable demise every passing second of every passing minute. So I ask you to hang in there, we will all be joining you soon to bolster forces in reconstructing the pillars that support the foundation of humanity. Goodnight and God bless."

The glass screen was again clear as the broadcast ended and Ness couldn't help but get shivers. He always saw the president of the United Intergalactic Movement to be a man for the people, someone anyone could relate to, but not all shared his-- perhaps naive-- view of their leader.

The crowd argued and bickered amongst each other following the announcement, forcing the guards to taze four rowdy inhabitants and haul them off to solitary confinement for a few hours.

The emotions of everyone were high-strung following the 'day one massacre.' Ness just hoped the military's plan of action would be quick and effective, so everyone could return to looking collectively forward to tomorrow.

He laid his head back down in his bunk and closed his eyes. In just a few short hours, the crews were again to set out and pursue construction phase, this time with beefed up security.

***

Just as sunrise approached, Leon, Kaito, and Tyler grouped up near the warp gate.

Leon dropped two large cylinders into the dirt. Their weight kicked dust up into the air. He then unholstered one of his pistols with his right hand and screwed one of the two smaller cylinders he still carried onto the barrel of his weapon. He followed up by doing the same to his second pistol.

"Suppressors; the larger one is for your rifle, Kaito, and the smaller for you, Ty. We don't have any for Aries's weaponry so it is important that, while in the cave, you do not fire your weapons," Leon said, looking up to Aries.

"Understood," The bot complied.

"Last time Kaito and I were in there, I was forced to pop a few shots. If we must engage, we must do so quietly, not foolishly. This is considered a recon mission and I would very much like to return alive. I am sure the two of you can agree with me on that."

Tyler nodded in confirmation as he screwed his suppressor to the barrel of his assault rifle, while Kaito just stared at Leon with a look of concern.

"Come here a second," Leon said, signaling Aries to descend closer to him. She drifted down to his level. He then pulled a small computer chip from deep within his pocket and inserted it into one of the bot's data trays. "Install this software update. That is going to rework your comm systems and allow us to communicate back to New Horizon despite the planet's interference."

"So, what are we looking for? We know there is some seriously creepy stuff in that cave. Why do we have to go in again, just the three of us?" Kaito asked. His pale face suggested he was well beyond the point of being afraid of going back in once more.

"Our primary goal will be to escort Aries in so she can ping down the tunnel and hopefully get a good sonar reading of what we are dealing with in there. Our hopes are that the bugs call that cave their one and only home. If we can confirm this, we will call in a smart bomb to travel down into the heart of the tunnel after we analyze the detailed map Aries ultimately draws for us."

It's as good a plan as ever, hell it better be... I worked it over in my head all night, Leon thought.

***

Abram opened his eyes to the throbbing pain coming from his wrists. He was tied up onto a wall via sharp, thick, thorny vines. Before him was a thin, pale, naked woman, hanging from a cross with a crown of thorns upon her head. Her feet and hands were nailed into the wooden crucifix. Her head hung down and hair obscured her face, but there was no denying that the motionless girl was dead and had been for some time: days, perhaps even weeks. In any event, she had been dead for far longer than human beings had been on this planet. Abram had to wonder who she was and how she got here.

A creature similar to a tall, lengthy, nude man and equally as pale as the girl was off to the side of her. He approached from the shadows with his grey, leathery skin and no actual genitalia. As Abram made out more of the man, he began to breathe heavy in panic. It had bits of bone sticking from open sores all over his skinny, frail body. His noseless face was warped and twisted about. "Oh my fucking God," Abram muttered in shock.

"Ah, a man of God I see?" the creature bellowed out in both pitches of high and low frequency, perforating Abram's stomach.

"You," Abram paused. His blood ran cold and sank far into his feet, "You speak English?"

"I am fluent in all of the tongues of man, even the ones time has long since forgotten."

Shock overtook Abram's face, "Who are you?"

"My name is Naberius. I am the utmost ambassador of God."

"God is dead," Abram spat.

"Indeed he is, or shall I say he was, for many eons. But like his son who rose to new life once more, so has our lord risen back from the dead." Naberius turned around to ponder and hide a twisted smile. In doing so, he exposed his back, where bits of spine broke through skin and excreted a black, gooey mixture of pus and blood.

Abram's nostrils flared in anger. "Why have you brought me here?" He roared with vigor.

"My, my, what brutality. I am sure you fought with equally as much. Why, if I still had genitals, I would almost consider fucking your skull just to watch and see you muster your might while I penetrate your eye sockets." Naberius's cheeks raised in amusement and blood began to drip from one of many open sores on his face.

"I instructed the Vai-Zik to bring me one of the mightiest of warriors mankind had to offer and they determined, amidst the chaos, that you were just that. Be grateful, my boy. It should be an honor to be considered as such among a race so prideful in the art of combat as the Vai-Zik," Naberius let out with a sense of sharpness about his voice.

"What are you talking about?" Abram sulked. His wrists stung as they bore all of his body weight.

"Our lord is weak from undergoing a recreation of self and he has instructed me to find and craft three generals to lead his armies to glory in the pursuit of regaining his seat on the throne."

"Why would God choose such a weak, disgusting creature to entrust with his armies?" Abram snickered.

"I like you, boy," The beast's voice was sharp, piercing the room. "Such as the rest of your sick species, I too am a sinner and I bear the heavy weight of my sins within and upon myself, but I have a gift. It is much useful in commanding and mustering vast legions to fight for the almighty."

Abram had heard enough. "A gift? To what, bleed from your *fucking face*?"

He pressed his wrist against the vine of thorns that restrained him. They dug deep into his skin and forced blood to trickle down. He had cut himself right down to the bone. Letting out a scream, he did not stop, not until the creature began to laugh, but this particular chuckle was one that Abram had never heard before. Though brief, the various pitches emitted from the cackle cut through the room like a blade through soft flesh. The sound pierced through Abram's armor as if he were wearing none at all. The lower portion of his spine twisted and turned and he closed his eyes, wincing in pain and fear.

In those seconds, he saw himself cast upon a long, wooden skewer. The vision was so vivid. He had no hands or feet, no legs or arms. He was merely a torso with a head--stuck on a spike that protruded from his belly to hold himself in place. All he knew was agony, all he felt was pain. As Abram struggled about the spear with what was left of his pathetic body, he saw what inhabited his surroundings: white maggots feasting on fresh corpses in a sea of blood and black. Endless death. Abram could hear the whispers of his mother. Long since passed, the words she cried were a reminder of something important she had once said to him, long ago. The woman then appeared in the sea of endless death. She was screaming, being consumed by fire. Her pleads for help were drowned out by her cries of agony and pain.

"Please boy, let us keep this conversation civil. I enjoy the culture and traditions set forth by your society. Now, you being my guest, I wish to honor them. Surely you could grant me the luxury of having an amiable guest, for it is not often that I have them." The beast smiled.

Fifteen seconds was all it took to bleed Abram dry of his soul. All that was left was the shell of a man. A once highly regarded soldier that had climbed to the top of the ranks within the UIGN was now a full-fledged, obedient corpse under Naberius.

"Tell me father, what does God ask of me?" Abram obliged with a blank stare.

Naberius smiled. "To act justly and to love mercy and to walk humbly with your God."

Chapter 6
On a Pale Horse

The excitement and ambition from the day before died with the hundreds slaughtered by the savage natives. All that was left was fear of what could be next. The crew of block sixty-five dug into the ground while hundreds of military escorts trained their weapons down into the hole of the dig site.

Every time Ness thrust his shovel into the dirt, he was uncertain if he would uncover a trap door and fall down into the unknown. He wouldn't be the first. Early that morning, three people fell into separate pre-dug holes. Luckily, the drop was not very far for the three and they were retrieved out safely with only scrapes and minor broken bone fractures.

A tall, dark skinned man with a bald head dug next to Ness. "How many of the guards do you think I could snap the necks of before they obliterate me into dust?" he inquired out loud as he peered over his shoulder.

"Excuse me?" Ness asked, thrown off by the question.

"I am sure I could cut through the neck of one with my shovel and grab his weapon," the man explained, as if he had calculated the scenario hundreds of times in the hours they spent working that morning.

Ness backed away from the man. "Are you crazy? They are here to protect us from those bugs!"

"If those bugs come from the ground once more, do you think these guards would swoop in and save us? Or reign fire from above--killing us alongside those creatures in this pit of *sweat* and *shit*?" Hatred burned in the eyes of the dark-skinned man who resented all forms of authority. His rant gained momentum and those around him slowed down in their work to better listen in. "Do you think these guards are here to defend us or slaughter us if we were to stop working? We have all made a grave mistake, selling ourselves for the empty promise of safety and freedom in a new world." He spit, throwing his shovel down and glaring at one of the guards that stood above.

The construction manager noticed the squabble and approached from behind. His oily, bald head profusely dripped sweat down into his bushy eyebrows. They collected the moisture and began to look like soggy, squishy worms atop his face.

"What's going on here?" the manager demanded.

Ness looked down at the dirt and continued to dig, trying his best to refrain from taking part in the conflict.

"I am done," The dark-skinned man stated, his nostrils flaring in anger.

One of the guards from above, seeing the argument below, jumped down into the hole.

"What the hell are you powder muffins doing?" he taunted the crew.

Thank God, Ness thought. *This will get resolved quickly so we can all just move along.*

The manager raised his hand with a finger extended and opened his mouth to take control of what he thought was his dig site, "I am in charge of these men, I can handle-"

The guard quickly cut him off with a hollered fit of anger. "You are in charge of nothing, you blob of lard. The sooner you motherfuckin' twats realize this, the sooner you can get back to work on this dig site so that we may set up a base to defend you spineless, worthless pigs with our own lives!"

He picked up a shovel and pushed the handle deep into the fat manager's stomach, forcing him to take the tool in hand. He raised his rifle, putting the end of the barrel against the fat man's cranium.

"I... I... I," The manager stuttered.

"Shut your fat ... fu...fu...fucking face," the guard said, mocking the man's stutter, "and dig," he finished with a hoarse whisper.

The manager, now standing alongside Ness and the darker man, began to dig, closing his eyes in fear of the weapon pressed against his skull.

Looking right at Ness, the dark-skinned man picked up his shovel and spat with a smirk, "What did I tell ya?"

***

Aisha woke up to bright flashlights being shined directly into her eyes. "Hey! What the hell?" she bitched in a temporary blindness.

"Looks like we are all set. You two are dismissed," said a woman's soft voice.

Aisha could hear the footsteps of two people walking out of the room. The sound of hydraulic doors closing behind them suggested she was aboard New Horizon.

Slowly regaining her sight, she could make out a blurry woman in a bleached lab coat. She was in a medical bay; luminous white lights above illuminated every square inch of the room.

"How are you feeling?" the woman asked as she tapped away on a thin glass tablet.

"What is it with medical lighting being so damn bright?" Aisha said, squinting and blinking her eyes back into full function. The lady doctor ahead was tall and thin with black, square glasses over her blue eyes. Her brown hair was pulled back in a ponytail and she had a strange scar across her forehead.

"We doctors like to see everything," the women joked.

"Yeah, what and ensure-" She paused, looking down to her left arm. It was silver and larger than before. It was seemingly similar to a regular arm of flesh yet consisted of cold, metal plating and strong mesh kevlar intertwined. From the ball of her shoulder blade, down to her five fingers, this new addition was foreign.

"I take it you can see just fine," the doctor said with a smile.

It was in that moment Aisha's memory of the events that landed her here returned.

"How long have I been here?" Aisha questioned--now in a much softer tone.

"You came in last night, after the attack, and the sun is rising now. So, you have been here all night. I am not sure exactly how long though," the doctor answered.

"What happened with that?" Aisha continued questioning.

"A lot of lives were lost, but everyone from above assures us that the situation is being handled properly, and so here we are, safe and sound."

Aisha sat upright and pressed the thoughts from her head. She looked back down to her arm as she raised it up and off the table. "It feels heavy," she said.

"You will get used to it when your muscles begin to adapt in the coming days," the doctor comforted.

Aisha slowly bent each finger inwards and rolled her knuckles. She gently pounded the metal table she was atop. What she thought was a gracious tap was actually a heavy smash, caving in and placing a large dent in part of the table. "Sorry about that," she apologized.

"It's ok. You will have to attune to your increased strength with that thing."

Aisha toyed some more with the prosthetic, swinging it around. The thing could be considered a weapon by most.

Aisha smirked as she clenched her fist and raised her forearm up and down. "This thing is better than the original one God gave me."

"Who is not to say God granted you this new and improved one?" the doctor countered. She was not paying much attention to Aisha as she fixated her gaze on the data stream that sped quickly across the screen of the glass tablet in her hands. The numbers reflected calculations in correlation to the new ligaments' performance.

"Everyone should get one of these," Aisha said with a laugh. "Hell, I am tempted to cut off my other arm to score a second one."

"Maybe if someday we could afford it," the doctor said with a chuckle. In a more serious tone, she continued, "You are very lucky to be granted such a piece of technology. Most civilians and military members alike receive very basic prosthetics to counter loss of limbs. Orders directly came from the vice admiral to rig you up with this. She had to pull some strings to have a couple military scientists strip some mech tech and refit it to be compatible with our stuff."

Aisha looked up to the doctor, "She did?"

"Mmhhmm. We had ya on the table, were about to cut you up and refit you with the basic stuff, then I got the call that said to wait a bit."

Why would she pull strings for me? Why would she care at all what happens to me, especially if she has to deal with the mess that happened last night? Aisha wondered.

"One of your comrades retrieved a piece of your companion drone that was apparently equipped with stealth tech," The doctor said as she pointed over to the other side of the room, where a large sphere sat cut in half on a counter.

Pisces had been Aisha's companion since day one of training for this mission. She had befriended that drone long before having ever met Tyler, Kaito, and the others. Originally, the drone consisted of three orbs that interconnected with a Y-shaped frame. All that was left was a single sphere that sat cut in half on the table with its internal wiring missing. The top of each half was melted away from the acid that consumed the rest of the body.

"Anyway, it was made important that some robotics specialists try to salvage the tech from your drone, which I guess they were capable of doing. So let's see if that works as intended," the doctor said eyeing Aisha, who looked at what was left of her robot friend.

"What do you mean?" she asked, turning back towards the doctor.

"Well, when connecting nerves and muscle to your new arm, we had to splice a few of the originals to fit properly and control what they rigged up here. So given our approach in wiring you up, the activation of this stuff should feel almost as if you are controlling an extra extremity. It *should* turn on and off when you try and make a fist, tense your bicep, and roll your wrist down and out."

"What will activate?" Aisha asked dumfounded as she followed the steps instructed.

Again and again she performed the sequence with nothing happening.

"Not so much doing that action in a literal sense, but your brain telling your arm to do it. There is a single piece of wiring connected into a spliced section of tissue and nerve," the doctor explained.

"I don't get it," Aisha confessed as she continued all the steps in randomized order.

Then suddenly, the girl felt her body go cold as her eyes bulged wide in surprise from the overwhelming feeling of a sharp pain. A brief shock overtook her entire body. She had fully cloaked herself. Just as efficient as Pisces had done for her, she had done for herself. She jumped off the table and appeared to the doctor only as a faint blur of movement.

"Excellent, we are the first human beings to successfully integrate stealth tech directly into a human being," the doctor chuckled triumphantly.

Aisha's cloak dropped and she returned to a state of one hundred percent parency.

The doctor continued, "It does draw immense power directly from your heart, so it can't last forever. Given that you just woke from being under, your heart can't keep it up for too long for now; but when you get back to feeling like yourself you should be capable of sustaining the power draw in much larger increments."

Aisha was speechless. *This is simply amazing*, she thought.

***

After hours of walking in the dry-yet-cool morning air, Leon, Kaito, and Tyler approached their destination.

"There it is," Leon said, pointing down into a valley at a black hole that rested in the side of a small mountain.

A lot of planet Flare consisted of hills and mountains on the outer edge of desert landscapes. Even the young mountains of Flare greatly triumphed in size over the largest ones found on Earth.

"At least we don't have to climb it," Tyler said as he looked up to the peak, which scaled up through the clouds.

"Never did scale Everest back on Earth. Always kicked myself for not doing it, but doing so would be a walk in the park compared to this terrain," Leon added.

"And just think, the kids of tomorrow will consider this the norm. You tell them about Earth back home, they will just laugh," Tyler pointed out.

The three of them continued towards the cave for a little over an hour until reaching the entrance. Eerie drips of water echoed out from the pitch black unknown with the steady rhythm of a heartbeat.

"So, why can't we just send Aries in there alone to grab the map. I mean, she even has night vision," Kaito raised.

"We can't afford to lose another AI drone. Let's go," Leon ordered with no hesitation to even consider Kaito's suggestion.

The three entered the cave and flipped their weapons' flashlights on. At first glance, the interior looked very typical of a standard cavern, but on closer observation Tyler could see hieroglyphics carved out above canals that were stained red.

Taking his right hand off his rifle, Tyler wiped a gloved finger along one of the aqueducts. The red stains were still sticky and wet. He smeared the substance against his pants and clasped his fingers again around his rifle.

"It stinks worse than I remember," Kaito said, covering his mouth as if about to vomit in disgust.

"Shut up and focus," Leon snapped.

Tyler scanned the cave which, aside from its grotesque stink, was almost a refreshing location to be. The air was much colder here than out in the open, under the scorching hot sun.

Stalactites hung from the roof and steadily dripped the condensation they collected from the air's moisture. There were even bats. Tyler froze. "Those bats are the size of a small child," Tyler said.

"Told ya," Kaito whimpered.

"If you want to be afraid of some bats, maybe you shouldn't have signed up for traveling to an unknown fucking planet. Hell, you could have ventured to Australia for big, scary bats," Leon threatened and blustered.

Kaito was obviously terrified of the things and rightfully so. They definitely gave Tyler the creeps. While the bats native to the country of Australia back on Earth were indeed big, they were infants compared to these monstrosities that hung suspended above. But in the end, he figured it best to stay quiet from here on, as Leon was clearly getting annoyed.

"Alright, Aries, start with the laser scan first. Then we will move on to sonar," Leon instructed Tyler's bot.

The drone flew up to the center of the large cavern room and began projecting small red lasers in every direction. As they moved throughout and forward, the strings of light lit up more of the bats--each one seemingly bigger than the last. No sign of the bugs that had attacked the night before. Tyler couldn't shake the feeling of being watched as the three of them and the two drones continued on deeper into the unknown.

Random pockets of a thick, tall, red, grassy-looking type of plant swayed back and forth. The air had a draft, but not so much that these plants should be flowing in the manner that they were. Tyler reached out and touched one. It quickly wrapped gently around his hand. It didn't seem to be any type of threat, but it was strange to say the least. One of the brown, spikey lizards he had seen the day before out in the sun was on the wall behind some of the brush. Tyler touching the plant frightened the lizard, and it ran fast down the wall towards Kaito.

A bat above silently swooped down and Kaito, for a moment, lost it. "Oh, fuck!" he screamed as he raised his weapon into the air to annihilate the bat that dove down towards his head.

Leon spun around. His flashlights lit up Kaito and his surroundings.

Tyler jumped towards Kaito, swatting his rifle off to the side so that it pointed to the ground as the bat latched on to the lizard and dragged it up into the air and off into the darkness.

"Relax, Man, it wasn't going for you," Tyler comforted. "Besides, if it were, Libra would have blocked it and probably fried the damn thing."

Kaito was breathing heavy. He shouldn't have yelled-- they were supposed to be quiet after all, and his drone was literally one of the best defensive units ever created. It was simply a ball of energy that could absorb damage and was capable of frying just about anything it touched to a crisp. Tyler figured if Aries were equipped with Libra's defensive tech, he himself wouldn't be afraid of much anything this planet had to offer, but she was not.

Leon became even more irritated and just continued on ahead.

For a guy always so calm, cool, and calculated, Leon is totally on edge. The vice admiral must have really dug her claws into him, Tyler thought.

***

Ness was unsure how long he had been digging. At some point in the day, his brain had just clicked into automatic mode. Tired, with no sweat left in their bodies to perspire out, the crew continued on, running off stimpacks and their canteens of water, which were consumed and empty almost as soon as the people were seldom allowed to fill them up.

He would glance over his shoulder every thrust of his shovel to see one mech patting down the earth, making the section they dug out smooth and flat while a second one mixed cement and began to pour it in. Another crew, from another block, smoothed out the cement foundation.

What I would give to be in that block, Ness thought. Though if he were, he would not be able to watch over his younger brother, who was still back at the ship doped up on painkillers for the day. Lucas was scheduled to rejoin the others in work tomorrow. Until then, Ness couldn't help but feel envious of anyone who didn't have to be out in this heat swinging at the dirt for however long he consecutively had.

Completion was in grasp as they approach the end of their designated day one zone. Ahead, a crew laid asphalt roadways interconnecting the multiple construction sites, while another one assembled large, metallic pillars with strange, flat, angular roofing. A pillar was placed at each end of every rectangular dig zone. Ness assumed the pillars were the basin to defensive magnetic shielding. When activated, they would project a transparent shield around the buildings, protecting them from the firestorms or any other incoming harmful assault for that matter.

Just a couple more hours and he would be done for the day. His crew would be the first to complete their task, and he was kind of proud of that. Not that there was any comradery to be found. Everyone working was too exhausted and afraid to engage in any form of conversation. They just kept digging.

The ground began to gently shake and Ness felt his stomach drop into his feet.

Another attack, he thought. He wasn't the only one to panic. Everyone around him stopped digging. Some even held their shovels as if to use them as weapons, to spear and swing at whatever was about to erupt from the ground.

Ness clenched his fingers so tightly around the handle of his shovel that he felt as though they were going to snap right off. He wasn't going to die in this pit today. He would decapitate every last one.

"Get back to work, you pussies," a guard called down, "It's just the warp gate," he taunted with a scowl.

Ness felt stupid. The looks on the workers around him were similar in their embarrassment, but Ness figured it was for damn good reason that they were afraid when the soil beneath their feet abruptly started shaking.

Even being a mile away, they could hear the warp gate begin to scream and howl up into the sky as the ground continued to rumble. It looked like it could explode at any minute and vaporize them all as its hum screeched louder and louder for about ten minutes, and then it just stopped altogether.

Up in the sky, silently floating, was a carrier: the second one to arrive. It sat there motionless for about five minutes before descending down behind New Horizon.

That's kind of exciting, Ness thought. *One step closer to having a city with people, and friends, and food.*

***

Aisha spent the day regaining her strength in a recovery medical bay after her night of being under surgery. All afternoon she forced her brain to accept the fact that her new arm was here to stay. She didn't dislike the new addition, but it was a radical change that she would have to embrace and get used to.

Restless to get back to work, she hopped out of bed and walked over to a pile of fresh clothes resting atop her armor and sword--all of which was set aside for her for when she was feeling a hundred percent. She was forced to drag along tubing that fed nanobots into her spine to travel up her body, fight infection and repairing tissue.

"Looks like you are doing well," said the voice of her female doctor, who had entered the room unnoticed. "You know you are supposed to be resting. You do not want to push yourself too far this early on and risk your body rejecting its latest addition."

"I feel fine though, and the more I use it, the more natural it feels."

Aisha picked up the clothing from the table with her dominant organic arm and used her artificial one to unbutton the uniform with precision.

"Very nicely done, I didn't think you would be capable of the precise stuff for a few days at least..."

Aisha's brain felt as though it was going to explode from her skull with the amount of focus she had to muster and strain to perform the task correctly. She didn't want to admit it and risk having to stay in the chamber any longer than she had already. Being bedridden was worse than dying to her. She had to get out and do *something*, anything.

Observing her struggle to put the uniform on over the tubing that fed into the basin of her spine, the doctor forced a smile. "What are you going to do? Wheel that nano injection machine out of here with you, too?" The doctor approached the girl and put a warm hand on her back. "This is going to feel," she paused, "strange." One after another, she quickly and painlessly pulled the long needles that ran the piping into Aisha's backside out. They disconnected with a sliding motion that felt cold and hollow. The doctor was right, nothing could prepare her for the odd feeling of something being removed from within her spine.

"What about the bots?" Aisha asked, troubled, as she realized any that were injected now had no way out.

"They are designed to dissolve in a matter of hours when their source of entrance is disconnected," the doctor comforted.

Aisha fixed her armor over her clothing, it was much easier than buttoning her shirt and, when she was done, she looked in the mirror and smiled in triumph for what she had accomplished.

Today I managed to dress myself a day after cutting my own arm off, she thought cheerfully. This was the first time she had looked at herself with the outside perspective a mirror provided and, in doing so, she noticed that her hair was shorter. She had been so preoccupied with her arm she hadn't even noticed until now the haircut she was given while under surgery. *Must of had to shorten it to make the procedure easier and more sanitary,* she figured as she toyed with the short, choppy brown do, *I kind of like it though.* She looked back over to the table where her sword sat in its sheath and picked it up with her right hand.

"I am told you are naturally dominant in your right hand. You are lucky you didn't lose the arm you swing that thing with," the doctor said with a wide smile.

She is right, Aisha thought. *I can't fire a gun accurately to save my own life, let alone defend anyone else's.*

"While I would like to see you rest a bit more, it is clear those are not your intentions. So when you are ready, the vice admiral requested you see her. She will be surprised to see you so soon, I am sure. I told her you wouldn't be ready to return to work for a few days."

She wants to see me? But why? Aisha wondered as she unsheathed her blade to inspect it for the first time since yesterday's gruesome fight.

There was dry blood all over its long, curvy body. Constructed with rare metals not of Earth, it was as close to being unbreakable as any blade ever constructed by man, and guaranteed to never lose its sharp edges. It was light, quick through the air, and all too devastating against the flesh of man. It held true even against those bugs in the conflict that served to cake the blade in blood. The blade was her companion in the thick of it all, and was a marvelous weapon indeed.

And to think I never gave you a name, she thought. Her eyes scanned the room and her attention was caught by the table furthest from where she stood where the fragments of her dead drone still sat scattered about.

"I shall call you, Havoc," she whispered to the blade, "And together, we shall avenge our old friend."

Chapter 7
Shadow Boxing

Leon glared down into the darkness of the tunnel ahead as Aries continued her scan. Her red lasers lit up various portions of the walls. Even the cracks and crevices of the cavern were absorbed into a master file that mapped out every detail of the cave they continued to explore.

The three men and two bots had gone deep enough in that they could no longer see the entrance. So far, they had only seen giant lizards and bats that mostly kept to themselves. This was okay with Leon, though part of him would love nothing more than to massacre more of those locusts and their maggot-looking friends. Keeping what was left of his squad safe in this dark and morbid place felt light years more important.

So far so good, he thought.

Aries's lasers would occasionally illuminate the men's faces: Kaito had a permanent look of concern and Tyler a look of wonder. Leon's own face harbored a scowl. His bushy brows slanted above his eyes, which squinted in an attempt to make out every shadow off in the distance.

He rubbed his forehead with his wrist in an attempt to comfort the splitting headache that had suddenly set in. The hair on his upper lip felt wet; he dabbed it with his forearm and looked down in the darkness. Blood. His nose was dripping a good amount.

"Tyler, take the lead," Leon said as he holstered his pistols and plugged the oozing faucet of blood with his gloves.

"Are you ok?" Kaito gasped.

"Just keep moving," Leon barked.

The men silently continued forward into unchartered territory. They walked for another fifteen minutes, straining to make out silhouettes. Their flashlights would dismantle the unknown into nothingness, yet spark more shadows in other directions. If fear were the battle, they were losing the war.

Aries broke their silence, "The tunnel ahead breaks into three separate paths."

"Stop your laser scanning and begin sonar pings," Leon commanded.

The three men stopped walking as the drone quickly followed orders. It pinged ahead using sonar to generate a rough idea of what was further down each tunnel.

"I am detecting a large opening a quarter mile ahead via the far rightmost tunnel."

"Is it an exit to the surface?" Leon asked. If so, then they had failed in accomplishing what they had set out to do. Exploring and generating a map of a cave filled with bats and lizards was far from the objective of discovering the hideaway of the creatures that attacked New Horizon the night before.

"No, we are a little over two and a half miles underground. It seems to be an opening that leads into a very large chamber."

LED lights along Aries's front side began to strobe as they changed from their typical blue hue to a red color that indicated her processing power was being bogged down. She was dedicating more CPU power and memory to the sonar pings to get a better idea as to what lay ahead.

"It is an enormous chamber," she informed, "perhaps multiple miles in width. I will not be able to get an accurate layout due to its size, but there does seem to be a lot of alien activity."

"This is it. We actually found it," Tyler said with enthusiasm.

"We have to get eyes on it one way or another," Leon said softly.

It was a truth none of them wanted to hear.

"If we call in the bombing of this cave and it proves to be nothing more than an ecosystem of plants and animals, then we will find ourselves in a world of trouble. The vice admiral will be the least of our worries compared to the crucifixion the political bureaucrats will sentence us to. Not to mention, setting off bombs underground would be a surefire way to piss off those giant bugs and provoke a second attack. We must be sure that this is their home before we call it in."

Aries disengaged her sonar pings and descended to the ground for a minute to recharge her power core.

"We have two ways of doing this," Leon explained. "Option A, we continue down in and check it out for ourselves, or Option B, we send Aries the rest of the way to confirm. She is linked into Tyler's nervous system, so he can see through her as long as they do not get too far apart. What do you guys think?"

Leon knew the answers both men would give before he asked the question. Tyler would not want to gamble with the life of his drone, while Kaito would rather that than bet with all of their own lives.

Sure enough, after five minutes of debate, the decision was a stalemate. Leon expected this and turned to the drone and asked, "What's your call, Aries?"

He also knew what she would say. Lacking emotions, robots had a sense of fearless heroism about themselves and Aries was not one to shy away from risk of death.

"Yes, I am ok with that," she agreed.

Sometimes that is how you lead, Leon thought.

This was an early lesson he had learned back in his training: to know who you are working with and how to set them up at times to do what you want them to do without them realizing that you had decided their fate already.

"That's bullshit," Tyler complained in losing the argument. "The entire reason we are down here is because you said we couldn't risk losing any more drones."

"And I meant what I said when I said it," Leon defended as he began stroking his beard. "But I don't see much risk in sending her the rest of the way to get eyes on a target on our behalf. What would be more dangerous is for us all to approach the chamber. If we did that, surely we would get caught. She can get in and out quickly and quietly. Different circumstances call for different actions."

Shaking his head, Tyler slung his rifle around his back and took a deep breath. "I haven't done this in a while," he added as he closed his eyes.

"It's ok. She will do all the work, just relax and observe. Aries, be sure to stay up and out of sight," Leon said, putting a hand on Tyler. "Grab hold of his other side, Kaito, so he doesn't fall down."

Aries drifted off into the darkness as Tyler let out a gasp, opening his eyes. They were purely white, rolled back into his skull. His vision was no longer his own, but entirely hers.

Usually, major advancements in the fields of science and technology were fueled by military research. Human history had always reflected that statement in a truthful manner. Their desires to kill one another was always one of the most powerful fuels man had stored within, but sometimes good things were developed by good people.

A Swedish chemist named Alfred Nobel in 1867 invented dynamite. Originally designed as a solution to use nitroglycerin in a safe manner for mining and construction, Nobel actually feared his legacy would be left tarnished in the history books as that of an enabler of human atrocities, for mankind would use his invention to kill one another. In his dying will, he set up a prize fund called The Nobel Prize, to give praise to inventors and contributors of greatness, in an attempt to keep the spotlight focused in a positive manner.

In the year 2045, a Russian man by the name of Vladimir Karkorov took ophthalmology to a whole other level when he figured out how to counter human-born blindness via fusing a human's eyesight with the cam feed of robotics. Eventually Karkorov won a Nobel Peace Prize for his works but, much like Alfred Nobel, Karkorov's invention was gulped up by the armies of the world for use in warfare. What Tyler and Aries were doing was an example of Karkorov's invention. An invention now actively used in the fields of warfare.

Impressive stuff, Leon thought.

"How you doing, Pal?" Kaito asked, breaking the moment of silence.

"Good. She has her night vision active and is approaching the opening. It seems very bright and obscure, though. Aries, turn off your night vision," he paused "Yeah, that's better. There is natural light in the opening. She is slowing down now as she gets closer... be careful." He hesitated again, watching as his vision led him closer to the opening with eyes that were not his by birthright. "Ok. She is at the entrance. Wow," he said with a dramatic pause, "It's an entire city! There are pillars of fire scattered about for lighting and hundreds, if not thousands, of buildings. This is incredible."

"The bugs?" Leon pressed.

"Yes, they are everywhere. It's a metropolis," Tyler said, amazed by what he was seeing.

"Good, get her out of there quick. We are going to cleanse that entire city by fire."

***

Kio-Kai entered a bar nestled deep in the city of Val-Muel with the help of Lai-Kai.

He could flutter his wings, but walking on his legs was shaky and unpredictably difficult. He was injured. The two of them found seats in the crowded establishment and ordered drinks. A twitcher drone approached them and offered them each a stone chalice of icor-- a mixture of lifeblood and a ground-up, intoxicating herb called leach.

"How you feeling?" Lai-Kai asked as she took a swig of her drink.

Kio-Kai's antennae and eyes both drooped in exhaustion. He had lead the assault the night before against the humans as instructed by Naberius and, in doing so, had collected a variety of minor scrapes and wounds as well as one slightly more pressing in concern. His legs had been bashed in and broken by the brute he helped wrestle to the ground and capture.

He took a sip of the icor and could feel the healing properties of the lifeblood get straight to work in repairing his injuries, while the numbing qualities of the leach soothed his aches.

"I will be fine," Kio-Kai said.

"I thought the assault would be easier," she said as she downed more of the icor and ordered another round for them. "I mean, we executed the plan well, but when we mapped everything out and went over it," she paused, "I don't know. It just sounded like it was going to be an easy win."

"Yea, that's how it goes. The plan always sounds better than the resolve," he said, sipping his second drink. "We suffered a lot of casualties, but we accomplished what we set out to do, I guess."

Lai-Kai tapped all six fingers of her left hand on the table. "There was no way we could have known they used projectile weapons...I mean, the one you found and captured yesterday morning, did it have weapons?"

"No, it was already injured and was an easy, quick kill."

The two finished their drinks and ordered a third round. At this rate, they would be drunk by high noon, but that was the plan: a day of drinking in an attempt to self-justify their actions of the day prior.

A familiar hunter approached the two. He was much darker in color compared to Kio-Kai and had a beard of spikes that hung from the sides of his cheeks down past the base of his chin. "Kio-Kai and Lai-Kai? I haven't seen you two since we were little larva in the spawning pools."

It was a common expression in Vai-Zik society, though not technically correct. Jek-Xio was approximately the same age as the two of them, but he wasn't born of the same queen and thus hadn't spawned in the same pools of creation. Not to mention that the last time the three collectively saw each other was two or three years back when a couple dozen members of their two clans were assigned the tedious mission of eradicating a stone giant intruder from an early Vai-Zik expansion settlement to the north.

"Hey Jek-Xio. Yeah, it's been awhile. How is Saf-Xio?" Lai-Kai asked of a member who had his entire body from the stomach down severed off on the mission they partook in together years back.

"Yeah, he is doing well. Not only did the bastard live, he regrew his abdomen and legs. He is getting better every day in strengthening them, too. I will never forget that mission, and we never did kill that damn stone giant," he said with a laugh.

"Yeah, well, we were supposed to get rid of it and we did. One does not simply kill a rock giant," Lai-Kai giggled.

"Aye... for a peaceful nomad, that damned thing sure has killed a lot of Vai-Zik," Jek-Xio said with a frown. "Anyway, what brings you guys to Val-Muel?"

"We just got back from an overlord operation to capture an alien species," Lai-Kai said with just enough sarcasm to make it sound unbelievable.

Jek-Xio laughed, "You take your orders from the overlords now? Does that mean you have become a queen already?"

Kio-Kai fired his eyes up from the table over into Lai-Kai's. He was not so sure that they should be telling others about the communication or commandments they had received from Naberius. Hell, he didn't know much of what she or he were supposed to do about the whole ordeal, period. They were so quick to abide and resolve that which was requested of them, that they never stopped to think about the consequences, let alone question the end result.

Such is loyalty, Kio-Kai thought.

Though Naberius's legion of overlords, or daemons as he called them, were secretive, the Vai-Zik bore no secrets, and so Lai-Kai did not care to begin doing so today. She ignored Jek-Xio's sassy comment and chose to talk about the assault.

"Yeah, strange little squishy creatures, sacks of flesh, meat, and bone. They seem to be pretty far technologically advanced--which I suppose is to compensate for just how damn hideous and weak they are," Lai-Kai continued. "They landed to the west. We managed to harvest a bunch and even brought one back alive."

Registering that she was being earnest, Jek-Xio couldn't help but confirm his realization out loud. "Wait, you are being serious?" He pulled up a stool from another table and took a seat between them to listen to her story of the assault.

***

Aisha made her way to the vice admiral's command chamber and was stopped at the door by two emotionless men in all-grey armor.

AI drones, Aisha thought. *I didn't know these things still existed.*

A nasty series of events caused public outcry years back that regulated that artificial intelligence drones were not to be constructed to resemble men or women.

Nonetheless, here they were, standing in front of her. Their armor being all grey was a sign that they were, in fact, robotic, as it was accustomed that their color reflect their personality: a clear slate of emotion.

"Good afternoon, Miss Sayegh," they simultaneously greeted her in a flat, monotonous accent as they moved aside to allow her passage.

How did they know my name? she wondered. *Are they that advanced in biometrics scanning?*

The hydraulic door they stood in front of opened and she was quick to scurry through to escape the uncomfortable situation of having to converse with them. They creeped her out more than facing a seven-foot locust. *That,* she could deal with. She could slice those bugs in half one after another for days on end, but an emotionless robot that looked like a man and was smarter than a thousand men put together was just a pill she could not swallow, at least not today.

She was unsure if being in this room was any better than being out with those robots as she looked around and noticed she was beyond out of place.

The vice admiral was sitting on a control counter, reaming out a woman below her, who wore a headset and relayed what was being shouted to her to someone on the other end of the call.

The room was large, but had a very claustrophobic feel to its layout. Hundreds of thousands of buttons, data servers, and LED lights filled the walls. Screens with hundreds of tabs of spreadsheets took up every square inch of spare space, and a handful of the ship's top engineers plugged away at buttons, keyboards, and voice calls.

Vice Admiral Fox noticed Aisha at the entrance of the data room and jumped off from where she sat, still chewing out the poor girl with the headset. She walked towards Aisha.

What can this be about? Aisha thought, nervous of the conversation that was about to transpire. To suggest that the vice admiral was intimidating was an understatement to say the least.

"When I requested you come see me, I was informed you would not be well enough to be out for some time," she said with a smile, extending her hand as a means of more personalized welcoming.

She was left handed. This meant Aisha had to use her prosthetic arm to abide by the means of greeting.

Aisha extended her hand and delicately shook the vice admiral's in return. She was careful not to squeeze too tight and risk ripping Fox's hand clean off. Aisha could actually *feel* the exchange of handshake within her fake arm.

Incredible, she thought.

"How are you feeling? You look well."

"I am okay," Aisha said. "A little tired, but I am getting used to the change and excited to get back out to work."

"I am sure you are," Fox said with a smile. "Anyway, you are probably wondering why I asked to see you. I am a little busy at the moment, but I could use ten minutes away from all of this, so why don't you come with me to the deck and we can chat."

Aisha followed Fox across the data room and through a door that led to the ship's deck. If the prior room felt claustrophobic, this one would be considered agoraphobic in its layout. The room was massive and three fourths of the walls were constructed with solid glass as to allow people the ability to see out ahead of the ship when piloting it. Only a small handful of controls resided in designated command stations throughout the room. A large, black table that looked to be constructed entirely of thick glass lay at the heart of the room.

"Have you ever been on the deck of a vessel this size?" asked the vice admiral with her arms crossed behind her back.

Aisha shook her head. "No. It's much bigger than I imagined."

"It is, and sometimes it doesn't feel big enough," she paused to glance around the large room. Its three enormous shatterproof windows allowed in so much natural light that the deck had a sense of warmth to it.

"I watched the tapes from the assault the other night," she continued as her eyes drifted over Aisha's face, as if reading tiny letters that were printed across her skin. "Do you know how many of those locusts you killed?"

Aisha felt she was being interrogated and quickly became very uncomfortable. She didn't think this was going to be an ambush of admitted guilt.

"I applied a thermal filter to the feed and watched you execute twenty-three. We counted over a hundred total kills and you were directly responsible for taking out a quarter of them by yourself. Impressive."

Okay, so maybe she isn't grilling me, Aisha thought, perplexed.

"This planet has shown to be more dangerous than anticipated. While I can deal with the challenges at hand, and am ready to confront whatever may be in store, the greatest danger I feel is what we brought with us."

"What we brought with us? I do not follow."

"Even though all the civilians are separated into cell blocks on all of the carriers, there still seems to be a unified uprising in the works. What little intel we have gathered shows a high percentage of chance that they will target higher ranking members of the military and assert themselves into the position of power, then spark a full-blown rebellion to overthrow the political seats within the UIGN."

"But why would they do that?" Aisha questioned.

"It's the ole saying, you give a mouse a cookie, he gets parched and will always follow up by asking for a glass of milk. We gave these people a future, a way off Earth in its hour of destruction, jobs and hope for a new life, but now they want more."

"What does this have to do with me?"

The vice admiral hopped up onto one of the command tables. They were not intended to be sat upon, but this was her ship and she could do as she pleased. In doing so, she came off to Aisha as being slightly more relaxed and welcoming: a feature Aisha did not know the vice admiral was capable of showing.

"I want you re-assigned as my personal detail. You won't serve me in errands or other petty matters, simply defend myself and the ship's bridge, which is the main access point to all of New Horizon's data and greater communication systems."

Aisha nodded her head. She knew this type of inquiry was more or less a command. She highly doubted refusal of this request was an option.

The door behind them opened and in walked one of the humanoid AI guards.

"Miss Fox, you have an incoming transmission from a recon squad led by Leon Fleisher."

"Patch it through in here," she said without breaking eye contact with Aisha.

The transparent glass that made up the walls came to life and before them stood Leon with Kaito to his left and Tyler to his right. It seemed so real, anyone that entered the room not knowing this was a call may very well be fooled into thinking the three men were physically present in the room.

"What's the report, Fleisher?" The vice admiral asked as she swayed her feet back and forth, sitting up on the table.

"We found the hive," Leon said with a scowl of determination and differentiation. His beard did little to disguise a faint smirk.

***

Tyler stood beside Leon and Kaito for minutes as Leon sold himself to the vice admiral. It was almost cruel the way she made him look so weak before his peers with her attitude and facial expressions. She had wanted them to go out and look for the insect hive. Perhaps she truly did hope they would not return from their journey.

The live video feed Aries projected in front of them was quite life-like, even in the dimming sun, where they rested just outside the entrance to the cavern they had mapped out.

The vice admiral hopped off the table, stood up straight, and folded her arms across her chest. "And you got eyes on them directly?" she asked.

"Yes," Leon answered with confidence.

"Have your drone send me the rendered map. I will forward it to a pilot. You guys have ten minutes to get away from there."

The session ended.

"Well, that wasn't as rewarding as I had hoped," Kaito chimed in.

Leon scratched his beard and wiped the sweat from his brow. The look on his face seemed to resemble a similar conclusion, as if let down by the lack of honor they had scored.

"So, what now?" Tyler asked, attempting to shift the mood in a different direction. Any would suffice, he figured, given the awkwardness of the situation.

"Well, when we send the data, she will forward the map to her pilot, then he will upload it to a smart bomb that will use the information to guide the missile through the cave and into the heart of that city. In ten minutes, it will be as if it never existed and then, I suppose, we move on as if *they* never existed."

The three of them called pest control. The service was approved and an exterminator was en route. It was not until then that it all sank in for Tyler: the absolute truth that an entire race of beings was about to be erased from history as they knew it.

Part of Tyler wanted to feel guilty and yet, should he feel so terrible for exterminating a nest of cockroaches?

What about a clan of primates? His conscious pled for reason.

Though these creatures looked to be bugs, they were clearly more advanced. Along their own evolutionary track, they would almost fit in a place somewhere between a chimp and a man.

"Come on. Let's get out of here," Leon said, walking ahead. "We should make it back by nightfall."

***

Fox exited through the single door on New Horizon's command deck, retreating back into the data center room, where engineers still plugged away, buried in a sea of controls.

Unsure what to do, Aisha followed.

"Did those two recon pilots that I sent out last night return yet?" Fox barked.

"They are on their way back now," a short man wearing a virtual reality helmet responded.

Aisha wondered what the man could be seeing inside the artificial world projected around his face. The workings of these ships were beyond intricate. Engineers practically had the technology to literally step inside of software, and so she figured he was doing something of the sort.

"Good, reroute them to the following coordinates," she paused, pulling up data on a touchscreen nearby, "delta charlie fiver zero delta orion niner fiver."

She swiped her fingers across the screen a few times and then double-tapped the glass. She concluded her actions via entering a sequence of encrypted code onto the device.

"Forward them this and have them upload it into the head of a nova missile, green light for execute, status change omega lion."

A whole lot of security jargon to fire a missile, Aisha thought.

***

After the longest day of his life, Ness and crew were done with their dig site. They were the first of any crew to accomplish their day one task and the sun had not even yet begun to set. They were rewarded by calling it a done day early.

Assured that 'half days' would never be anything close to a regularity, it felt all the more sweet to be returning to the ship for a shower and some sleep.

Though they came back with a sense of triumph, they were all well past the line of exhausted. There was no cheering or laughing, just long, blank stares as they shuffled back towards the ship in formation.

They returned that late afternoon with twenty-seven fewer a number then they set out with that morning. Heat strokes claimed all twenty-seven lives. While all but eight died to the hypothermic tragedy within minutes, the remaining initial survivors passed away shortly after being transported to a medical bay.

Ness did not know any of them, but he did watch one of the victims fall to the ground and begin seizing around in the dirt like a fish out of water. It was a girl about his age. She was blonde and, if not covered in dirt and filth from a day of digging, she would probably have been quite pretty.

Two days in a row now he had seen death.

He entered the ship. The dramatic difference in temperature of being indoor with the shade and out from the sun's blistering oppressiveness was well beyond the means of refreshing.

They entered their living quarters. Block sixty-five was printed in large red letters above the doorway and as soon as they had entered, people made way to the showers in haste. A line quickly formed and, while Ness would love nothing more than to cleanse himself of the thick layer of dirt and dust that caked his skin, at this moment he would much rather simply sit down. And so he did just that, walking over to his bed, he climbed up into his bunk, fell back, and stared off into the nothingness that was his future.

In that moment, he didn't care about the city they were building or just how 'valuable' and 'necessary' he was to the mission at hand. He didn't give a shit about the families of tomorrow or their children, let alone their children's children. All he wanted was to close his eyes and keep them closed for eternity.

"Hey, Ness," said his younger brother in excitement as he approached the bunk.

Ness rubbed dirt from his eyes and reopened them before forcing himself to get up and climb back down to reality.

"Hey, man," he said, forcing his sore, exhausted body to descend down from the bunk. "You are looking better," he continued as he inspected Lucas' wounds.

"Yeah, I feel better too. Wish they didn't shave my head, but it will grow back. How was work? You look filthy. Why don't you shower?"

Ness forced a smile. "You think that gross water can wash away this dirt from my bones?"

The water used for showering and drinking purposes was endlessly recycled and reused. It was never truly fresh, as carrier ships could not afford to waste a single drop of the liquid that sustained all life.

"Better than nothing," Lucas said.

It was then that Ness noticed a boy about the same age as Lucas was standing beside him. The boy was dressed in fancy, expensive clothing and had a purple electronic wristwatch on his left arm. This signified he was free and paid, or rather his parents paid for his ticket to be aboard New Horizon. Working civilians were assigned to their designated blocks and could not leave, but the rich, free civilians could come and go as they pleased almost anywhere they desired.

His slicked-back blonde hair made his forehead look big compared to the small frame of his body. His eyes scanned Ness as if in disgust for how dirty he was.

"And who are you?" Ness asked.

"Oh, this is Ryan. He is my friend," Lucas cheerfully admitted.

"I heard that a second carrier landed today. Is it true?" The kid asked.

"Yeah," said Ness.

"That's good. Mom says when the city is complete we can go outside. We will have an apartment with a pool and maybe even a dog," said the small blonde boy as he smiled from cheek to cheek.

Is it wrong of me to hate this kid? Ness wondered.

"That's great," Ness said sarcastically. "Looks like the line for the showers is dying down, so I am going to go do that." He listened to the boys converse while he grabbed his bar of soap, a towel, and washcloth.

"Maybe someday, me and my brother Ness will have a dog, too!" Lucas said with excitement.

The harsh reality was, neither Lucas nor Ness would ever own a dog, or an apartment with a pool, for that matter. Hell, Ness didn't even know if the two boys were even going to survive this construction phase, let alone whatever shit future may be in store for them after the city was fully built.

I should cut his arm off and take his data watch. Maybe I could pass as some rich kid and buy me and my brother a peaceful life of ignorance, Ness thought as he bitterly walked off towards the showers.

Chapter 8
Stitches

Kio-Kai crawled out from under what seemed like an endless pile of rocks and debris. His body was broken and his antennae were gone. His face was only partly intact, and he was left crying out in pain.

The city around him was in ruins. All the buildings were gone--even the great colosseum which towered over all the rest, sculpting the city's historic skyline, was replaced with smoldering rock, ash, and smoke. Fallout winds howled and wailed about as sand, dust, and fire obscured any visibility ahead.

His head throbbed and his face stung. Bits of sharp rock were stuck in his chest and he was bleeding badly from the sockets where his antennae once hung. Attempting to remember what had happened, Kio-Kai closed his eyes and tried as best he could to tune out the chaos around him.

I was with Jek-Xio and Lai-Kai. We were in a bar. The last thing I remember was laughing at something Jek-Xio had said about... I don't know... then... a bright light? He thought as his brain frantically tried to make sense of it all.

He spun around and looked down at the pile of wreckage he was buried under merely minutes ago and began digging as if he had gone mad.

"Lai-Kai, Jek-Xio," he called out.

As he dug he began to weep for his friends, fueling him to unravel the earth below at a faster rate. A few minutes passed and in the time he spent digging, his fingers were shaven down to nothing more than bloody stumps from clawing away at the rock below.

At last, he found the twitching arm of a hunter and grasped it.

"I've got you buddy, hold on!" he cried out as he scraped away at more rock to better unearth the survivor.

The wrist of the buried Vai-Zik snapped clean off. Kio-Kai fell backward and screamed out in anger and frustration as the world around him continued to burn.

***

The man wearing the virtual reality headset called out to the vice admiral, who was standing resolute with her arms crossed, staring at a screen that announced the progress of various construction units from the day that were coming to a close.

"It looks like the missile successfully navigated its way through the cavern and reached its destination in the heart of the insect hive."

"Good, one less thing on my plate. I need to see the

pilots. They have been gone almost an entire day and I want to know what they found during their initial recon mission."

Aisha stood watching over the inner workings of the busy room for a few minutes. She tapped her foot, trying to hold in the fact that she had to pee.

Should I just walk off and go? Do I need to ask permission? What do these people do when they have got to go? Do they ever even need to go to the bathroom? Maybe they just wet their pants and continue working throughout the day.

Finally, feeling as though her bladder was going to explode at any given minute, she walked towards the exit. In the hallway just outside the door was a restroom. She prayed either no one would notice her having walked out or, if they had, they would not care in the slightest.

In the stall, she realized going to the bathroom may very well be one of the more uncomfortable tasks she had to endure with her robotic arm. Silly really, that she was equipped and capable of performing some truly incredible feats, but using the restroom was not one of them. When heading back to the data room, she noticed a man and women in aviator uniforms walking towards the doors.

"Woah, look at this," the man said staring at Aisha's arm. "That thing is crazy."

He wasn't just skinny; his entire frame of build was small. His fellow pilot, a female accompanying him, was equally as small but she stood quiet. She started to look Aisha up and down, trying to figure out just what was going on with this tan girl in white and orange armor who had a bionic arm and a sword draped down her side.

"What other robotic parts you sportin', Cutie?" the male pilot said, picking fun of her.

Typically, Aisha would combat insecurities with sarcasm, but her mouth was dry and wordless.

"Your armor is not grey, so you are not AI," the man observed out loud, squinting as if trying to figure out just what exactly she was.

Aisha simply walked back into the room as the two pilots followed her in with awkward stares.

The vice admiral caught eye of her entering the room, "Christ, where have you been?"

Aisha became warm and uncomfortable. How could it be that telling someone you had to go pee could be so nerve racking? She wanted to lie, then stopped herself. She questioned in her head why she would lie about something so insignificant and stupid.

The two pilots approached. "You told us to scout and so we ran until our burners were close to overheating. Lots to see out there."

She wasn't even questioning where I had been. It was a question directed towards those two, Aisha thought, feeling daft.

"Then you had us bomb a cave," the girl reminded.

The two were not afraid of the vice admiral and yet, here Aisha was cowering at the thought of going to the restroom.

"Well, give me the rundown. I have a briefing with the president in ten minutes."

The three left the engineers and the data center and went ahead into the bridge of the ship. Aisha followed and lingered near the doorway as the three talked quickly, just out of ear reach. They leaned over the glass table, which came to life with images they had apparently captured out on their recon mission.

A few minutes passed and then one of the grey, robotic men entered the command bridge, "The president is ready for you."

"Patch it through in here and leave us."

Aisha turned to walk out.

"Not you," Fox said motioning Aisha to come closer.

The door automatically shut behind the drone after he left the room. One of the clear glass windows sparked up, illuminating a perfect image of the president sitting in a chair with one leg over another. He wore black, square glasses below his bushy eyebrows. He held a tablet in one hand and a glass of scotch in the other. Well dressed in a suit and, for the most part quite handsome, he had broad shoulders and a long, muscular neck. An unshaven face and black circles around his eyes suggested he had not slept in some time.

The two pilots backed away from the vice admiral and stood up straight with their hands behind their backs.

Aisha tried doing the same, but she couldn't get her muscles to execute the motion in her bionic arm. So instead, she held it in front of herself in an equally professional manner.

"I hope that you have better news for me now than the last time we spoke," the president said, his voice thick with authority that even the vice admiral could not undermine.

"First and foremost, President Walker, the insect hive was found and destroyed. If any more are found, we will be just as quick in dismantling them."

"Just what I wanted to hear. Now what of the scouting?"

"We found a cluster of active volcanoes that form a ring around the planet's single great sea. Given that the great sea on Flare is composed of mostly lava, the volcanoes that were discovered in a ring around it were not really a surprise. To the east, roughly four hundred miles, lies quite possibly the largest volcano ever discovered in human history. It seemed to be inactive, but hot springs and geysers surrounding the great mountain for many miles suggest perhaps otherwise. We will have to run some tests to fully determine the level of threat it presents, if at all any. So that is on the agenda."

"Did you find running water?"

"We did. We pinged positive for streams, lakes, and ponds, but they were almost all exclusively underground. The few that were discovered above ground were all at the pits of canyons, so they will be equally as difficult to reach and harness."

Next on the screen was the four-legged stone giant that

Aisha had seen the day that she had arrived on Planet Flare. The pilots must have gotten quite close to the beast, as the detail of his being was immaculate. The plants along its backside were truly the most incredible collection of vibrant colors Aisha had ever seen.

"We also discovered a new species."

The screen changed to a distant shot of the giant, one that could capture it in entirety.

"Now, in the background there is a mountain range whose elevation is in the thirty to forty-thousand-foot range that certainly helps in comprehending just how massive this creature is. It appears to be standing upright at just shy of fifteen thousand feet."

The president removed his glasses and rose to his feet with the look of wonder upon his face, "Does it pose a threat?"

"We are unsure. It showed zero interest in our jets, but there is no denying that if this creature approached a city, it would trample right through it with no resistance. Our energy shields were never designed to stop something of this scale."

Walker let out a sigh and began to rub his head.

Hunched over the table, Fox maintained a stare into the eyes of the president. Despite his uncertainties, she was uncertain of nothing. "I know it is difficult to accept, but I think we both know what needs to be done about this. Even if the creature has no interest in us, it is only a matter of time until it accidentally levels a city."

"Who knows that it exists?"

"Just us five," she said implying herself, the president, the two pilots and Aisha.

"Label it as highly classified and handle it as you see fit." He fixed his lenses to his face. "What of the workforce?"

"While the civilian workforce of our carrier is mostly construction units, the populace of the second ship that arrived today are crews that specialize in satellite tech. They are getting to work in the morning constructing and launching the first fifty probes, with an end goal of total planet coverage within two months and six hundred and eighty satellites total. After that, they will move on to small space stations and progress eventually to much larger ones. This puts a little more pressure on acting quickly to handle the giant quietly."

"I will leave you to it, then."

She nodded, stood upright, and saluted. The two pilots did the same and Aisha was slow to follow through, but no one seemed to notice.

The glass returned to its transparent state and the president was gone.

Fox looked down at the table and sighed. "Ok, let's figure out just how we are supposed to vaporize a walking mountain."

"We could do the ole snow speeder harpoon tow cable trick," the male pilot said with an overabundance of sarcasm.

The female pilot raised her eyebrows, "I don't follow."

"You know, against the imperial AT-AT walkers?" he continued, taking a seat at the large table and throwing his feet up on it.

The female pilot stayed silent with a dumb look of confusion.

"Star Wars?" he said, slightly annoyed.

She shook her head, clueless as to what he was rambling on about.

"Late nineteen-hundreds classic? No way, have you not seen it?"

Fox turned to face the two, "How long do you think it will take to find it again?"

The male pilot looked at the vice admiral in horror, still perched back with his feet up on the table, now throwing his hands in the air, "Can you believe this girl has not seen Star Wars?"

Fox was getting annoyed. Flaring her nostrils, she took a

tone of anger, "Focus, you idiot. We are not dealing with some twentieth century fictionalized threat This is a real life monolith-- a living, breathing mountain. Now, we need to act quickly. How long do you think it will take you to track it down again?"

He did not seem to care for her outburst, rather, he took pleasure in watching her become unhinged. "Listen, Aunt Natalia, as you said, it's a moving mountain. It's not going to take long for Lanfen and I to find it again. Let us grab a meal and shower. We have been out flying since the early morning."

He is related to her, Aisha thought, *that makes sense. Explains her toleration towards his asinine personality.*

"Just because I granted my late sister her dying wish of getting you assigned to my command does not mean you get to address me by my first name while on duty-- especially when aboard the bridge of *my* ship."

Aisha looked to the floor and felt grateful she played zero role in this conversation.

"Are you taking out your aggression on us because the rumor is true," he paused looking up from the table and over to her, "That there was an attempt on your life shortly after landing?"

The vice admiral's face maintained its cold stare for a moment as the gears in her mind tried to churn out a reasonable response. "Jason," she said calmly, "If you and Lanfen were not the best two pilots of the thirty aboard this ship," then her tone ruptured into that of anger, "I would be half tempted to strip you of your rank, throw you into construction crew, and see how long your attitude lasts in a life of physical strenuous labor! Don't think I cannot groom two of any of the thirty pilots aboard my ship to take your place. Now get your feet off *my fucking* table and go attend to that giant," she snarled, turning her back to them.

"And how are we supposed to do that?" he asked, folding his arms.

"I don't care, but I do *not* want to see your face again until either *you* or that behemoth is dead," she finished coldly.

***

Kaito, Leon, and Tyler made their way back to base. Aries had informed them that they had a new mission and that there would be a group of soldiers waiting for them at specific coordinates back near New Horizon.

"No rest for the wicked," Kaito remarked as they ventured back.

After hours of walking, the carrier was within eyesight and it looked as though there were now two of them.

Thousands of crews worked away as the sun began to drip out of view from the vast sky. They began to set up their lights for a night of continued labor though, given the brightness of the colossal moon, they really didn't *need* extra lighting.

Tyler was not envious of their work in the slightest. There were plenty of men and women, adults of his own age and older, but the amount of kids and teenagers that ran off of stimpacks for hours upon hours-- tricking their minds into accepting the work as a regularity-- it was something sad that Tyler had never really ever seen before.

The three men and their two drones passed a mech in a pit below who held together steel beams so that a crew of teenagers could weld them into place. Tyler stopped, his rifle slung across his chest and pointed to the ground as per custom of a non-combat zone, and watched them work for a moment.

His gaze was caught by a girl who couldn't be any older than twelve. She dripped sweat in her filthy clothes and was being yelled at by a soldier who pointed a rifle into her belly.

"Since when do soldiers command civilians?" Kaito questioned, then continued, "I don't know about you, but this is not what I expected when signing up for this."

Leon walked on, not noticing the scuffle below or that the other two had stopped to observe it. He had been quiet the whole walk back, as if stuck deep within his own mind in thought.

The soldier struck the girl with the butt end of his rifle. She fell to the ground as he continued screeching above her, showing no sign of mercy towards her as his peers began to laugh, which served to ramp up his outburst of rage even further.

"What could have she possibly done wrong to deserve that kind of treatment?" Kaito asked Tyler.

"She is just a little girl, what could they expect her to possibly do right after twenty hours of working?" Tyler said inaudibly, with his eyes fixed below.

On the ground, the girl cupped her face, which now bled. The man that had struck her knelt down to whisper something in her ear, then he groped the young girl's chest.

Tyler raised his weapon in the air and looked down the rail, taking aim at the soldier just below the neck. No one noticed. The conflict was too far away for any of them to see himself or Kaito standing on the ledge above them. He flipped off his safety.

"What the hell are you *doing*?" Kaito choked out.

Tyler ignored him. The honest truth was, he didn't know. It was as if his soul had left his body and another resided in his flesh. His muscles moved without command from his brain and without hesitation he burst three shots into the soldier's face.

***

The two pilots walked alone down a corridor after leaving Vice Admiral Fox irate on the bridge of the ship.

"You know, you don't have to be such a jerk to her," Lanfen lectured in her broken English accent.

"How was I being a jerk to her?" Jason snickered. "She has been on some psycho power trip ever since the president put her in charge of Project Salvation."

"Well, she does have a lot to deal with and your attitude doesn't help things, especially when she was helping us brainstorm a game plan."

"Still, no excuse to act like a total cunt."

Lanfen shook her head as they continued walking. Reasoning with Jason was futile. His ego was in control of his actions and everything he did was justifiable in his eyes one way or another. It made for a dangerous partnership between herself and him as far as piloting two hellcats went. Her actions were calculated and precise, while his drastic and risky. But there was no denying the guy had a sixth sense in the pilot's seat. They had escaped some close calls together back on Earth fighting in the Onyx Wars that lead up to the Project Salvation launch.

In their mid-twenties, they were perhaps the most experienced pilots in the entire fleet; or at least that is the line Jason would feed Lanfen on a regular basis.

The two entered an industrial elevator shaft made of a solid piece of sheet metal for its ground platform and a few thin steel beams for walls. Jason pounded one of the buttons with the base of his fist, then crossed his arms.

"So, how do you want to handle this giant?" he asked as the elevator whined and moaned to life.

"I really do not know. It's bigger than anything we have ever faced, but as long as we keep our distance we should be okay, I guess, right?"

"Suppose we just go in hot and hope our weapons are good enough," he said with his eyes closed as the lights cast shadows across his face in a strobe like speed from the elevator descending to the ground floor.

The truth was Lanfen was terrified, not of the giant but rather of failure. If they fired upon the giant and failed to kill it, they would surely piss it off. What was to stop it from rampaging towards the newly established colony?

The doors opened and the two exited down into the hangar where their hellcats were undergoing standard minute maintenance. Other than the chipped paint on Jason's from a dangerously close scrape a few years back, both vessels were identical in construction and appearance. Three sets of wings, all various in size and position, were fitted on the small vessels. The six wings total were equipped with additional thrusters and boosters that could be repositioned in the air and accurately controlled to allow for superior directional manipulation.

Both ships had similar weaponry: light lasers attached to their underbellies for dogfights, missile launchers fixed to the smallest of wings, rail guns on the larger ones, and anti-gravity grenade launchers rested in a line on the mid-sized wings that were refined to fire an impressive distance of up to two miles before impact. The small handheld grenades were some of the most devastating in the arsenal. The bomb bay, being able to harbor four nova rockets, contained some of the most advanced and expensive explosives known to man. Guided by a digital mapping to the entrance of the cave, one of these explosives had been fired off into the heart of the bug hive just a few hours earlier.

"Systems good?" Jason called out to one of the chief mechanics on deck as they approached their ships.

The mechanic looked up from his tablet where he scribbled a few notes for himself. "Hmm? Oh yeah, you guys ran them a little longer than recommended, pushing their cores to their limit, but everything seems to check out."

"Good, we are undocking."

"Uhm, well you guys really should let the cores cool a little longer," the mechanic suggested with unease.

"Not an option," Jason said as he climbed up into his cockpit and fit his hololens helmet over his messy hair.

Lanfen scaled up into her vessel and squeezed her helmet over her long, black hair. She strapped herself in then ran her fingers across a line of switches, flipping them into the 'on' position

The light hum of the engines roared to life. Hellcats had some of the quietest engines man had ever conceived, which was especially impressive given just how powerful they were.

"Where are you guys going?" The head mechanic called up.

Bureaucracy dictated he had to record every little thing these beyond expensive aircrafts did.

"We are off to see a man about a horse," Jason called down before sealing off his cockpit.

Lanfen closed the cockpit to her aircraft and engaged a row of switches within the cabin. A full and intricate holo display quickly appeared and surrounded her. A fully digital array of colors and lights laid out the complex navigation controls of her hellcat. She clenched two multidirectional levers in each hand. As the blast doors to New Horizon's shuttle bay opened, Lanfen punched her thrusters forward, sending her aircraft out of the hanger at high velocity, in search for a walking mountain.

***

The soldier that Tyler shot spewed blood quickly from the veins split out of his open neck. His head was gone. Bits and pieces of brain and bone lay scattered on the ground in a pool of red.

His comrades, no longer laughing at the girl, were now panicked--pointing their weapons in all directions. No one but Kaito knew it was Tyler's doing; he still had his suppressor attached to his rifle and they were a good distance away.

He could go, slip away, run and no one would know of the atrocity he had just committed. All he would need to do is shut Kaito up. Hell, Kaito was a coward. He could even kill him if he really had to. Kaito looked on, frozen solid in a state of complete shock.

Tyler drifted the aim of his rifle onto another soldier, who shakily scanned the dusky horizon for the assassin. With a blank slate of emotion, Tyler dropped the soldier with two shots to the chest that tore open his ribcage and sprayed chunks of his insides onto a comrade, who Tyler then fired upon next.

What am I doing? Tyler thought in horror.

Only two soldiers were left of the five that had laughed at, beat, and groped the girl. They now figured out which direction they were being assaulted from and began to return fire. Kaito's bot, Libra, activated her energy shield, absorbing the incoming projectiles, which would have certainly killed both Kaito and Tyler. Tyler's heart felt as though it was pounding so hard it might blow out from his chest as he took his time aiming at the remaining two. He hit them in the limbs-- severing them clean off as if toying with them-- before ultimately ending their lives, insuring his final two kills in his murder spree were as brutal and vicious as possible.

Libra disengaged the shield that granted their safety through the ordeal. Tyler dropped his rifle in shock. Falling to his knees, he looked down at the gore he had created: five bodies turned to chunks of meat like pigs to a slaughter.

At this point, everyone in the nearby vicinity was now looking at him: workers, Kaito, Leon, and soldiers who approached to take him down.

They will end my life. I should end it first, he thought. On the ground he outstretched his arm, reaching once more for his weapon, but felt the blunt impact of force to the back of his head.

Kaito had struck him so hard with the butt of his rifle, Tyler quickly fell forward and passed out.

***

Leon, now standing by Kaito, watched as soldiers placed Tyler in electronic handcuffs and dragged his unconscious body away. Aries drifted behind him, accompanying her now-murderous master.

"What the hell happened?"

"Well," Kaito paused, still in awe over the bloody scene, "He just snapped, I guess."

Leon's eyes were cold and tired. Being unsure of when the last time he slept was, he unslung his backpack and withdrew two stimpacks. After handing one to Kaito and injecting himself with another, he rose to his feet.

Two men in the large pit below loaded the dead bodies of the fallen into a truck as their blood still dripped warm. As they drove off with the carcasses, they left behind bits and pieces of unidentifiable body parts in their scattered pools of respective red blood.

The construction men and women were back to doing their grind and the little girl who was assaulted was pulled to her feet--cast back into her line of work as if nothing had ever even happened.

Kaito was stuck in a daze, staring at the blood on the ground. "Will they kill him?" He asked, saddened and already knowing the obvious answer to his question.

Leon had never thought Tyler was capable of such a brutal, heinous act of treason, but whatever was to happen next to his comrade was well out of his boundaries of control. He had no idea why Tyler did what he did, but the UIGN would, without question, execute him for his crimes.

Leon put a hand on Kaito's shoulder. "Come on, let's go," he said, and the two men, with their single drone, quietly pressed on.

They ventured for another fifteen minutes, crossing through multiple labor forces where men and women of all ages shared the same miserable look of sadness as they labored away in the light of the setting sun. Some dug into the dirt with shovels and pickaxes, others lay and evened out liquid stone, while some welded steel pylons into the setting cement.

A handful of mechs joined in the labor, performing the tasks too great for man. Leon could see someone inside one of the mechs. The control panels for the machines were a hotbox of radiated heat and the driver poured sweat, looking as though he were about to melt away at any given minute.

They approached New Horizon, where a short, brutish man, an officer to his peers, flagged Leon and Kaito over. They had been waiting for them, surrounding a large vehicle that they had been collectively working on.

"I thought there were supposed to be three of you," the man pointed out.

Our third got tied up. What's the word?" Leon countered, sidestepping away from the awkward question.

"I am not sure of the particulars. It was relayed that whatever you guys are doing is highly confidential. We were just informed to ready up an armadillo for you. Apparently, the details will be relayed when you are aboard and biometrics confirms your identity."

An armadillo was an all-terrain armored vehicle with six wheels and was suitable for nearly any situation. It had a massive high-powered railgun attached to the top that reached from the rear to the front and two sets of missile launchers fixed to each side.

"Well, at least we get a vehicle this time," Kaito said, forcing a frail smile. He was astonished by the armadillo.

It was the first time Leon had ever seen one in person and it was much bigger than he had previously imagined.

"These things are crazy expensive," Kaito said.

"Which is exactly why you won't be driving. You will take control of the weapons, I will drive. Plug Libra into the exterior so that if we need her to, she can project a shield over the entirety of the vehicle and provide an extra layer of security," Leon said, forcing Kaito's imagination back down into reality.

"Extra security?" The officer before them questioned. "These things have been rolled down cliffs and landed upright without so much as a scratch."

The two approached the vehicle to get a closer look as soldiers finished packing it full of crates labeled 'explosives.'

"What are we car bombing now?" Kaito said, wide-eyed.

The men laughed.

One of the young military noobies smiled. he was skinny and awkward with little to no muscle about him.

"That's what I said when we got the orders to load you up. That whoever is taking this thing out doesn't plan on coming back in. They are off to see Allah about seventy-two virgins," he conveyed with an awkward laugh.

The young man clearly looked up to the unit of specialists. He had taken the idea of a joke and used it as a bonding experience, as if it would justify him as worthy to his peers. For a split, insignificant moment in the history of his existence, the almighty recon squad that was Kaito and Leon thought one in the same.

What a moron, Leon thought. *Probably best to let him have his moment though, sadly, that will probably be the first and last positive interaction of friendship with his peers he will have. Who am I to take that away?*

Leon entered the vehicle and took the driver's seat and Kaito pushed his way past the explosives, squeezing into the gunner.

"For such a large vehicle, it sure feels crowded with just two people. I can't imagine cramming this sardine can full of its recommended number of personnel," Kaito called out to Leon, who sealed the doors with the push of a button.

"Hot as the beating sun on this planet too," Leon mumbled as he fired up the vehicle's engines.

Red lasers scanned his face from the dashboard before him and then turned green. The same sequence played out for

Kaito in his gunner's seat. After both of their identities were confirmed, the armadillo projected the holographic image of a woman, whose robotic voice simultaneously came to life within the vehicle's hull.

"Hello Leon Fleisher and Kaito Shimizu. I am Arma Thirty-Seven, but you may call me Amy."

"Holy crap," Kaito gasped, "This thing is embedded with AI."

"What's the word, Amy?" Leon called out over the faint rumble of the armadillo's engines.

"I have a set of coordinates," she began. "We are to make way towards that location, where there are two hellcat pilots searching for a living obelisk. The giant is considered hostile and dangerous, so we are instructed to eradicate it via any means necessary and ultimately halt the threat it presents. We are to launch explosives onto targeted zones of its exoskeleton while the hellcats engage it directly. The target area will be first the legs. If we can blow them off, we will find ourselves in a much easier position to handle destroying the rest of the giant."

On the heads up display, an image of the giant mountain-like creature was displayed.

Leon glanced back to see Kaito squinting to make out the imaging. He was squished in back in between boxes of explosives and the large control panel that controlled the vehicle's main railgun.

"Kaito, come on up here and get a better look at this thing," he called out.

Together, the two watched the video of the beast. Amy zoomed in on the pressure points of the legs and projected lasers onto the areas they were to shell. The feed stopped and Amy's frame again materialized. Seemingly human, her holographic lips moved as she continued on with the briefing.

"This is a highly classified mission that will result in considerable corrective action if leaked," she warned.

Leon never understood the need to portray artificial intelligence in a human like form until now. One might feel helplessly entrapped in this box of steel controlled by a greater presence, but looking into the eyes, even though artificial, of the being who controls your fate, was a feeling of comfort.

Chapter 9
Dominos

Aisha stood by the doorway to the bridge of New Horizon as the vice admiral leered, hunched over, plugging away at the holographic computer embedded within the table. They were the only two in the room since the pilots had left a little over an hour ago, and all was inaudible.

After finalizing her lengthy commands via the table's computer software, Fox stretched her back and let out a sigh. She then turned to face the exit where Aisha still stood silently.

"I forgot you were even here," Fox tittered, stopping before the girl.

"I suppose that's a good thing," Aisha said. Unsure of what she even meant by the phrase, she quickly felt foolish in second guessing herself.

"I suppose it is," Fox said with a smile. "You hungry?"

Aisha nodded her head. She was famished. The last time she remembered eating a meal was years ago, just before going under cryosleep. Since she awoke, her diet had consisted of nothing more than vitamin injections and stimpacks.

Fox leaned over to an intercom on the wall by the door and pressed her long, narrow fingers on the touchpad, entering the numeric code of six, four, seven.

"Linus, bring in some food for myself and Miss Sayegh." She let off the comm system and turned back to Aisha, "I don't usually eat in the bridge. Hell, I don't usually eat at all, but the solace of this empty chamber is something you will find nowhere else on this ship, or perhaps even on this planet." She took a seat and ushered Aisha to do the same across from her.

One of the greys entered the large room. His blank stare reminded Aisha that he was not a human being but rather a robot. So near perfection as to replicate a living breathing man, the human eye would understandably mistake him as such if it were not for his grey armor.

"A man has just shot and killed five soldiers," he announced in a monotone.

Fox shot him a look of disgust. "Has he been apprehended?"

"Yes."

"Who was he?"

"Tyler Flynn, one of the specialists you delegated the task of mapping out the enemy cave to."

Fox shot a look of confusion to Aisha, whose face shared the same emotion-- only coupled with concern. She had no idea what this could all mean.

"What of the other two? Leon and the Japanese kid?" Fox asked.

"They are heading off to begin the next mission you assigned to them."

"They played no part in the killing?"

"Seems not."

Another grey, humanoid robot entered the room. This one carried a tray piled high with roast beef sandwiches cut into perfect little triangles with the crust removed. Pieces of diced fruit: oranges, apples, and mangos lay sprawled out neatly on the outer edges of the silver platter.

Fox picked up one of the sandwiches and bit into it with a look of pure bliss on her face. "Leave us," she said before taking another bite. The two greys left the room and Fox looked to Aisha once more. "Eat up, it is quite good. Roast beef is a delicacy; given we have no cows here on this vessel."

Aisha's mind raced with questions of what had happened to make Tyler kill five soldiers. With little information on the matter, she forced herself not to think about it for now; she knew that if one dwelt too long on the unknown, the mind will fester the unease quickly into an emotion of terror and fear.

She picked up one of the perfectly cut sandwiches and bit into it: tomatoes, lettuce, mayonnaise, and roast beef all delicately encased in bread that tasted of honey. *Incredible,* she thought as she moved on for a second bite.

"You know; I am only second in command to Admiral Vetrov. He has to stay out in space guarding the president with the fleet while we warp in a carrier a day and try to establish a safe, livable city before the majority populace can arrive," she paused and took a deep breath. "They don't think that we can do it. They want to use the warp gate to shoot out further into space and find a more desirable planet."

"Do you think we can do it?" Aisha asked with a mouth full of food.

"I have spent years planning with my peers on how to live and thrive on this planet. I think we are coming along just fine while they cower at the thought of residing in a place so distant from the one we come from. The reality is, we must accept change, because that is the only thing the universe is selling right now. I do not know that we will ever find another planet as close to Earth as this one. The odds of this one existing within grasp to the technologies that limit our reach is astonishing in and of itself."

"People hate change," Aisha said, stuffing her mouth with another sandwich.

"Aye, that they do. Tell me Aisha? The girl who cuts off her own arm in order to live, what does that girl hate? What does she fear?"

Aisha's stomach wrenched, upset with the rate that she had practically inhaled the sandwiches. She was not even sure that she chewed them before ingesting them and her body become irate for it.

"I don't know...I mean, fear is a useless emotion that only presents you submissive to another, granting them alpha male status."

"And where did you learn that?" Fox asked with a chuckle.

"My father," Aisha said, her eyes suddenly dropping in sadness.

"Interesting advice for his daughter, but from what I have read, you were an only child, so perhaps he saw you more as a son than a daughter. Maybe that is why the man from Mars, a common miner, spent his every last penny saved in obtaining the rare materials that your sword is composed of."

Aisha's sword was not only an extension of her body, but at its core rested a fine piece of her soul. It was as much a part of her physically as it was mentally.

"The man crafted a masterpiece and passed it on to his beloved daughter before passing away himself, but was his master work his creation of the blade, or his creation of you?"

Aisha stayed silent, unsure what Fox was getting at.

"While on leave, he went to Earth for a year, met and married a dancer-- and not just some pole slut, but a world-renowned, award winning theatre act. In finding out his wife was pregnant, he extended his leave of absence from his work on Mars an extra year and soon after you were born, he reshipped off to work."

Aisha remembered dancing with her mother when she was a little girl. She had enjoyed it up until her mother's tragic murder. She had cast out the joy of dancing, for it bore a constant reminder of her late mother. "How do you know so much about me?"

"I have read a lot on your history. It is interesting to say the least. After your mother's passing, you were sent to Mars to live with your father, who began training you in various types of ancient swordplay in his off time."

She had always hated Mars; dramatically cold with nothing more about it than a collection of depressing outposts and refuel stations. Its small, controlled population was nothing more than mechanics and miners whose only true love was that of alcohol and hookers. Certainly no place for a young girl to be raised.

"The life expectancy of a Mars miner is only thirty years. Your father lived to see the age of thirty-nine, but never got to see you join the military, let alone climb the ranks wielding the sword he crafted for you," she paused for a moment in thought. "An interesting life indeed. Anyway, I am sated. Suppose it's time we take a look into the actions of your comrade... see why he found it necessary to gun down five of my soldiers."

Aisha had forgotten entirely about the situation with Tyler. Her mind began to fill with murky clouds that beckoned with ideas of reason and forced her stomach to feel sick with anxiety. Nevertheless, she mustered the strength to stand to her feet and cast out the feeling of unease as she gave the vice admiral a forced nod in acceptance.

***

Ness stared helplessly over a three headed dog as it

feasted on the mangled corpse of his younger brother, Lucas. The animal was missing its skin; exposed muscle dripped blood onto a ground powdered with fresh, cold snow that quickly turned from white to red. Each head snapped and fought with one another for a chance to sink teeth into the little boy-- ripping apart his insides and consuming the flesh with little effort made in actually chewing the meal.

They were atop a mountain where the wind howled and stung Ness's face, but he did not feel afraid or confused as to what he saw. He merely watched the beast ingest his younger sibling alive as if it were a normal day and all was well and right with the world.

Lucas squirmed in the crimson snow, covered in his own mess. He reached out to his older brother for help in his hopeless state. His legs were gone and his insides emanated out his open belly.

Ness closed his eyes for but a second to blink. He opened them to now see life from within a glass cage. He was a bird, shrouded in leaves, perched on a branch within a tree. Inside New Horizon, he watched as military men and women walked past his cage with blank stares, entering into a large open room where they collectively laid flat on the ground, submitting themselves to their fate--which was of death to a woman in a white trench coat.

She was tall and thin with black hair pulled into a ponytail, exposing a scar on her forehead. Her lab coat was covered in blood. She walked over their bodies, wheeling a small corroded cart that pulled hundreds of very fine, razor-sharp wires. As she pushed her cart, it gave off a sharp squeal with each minute turn of the rusty wheels.

The wires dug into the sea of flesh as the bodies quickly began to drown in a bath of their own blood. A line of people had formed at the entrance, patiently awaiting their turn to enter and die. The room now stunk of death and decay.

Ness awoke drenched in his own sweat, frantically gasping for air. He felt as though no matter how hard he tried to intake oxygen, it simply was not enough. He began to feel dizzy and woozy as he tried to make sense of himself slowly coming into full consciousness. Unsure as to how long he had been asleep, he tirelessly rose from his soaked cot and looked around to be sure no one was watching as he peeled off the wet clothes stuck to his skin.

He dropped his soggy apparel to the floor below. His bed was a bunk that set atop other sleeping civilians. The clothing hit the ground like a sponge full of water and he immediately regretted dropping it so carelessly, as he now realized it was the middle of the night and that most people in his block were fast asleep.

I wasted my half day sleeping, he thought as he headed for the showers with a fresh pair of clothes in hand.

Two guards passed a flask back and forth as they watched Ness scurry off to the showers in nothing but his skivvies and his face dripping with sweat. Firing him the stink eye, one of the guardsmen drunkenly mumbled something under his breath, but he was far too gone to stand, let alone exert energy communicating with the boy. The other slumped over in laughter after hearing whatever was said. He whispered something to his comrade, then vomited chunks of brown mess onto the floor. They looked at each other and continued laughing and drinking.

***

Tyler gawked dejectedly at the wall as he sat on the edge of a steel cot in a small jail cell aboard New Horizon. His face was pale and his stomach wrenched in sickness. He wanted to continue vomiting, but there was nothing left to heave up after doing so for the first few hours since awakening in his new found cage. A hydraulic door to the jail room opened, but he did not bother turning to see who entered into the room.

"To your feet, soldier," said a firm voice.

He glanced over to see Vice Admiral Natalia Fox looking through him with her piercing stare and he sluggishly shot up to his feet. Behind her stood Aisha.

She is alive, Tyler thought in relief, *and she even has a prosthetic arm.*

"You do not look at her, you look at me," Fox shouted.

Falling back down to the reality of the situation at hand, he slumped in horror as his eyes drifted back to meet the vice admiral's.

"I watched the video feed of the slaughter as I walked over here. You do realize that given the salvation space treaties, the act of killing military personnel is not only considered a crime against humanity, it is also treason. You are facing these charges on five accounts. Rotting in a cell will not be an option, nor will the death penalty. You see, Tyler Flynn..." Her eyes locked onto his as she got closer to his cage. "Life is not wasted in this day and age. Your body will be donated to science, the kind of science requiring the body to still be alive and functional, to perform brave new extensive testing."

His face maintained a blank stare of emotionless display. There was nothing he could do or say to alter the situation even slightly in his favor, let alone ease the fury Fox had towards him.

"So tell me, Flynn, why did you do it?"

His lips were dry and stuck together. He managed to peel them apart and open his mouth, but no words formed. He had run the event over hundreds of thousands of times in his head. Again and again and again, yet still refused to accept that he was capable of doing something so barbaric and cold.

She raised her eyebrows, wordlessly expressing the fact that she was awaiting an answer. A few minutes passed and she turned her back to him. It was then that he realized that *this* was as good of a trial as he was ever going to be granted.

"They were assaulting a civilian, sexually, verbally, and physically," he mustered in a low, raspy voice.

"And so, you decided, then and there, that they should die? Be slaughtered like pigs?" she said, her back still facing him.

"She was just a little girl," he said looking at the floor as he replayed the image in his head of their deaths at his hand. "Maybe they did deserve to die," he continued coldly. "Maybe they deserved to be put down like the rabid dogs they were."

Realizing that what he had just said could be taken as an admission of guilt, he fired a wide eyed look up to Fox to see her response.

With her back still facing him, she did not bother to turn. She simply nodded her head and, without saying a word, she left the room.

***

Fox and Aisha left the jail room and walked halfway down the thin corridor back towards the front of the carrier. Aisha couldn't believe it. On the walk down to see Tyler, she had watched the video feed with the vice admiral on a tablet and was perplexed in just how exactly Tyler was capable of performing such an act of horror. In his jail cell he looked disgusted in himself, but in the video it almost looked as though he had enjoyed killing the soldiers.

"You know something, if I were in that boy's shoes, I don't know if I would have acted any different, in all honesty. But there is a chain of command, respect, and rules that we must adhere to if we are to carry on our way of life. If we fail to do that, we will be no better than primitive animals, and the legacy of our species as a whole will be a red stain in the pages of history."

"So, what are you going to do with him?" Aisha asked.

"I don't know," she sighed as she pressed her temples in with her fingers and closed her eyes. "You let this sort of thing slide and you see repercussions, not only from my peers, but the civilian population. I mean, how does it look when the workforce population sees military personnel killing each other?" She paused for a moment and then continued with the answer. "We will give him a day, a final meal and such, then put him down with a bit of dignity intact via lethal injection."

Aisha had no comment, though it seemed the vice admiral wanted her opinion. She did want to save her friend, however; she did not want to say something out of place. She was after all only a personal bodyguard, and while she thought of Tyler as a friend, maybe she really didn't know him as well as she thought she had. They met in their training a few years ago and most of the time between then and now was spent in cryosleep.

The visual of him smiling as he gunned down those soldiers was a vision that would reside with her for the rest of her life. It was as true as ever a display of character: portraying sheer ruthlessness, cruelty, and insanity. She didn't question his reasoning, but the act depicted him a true infidel at heart.

Tyler's robot, Aries, drifted down the hallway towards them and silently passed by as she headed into the jail room to visit her imprisoned friend.

***

Tyler slumped back on the metal cot and slammed the back of his head down. The dry, coagulated blood from the wound given to him by Kaito re-opened. Warm blood ran down the back of his neck and smeared onto the cot. The hydraulic door opened again and, without moving his head, his eyes crept over to see Aries come into the room.

"Hey, Tyler," she called out to him in her usual tone.

"Hey, Aries," he responded flatly.

She looked him over from outside the cell. "You are bleeding," she exclaimed.

"Yeah. It's fine," he eased.

A few minutes of silence passed while she hovered up and down, continuously watching him as if waiting for something. "Are you afraid of death, Tyler?" she asked.

He thought about it for a minute. He knew he was going to die, but it wasn't until then that the emotion of it all really seemed to sink in. "Yes."

"Do you know what death is?"

"I have a pretty good idea."

"Do you think that you will meet God?"

"I'm not so sure God exists," Tyler said with a sigh.

"Well, the universe as we know it is endless. Realities and dimensions exceed that which your mind, or my processor, can even begin to imagine. Cats, dogs, robots, and man alike, we all live within our own reality which exists on the same plane of laws and physics we are programed to perceive. Given that intelligent life outside of our own native galaxy is now known to exist, one can draw the mathematical conclusion that a being transcending in power well beyond that which we could ever truly comprehend not only exists, but could also very well know of our existence in great detail."

"Wow," Tyler frowned, "That was quite the answer."

A few minutes of silence passed as Tyler thought about what she had said.

Most all of humanity disregarded religion when life was proven to exist elsewhere in the galaxy, but her theory is one backed by math. If life exists in endless space, there is no reasoning for the intelligence of that life to ranges from a single celled organism to a form of life so far progressed into its existence that it transcended multiple dimensions and realities. Perhaps a being even existed with the ability to craft, shape, and manipulate elements--the very pillars of all creation as we know it. The notion scared Tyler beyond belief.

"That girl you saved, you did not know her?"

Tyler paused in answering as he tried to shift his thinking away from endless space and back into the room he resided within. "No, I did not," he said with a sigh.

"Then why did you save her?"

"I don't know."

"Yes, you do."

Tyler could not believe it. Since meeting Aries, he had grown highly affectionate of the bot. Though it was artificial, something about its level of intelligence and morality had led him towards holding her in high regard. But now, she seemed abnormally cold and heartless. Perhaps that was because she indeed did not have a heart to feel anything at all.

He remained silent, not knowing what exactly she wanted of him. A few minutes passed and, with time, a tear quietly began to drip down his cheek.

"I should never have overstepped my bounds, Tyler. I was not instructed to interfere with your situation, but I did anyway." Her LED lights increased in the speed in which they blinked, suggesting her processor was under tremendous stress.

Tyler slowly repositioned himself to sit upright to face and pay attention to her.

"You are my friend, Tyler. You expressed an emotional desire and I fed into your aspirations."

"I do not follow," he said, squinting his eyes and lowering his brows.

"Maybe I am as much to blame for killing those soldiers as you are, but you wanted to do it. Your mind begged for the courage," she defended.

He stood to his feet, walked over to the bars that separated him from the bot, and spoke very carefully. "Aries, what are you talking about?"

"You wanted to kill that man and his peers, but your conscience acts as a safety switch. I merely flipped it off and allowed your instincts loose."

Tyler's heart sunk into his knees. He couldn't believe it. How did the thought not cross his mind that the robot, synched into his nervous system, could have played a role in his outburst of character? "What right did you have?" he said softly in disbelief.

"I'm sorry Tyler, I-"

Tyler placed his hands on the cold steel bars that entrapped him and cut off her attempted apology with a fit of animosity, "Who gave *you* permission to alter my psyche?"

Aries said nothing.

"Who said you could fuck with *my* mind?" he continued as he submitted himself into a full blown tantrum: shaking himself into a fit of rage against the steel bars that did not move or care for his agitation. Ceasing his outburst, he slid down to the ground and began to sob. "I am going to die in here because of you."

"I will never let you die, Tyler Flynn."

"You sentenced me to death," he huffed as his eyes filled with water.

"I helped you save one of your own, and now I will ask you do the same for me."

He shook his head like a child combating inconvenient truths. He did not want to believe that the series of events that had landed him in this cell had ever even truly occurred. He wanted to confess to Fox that it wasn't him. It was really Aries, but in all reality, that would be a lie. Killing those soldiers was his desire and he was the one who murdered each and every one of them.

"Scorpio is alive. I want to save him," she said.

Tyler said nothing as he ignored her. Instead, he reflected on his own fate. He was going to die. The fear of nothingness in death was one that knotted his gut and wrenched his soul.

"So, will you help me in recovering him?"

"Who?" he questioned, coming late into her new conversation.

"Scorpio."

Leon's drone, Tyler thought, *so what about a stupid, worthless robot?*

"I will get you out of here and we can go save him together, okay?"

"He is software. Can't you just redownload his spark into another vessel?" Tyler spat.

"I cannot do that without him being present and alive to transfer his essence into another. Not to mention, his current hardware is far greater than most artificial beings in existence today. We need him if we are to survive on this hostile planet. The last time he had a full systems cloud backup was almost a decade ago. Re-downloading his consciousness would be like reincarnating him as a child. And cloning AI is not like copying and pasting software. There are unique keys that bind to each drone that, if replicated, would lose the data packs that make them supreme in thought. Without our encrypted spark keys, we would just be choice computer powerhouses, but we would not be artificial intelligence."

On his knees, Tyler glanced up to her. She hovered on the outside of the cell, watching him with the steady pace of her LED lights blinking, awaiting his response.

He sniffled back a set of tears. *How could she be asking me for help right now, after she allowed me to commit the heinous acts I was never hardwired to commit?*

"Tyler?" she pressed for an answer.

"And what if I don't go?" he said as he looked again to the floor.

The levees broke and the water contained by the floodgates began to flow freely from his eyes. Tears streamed down his face at an indiscriminate pace. They weaved and turned about through the hairs of his unshaven face and dripped to the cold, hard floor.

"Then they will kill you, Tyler Flynn."

***

"Looks like an armadillo tank with a couple special ops guys are going to be helping us out," Lanfen called out over the radio to Jason.

"Toss them the coordinates to where we are heading. I am sure if we head in the direction the monolith was venturing to from the location we last saw it, won't take us long to spot it once more," he commanded.

"They are already en route. I guess they are packing enough explosives to vaporize a small country, too."

"Sweet, a private late night light show," he said with a chuckle.

The two pilots flew mid-speed for about fifteen minutes, scanning the eerie night sky, which was lit up due to the size and proximity of the planets' colossal moon. Lanfen mostly throttled back and forth while Jason made a spectacle of unnecessarily dips and dives through the canyons and between mountains.

"Is that him?" Lanfen called out, breaking the silence.

The details of the faint silhouette were filled in clearly as they approached. Sure enough, there it was, the largest living creature known to man. And here they were, about to get rid of it like some rabid, infected animal. The flowers on its back had turned white under the moonlit sky, and tiny, illuminated orbs drifted out from them. Glow-in-the-dark pollens trailed out into the desert landscape, spreading life in a lifeless wasteland of hardship.

"Yea, that's him. What channel is that armadillo on?"

"Delta Sixer Charlie," she answered.

"Alright, switch over to that with me," he said, punching the three-digit code into his comm system.

"Hey, ground grunts, we found the target. So on me double time."

***

"Looks like we are about ten minutes out," Leon said into the radio.

Kaito was stuck in the back, glued to the controls of the vehicle's weapons system, encased in what felt like a sea of explosives while they navigated through a jagged, rocky terrain.

"There is a canyon approximately two miles ahead," the vehicle's AI bot, Amy, called out, "Going around it will add nine minutes to our ETA. Shall I reroute?"

"Can we jump it?" Leon asked with a spark of madness in his eye.

"If we disengage gravity stabilizers and punch vertical thrusters to their limit for twenty seconds, we should be able to float right over," she informed.

"You sure about that?" Leon asked, scratching his beard with one hand while he controlled the vehicle with his other.

"Yes, I had a systems update with current known geographical layouts before our departure."

Holy shit, Kaito thought as he closed his eyes.

It was bad enough he felt queasy at every jerk of the vehicle, and now they were just going to stroll off the ledge of a canyon, completely ignoring the fact that they were carrying an insane amount of highly explosive crates.

***

"Could there be other survivors?" Tyler asked.

"There may be. Scorpio is too far under the surface of the planet to establish reliable communication, but we did ping back and forth successfully a couple of times, confirming his well-being. He overloaded his power cores getting the messages out."

"So, the bugs did not die?"

"I am sure a large amount of them were killed with the bomb, but my guess is that their network and population may very well exceed that which we previously assumed by a very large margin."

The thought terrified Tyler, though it made sense. Even today, earth harbored a population of ants and insects that exceeded a number well beyond comprehension by human beings. But these were no ants. They were bugs the size of men who were proven to be brutal, savage killers.

"As soon as you free me from this prison, the alarms will sound and we will be hunted like game for slaughter."

"I can disable the alarms while you escape."

"And I am just supposed to walk out of this carrier while no one pays me any mind? Pay no attention folks, just murderous scum walking freely about," he mocked.

The cell door clicked, swung open candidly, and Tyler's heart sunk into his stomach. He couldn't just stay. She was right in that they would kill him, but walking out the door and navigating this unfamiliar carrier in hopes of finding an exit was suicide. As if that were not bad enough, even if he were to make his way out, slipping past workforce sites guarded by armed militants would prove even more difficult.

Aries began to drift towards the door. "The vice admiral and her personnel have just departed back towards the command bridge. No one will recognize you, and given that your uniform colors reflect your outranking of most military personnel along the way, I would say things should work out for the better."

Tyler exited the cell and raised his wrists in the air which were bound by a set of electric-pulsing cuffs. "What about these? They require an electronic encryption key that-"

Before he could finish his sentence, Aries did something that was naked to Tyler's inferior human eyes. The cuffs simply turned off and fell to the floor with a thud.

"I wish I could see into the dimension of electronics," he muttered.

Taking him seriously as per usual, she answered logically. "The human mind in its delicate state would be overwhelmed and begin seizing if exposed to a sense of alternative complex dimensions. It is theoretically possible, but it would require the mind to receive proper conditioning over time."

"Shut the hell up and let's go," he said, walking past her and out of the room.

The hallway was empty, and so the two quietly strolled down it towards a set of elevators. While waiting for one to arrive, Tyler began to feel sick with anxiety. *What if this door opens and there are soldiers inside? I will have made it a whole twenty to thirty feet from that prison cell before being gunned down*, he worried.

The elevator was loudly approaching and Tyler looked up to see cameras beaming straight down at the two of them.

"We are screwed," he said

"We are fine," she comforted.

"What about those?" he questioned, pointing above.

"The cameras?" she asked, looking up to them as if surprised by his concern. "They said that no one is watching currently," she eased.

Of course she can communicate with a camera like an

old high school pal, Tyler thought, still feeling uneasy about his chances of escape.

The lift finally reached them and they entered the simple metal crate.

"Ground floor, I assume?"

"Yes," she confirmed.

He pressed the button and they began descending from their current status on the eighth floor. They could see into every floor they passed by, given the basic construction of the elevator was nothing more than a thin and fragile cage.

On the fifth floor, a man in uniform stood waiting to enter. The elevator stopped to allow him entrance, and Tyler again felt afraid that he would be noticed.

"Going to third pal," the man said.

As if grasping an alarm in an emergency, Tyler awkwardly threw himself at the button labeled *three*. He was sweating and knew the way in which he handled pushing the button was suspiciously odd.

"You okay, man?" The soldier asked.

"Yeah, just feel a little warm."

"It's heaven in here compared to outside," the man laughed.

"Tyler, you need a weapon. Take his," Aries said, throwing Tyler completely on the spot.

"Um, what?" The soldier said, looking confused.

Tyler looked at the man and then back to Aries. She was so to the point that he had no option other than to oblige. "You heard her, son. I need that weapon."

Son? Really? This kid is eighteen or nineteen at best and I am in my late twenties. I don't think that qualifies me to call him son. Just go with it Tyler, you outrank him, instill dominance and the fear of repercussion, he frantically thought.

"I ... But," the soldier stuttered trying to form words with his twisted tongue.

Tyler put his hand on the barrel of the weapon, lifting and pressing it to his own chest while exerting a strange and devious smile.

"Trust me, you do *not* want the headache of being tried for treason and murder, kid," Tyler said as he firmly held the barrel in place.

"Woah, man, chill out," the novice teen said as he let go of the firearm and raised his hands in the air in an act of surrender.

The door opened as the elevator reached the third floor.

"Your grenades," Tyler said, now pointing the rifle at the rookie soldier.

"But if I-" the boy's excuse was cut off mid-sentence by the clicking sound of Tyler disengaging the safety of the weapon. Quickly, the soldier removed his belt of five grenades and handed it over.

"Now get out," Tyler pressed, introducing a serious side of himself to the boy as he held the door open with his foot to prevent it from closing. After the soldier exited, Tyler let the gate close and then the two continued their descent to the ground floor.

"Funny how terrified and uncomfortable people get when you act a little crazy," Tyler laughed while fixing the belt of grenades to his waist. They were not the special grade antigravity ones he was used to, but a compact laser-based explosive that he had never physically seen before. Apparently, when detonated, the devices would barrage a cluster of lasers and shrapnel in an effective radius of fifteen feet.

"I am afraid that maybe, perhaps, you were not acting, Tyler," Aries said.

"Maybe," he paused, "maybe not."

He looked over his new rifle. It was nice and looked to have never been fired--a lightweight energy rifle that paled in comparison to his old one, but a solid piece of equipment nonetheless that would hopefully suffice the task at hand.

"Maybe that is why you asked me to escort you through a hive of insects," he added as they reached the ground floor and the gate opened before them.

Chapter 10
Over and Out

Ness stood in the shower staring at the tile floor beneath his feet as hot water flowed down from the spigot above. The water felt like an aggressive but much-needed massage. His back, neck, and shoulders were sore. Despite sleeping his half-day away into the wee hours of the night, he still felt exhausted. He knew the aches and pains of his body meant that, in the long run, he was building muscle that would make him stronger in the days to come. If the glass was half full, that might be something of value to him, but the thought lingered for only a short time.

Another man entered the large shower, which was equipped to accommodate ten at a time. Ness did not turn to look at him, feeling awkward to be naked and alone with another man in a shower. He forced himself to outweigh the unease with the simple joy and cleanse the hot water brought him by washing away his filth. He rubbed his face down with soap and gargled a mouth full of the wretched-tasting recycled water before spitting it out and then going back for more to drink. He turned off the shower and, in doing so, noted the silence in the room. The man who entered had never turned on his water. Ness turned around slowly to see a fully clothed man with greasy hair who harbored a sick, twisted smile as he looked over the boy's naked body.

Ness quickly wrapped himself with his towel and shuffled past the sick pervert. No doubt he would be able to defend himself against such a frail old man, but conflict was not his strong suite. He returned to his bunk, periodically looking over his shoulder to be sure the man was not following him as he walked.

After clothing himself, he laid himself back and looked over to the big, red clock in the center of the room. Four hours until he had to be awake for another day's work and here he was, now wide awake. He perched over the ledge of his bed to see the two drunken guards passed out, slumped against the entrance wall twenty feet away.

He climbed down and made sure his brother was asleep. After confirming Lucas was indeed out, he walked over to the block's entrance, where the guards sat covered in the stench of vomit and piss. Ness couldn't help but gag as he walked past them to poke his head out in the hallway. Mostly dark, the corridors were only lit in small pockets where emergency lighting illuminated at a low night setting.

Smelling smoke, he began to walk down the hallway towards the source, where he quickly found a civilian man propped against a wall, smoking a cigar with a guard. They were just outside a block of their own, identical to Ness's. He couldn't make out the numbers above that would indicate what block it was. He leaned in to listen to their conversation.

"Listen, Frank," said the civilian, pausing to puff his cigar, "We were friends for a long time, well before you ever joined the military. I knew your father back before Project Salvation was ever even conceptualized. You *know* me and can trust me."

"Roger, you know I have always valued our friendship, but what you are asking of me is suicide," the guard said in an honest tone of fear.

"You trap a dog in a corner, he gets scared. You can only beat the living shit out of him for so long before he bites and, when he bites, he has already made up his mind to sink them teeth in until he tastes him some blood. We all know an uprising is inevitable, and the civilian workforce outnumbers the military ten to one. What side do you want to be on here, Frank? The one that beats and enslaves the dog, or the dog that bites back?"

"I agree with you, man. A good amount of the military does. We are not all so bad. Hell, most of us were civilians before all of this went down just a few years ago. You are willing to kill the innocent members of the military along with the guilty? And what of the government? As soon as this goes down, they will either stop sending carriers and let us starve out here or they will send more carriers, the ones loaded with the heavy weapons, and they will vaporize us off the map. If you think they will just roll over and play dead, you are a fool. They will kill every last one of us to stay in control, and you of all people should know just that!"

The man, Roger, puffed his cigar as he pondered the statement. He was muscular with a thick, brawny build. He had short, messy brown hair, coupled with a short, unkempt beard of the same color. His appearance was rugged: a handful of scars across his face accented as such, and an eyepatch over his right eye.

Quite the character, Ness thought.

"Frank, it is going to happen regardless of what I, you, or your friends here decide to do. Now you said it yourself, they will kill us all without picking or choosing who deserves life or death, so why should I exert anything less than the same standards of judgement?" He paused for a second to give the guard a minute to answer, but received no acknowledgement and continued, "You *have* heard that there was an assassination attempt on the vice admiral, right?"

From the shadows emerged a man in white and orange armor, wielding an energy rifle. He was accompanied by a drone that drifted by his side. Roger looked to the floor and covered his face as he ran his fingers through his hair, and the vocal guard who engaged in the conspiratory conversation, harboring a look of terror, simply watched as the man and his robot strode on by.

Ness panicked, wanting to run as to not be seen, but he would never make it anywhere with the man swiftly approaching. He was in full-stride down the dim hallway. Ness jammed his hands in his pockets and hunched over, propping himself against the wall as if he were there with purpose.

The man walked by, paying no more mind to the boy than a slight glance in his brisk walk to get somewhere. When he was out of eyesight, Ness let out a long sigh.

The guard conversing with the civilian heard Ness. Raising his rifle and pointing it down the hall, he clicked on the attached flashlight. Like a deer in headlights, Ness stood feeling foolishly trapped and terrified.

***

Kaito felt butterflies in his stomach as the lack of gravity's constant constraint on his organs dissipated. He quickly realized he was in freefall. Himself, Leon, and the armadillo they were in was making its leap of faith high over the desert canyon. He pinched his eyes shut and took big, deep breathes as they flew through the air.

"Punch thrusters," Amy informed Leon.

Kaito forced open his eyes to see multiple controls in the cockpit before Leon were flashing--some warnings and some indicators. Leon slapped his right palm against a blue button and then thrusted a throttle lever to its peak of acceleration.

The armadillo's engines gave off a high pitch squeal as if debating whether or not to explode at any given second. Gears sounded as though they were crunching and grinding together somewhere. Kaito had to wonder if Leon had screwed something up mid-air.

Finally, bracing himself to snag a peek outside, Kaito looked out into the gorge. They were still soaring, a little over halfway across so far. It was similar to the Yarlung Tsangpo Canyon in Tibet, back on Earth, which is the largest to be found on the little blue planet. But this one was much wider and deeper. It was as if the distant relative of a ravine back on Earth had a much older and much darker cousin. The details of what might lie below were shrouded in darkness. The shadows twisted and warped as Kaito's angle of view shifted in passing. The shades played games with his mind and added to the already abundant amount of fear he felt over heights as they flew through the air with their jump.

Ahead, Kaito could see the edge they were shooting for. It looked like they were going to clear their jump with plenty of room to spare. Leon had overshot the distance to ensure they would, and the armadillo hit the ground hard, bouncing up off the planet's rocky surface with a foot of clearance while the vehicle's shocks tried to absorb the blow.

Kaito's heart was pounding through his face. He never was a fan of heights and, as his fear was subsided by the success of clearing the jump, his panic became a rush. A thrill he almost felt as though he wanted to experience again.

The desert landscape appeared vastly different under the moonlit sky as they sailed through the waterless ocean. Kaito could see clearly across the sea of sand and rock in the dead of night. Above was a clear shimmering display of stars and galaxies that churned about in their little corner of space. If ever you could find a spot back on planet earth with minimal light exposure, it would fail to come even remotely close to the view before him now.

Flare was in the thick of a vast galaxy that humanity knew nothing about. The scouting drones and rovers had mapped out so little that what was known could not even be put into terms of a numerical figure. In all technicalities, point zero two percent was the amount of information known about this galaxy. But such a comical numerical figure ignited the human race to venture deep into space, colonize, and expand its footprint into the history books of eternity. Kaito chuckled at the thought.

All of these views, of course, were through the optics of the armadillo's railgun system. Crammed in the backseat, buried in boxes marked 'explosives', he couldn't help but feel claustrophobic as they sped through a tiny fraction of what the barren planet potentially had to offer.

In his view finder, Kaito could make out what looked to be a mountain on the move.

"That's it," Leon called out when laying eyes on it himself from the cockpit ahead.

Amy confirmed the stone goliath as their target and Kaito almost wished she hadn't. The true nature of the creature's size blew Kaito away. Nothing in man's deep banks of knowledge knew of anything to have existed even remotely similar in size. It looked as though it could pick up a whale with one hand and smash it against a brontosaurus with another without so much as batting an eye.

As they got closer, Kaito could see the two hellcats weave ahead of the beast at a safe distance. They looked like flies circling an elephant, and it was then Kaito realized that there was just no way this was ever going to work.

***

"What are you doing out here, kid?" asked the guard, who had caught Ness eavesdropping.

Ness covered his face with his hands, blinded by the flashlight and scared of the rifle: both sticking in his face.

"I swear I will tear your head from where it rests upon your neck, boy," the soldier growled. "Who are you?"

"Turn off that light before the kid loses his eyesight permanently," barked the unarmed civilian man with the cigar and eyepatch, who snatched the weapon from the soldier's hands and turned off the light.

Ness painfully blinked his sight back into functionality.

"Roger," the soldier said coldly as he shot a glare so serious, it perhaps was a prerequisite to his intentions to do something harsh and rash, "*Give* me back my weapon."

The man with the eyepatch removed the cigar he had been mouthing on for the past twenty minutes and looked it over as if it were a dear friend that had somehow greatly disappointed him. He then abruptly flicked it at the soldier; the embers spread harmlessly and fell to the ground on contact, but the initial sprinkle of fire caused the soldier to flinch and, in the time it took him to do so, the man Roger raised the rifle and engaged the flashlight, turning the tables, so to speak, on the soldier.

"What the *hell* are you doing, Roger?" the soldier squealed.

"How does it feel, Frank?" he taunted. "How does it feel to be on the other end of the oppression and the tyranny of a man with a gun?" he hissed.

"Roger, let's not do anything crazy here. You don't want to do something you will regret. Something you will never be able to take-"

Cutting him off, the larger man slammed the butt of the rifle into the soldier's face. As Frank fell to the floor, Roger shoved the rifle into Ness's chest, forcing him to grasp hold and take the weapon. This freed up his hands to quickly wrap them around the soldier's neck and begin choking the life out of him. "How does it *feel*, Frank?" he shouted, "To feel something such as fear!" His strength allowed him to hold on with ease while his victim flailed about helplessly until falling limp.

An awkward minute or two of silence passed before Ness decided to say something. "He is passed out."

"I know," Roger said, still squeezing the man's throat.

Then Ness realized that this man, Roger, had no intentions of apprehending the soldier. He was not going to simply let him go now that he was unconscious. Rather, he kept him in a firm grip until all the oxygen and life left the soldier's body.

The cartilage in the soldier's neck cracked as Roger suddenly snapped it like a carrot. "He was not going to give me what I wanted, anyway." He seemed to find satisfaction in hearing the loud crack pulse through his fingers as he claimed the life. After the body was limp, he dropped it to the floor. He then knelt down to the dead soldier and removed his security card: a small chip-embedded passport for unlocking doors within New Horizon that civilians would otherwise not have access to.

"Take that," he said, pointing to the rifle that Ness still held before lifting his eyepatch and painfully stuffing the security keycard deep into his empty eye socket. "Sneak it back into your cell block and hide it. They will turn my block upside down looking for it, but won't think twice to check yours."

"*What*? I don't want this," Ness screeched, trying to hand the rifle back.

"Trust me, kid, in due time you will be grateful to have one. Its value will be on par with water and food on this planet. Now get out of here!"

Ness stumbled backwards through the darkness towards his block. His heart was pounding against his chest and he felt nauseous. He wanted to ditch the gun and just run but was afraid his DNA could somehow be extracted. Walking cautiously into the dark room, he harbored the weapon behind his back. Up in his bunk, he had a cubby for clothes, just big enough to stuff the rifle underneath his linens. He climbed up into his bunk and hid the weapon away. In the coming days, he would figure out how to dispose of it safely, but for now he just wanted to lay down in the safety of his bed where no guards would scream and yell at him, no perverts would eye him over, and no insane killer with an eyepatch would *strangle* him to death.

Ness laid in his bunk for hours before his long strenuous work day began, crying silently. He missed home, his mom, and the simplistic nostalgia of his long-gone youth, left behind on Earth abandoned to a tumultuous fate. In this new world he had to be strong, not only physically to survive for himself, but mentally to try and be a positive inspiration for his younger brother amidst the world of selfishly spawned chaos and hate.

***

The tiny holographic image of Amy, who had spent most of her time up towards Leon advising him on various aspects of the armadillo's control system, vanished and reappeared beside Kaito. She was being projected from his control panel and began explaining his custom system's capabilities.

"Alright Mr. Shimizu, the railgun has been fit with a tartan twenty-seven explosives adapter. Via flipping the red switch on the right side of your control panel, you shift over to firing from your explosive rounds reserve. These must be manually loaded via attaching the forty round magazines underneath the tartan adapter and, when attached correctly, they will fire with semi-automatic ease.

Wow, that mouthful to explain that this thing accepts magfed explosive rounds. Kaito thought as he cracked open the crate next to him and heaved out one of the many magazines. They felt as though they weighed a ton. He assumed that under regular circumstances, two men would typically work together in attaching full magazines and detaching empty ones while a third man would fire the weapon and the fourth drove the vehicle, but it was only the two of them and Leon had to keep them on the move and away from the goliath.

Struggling to lift the magazine high enough to fit in the magwell, he stopped to catch his breath before thrusting the encased steel up into place. A loud click confirmed it was attached and he fell back into his seat.

Forty rounds before I have to do that again, he thought. *Better make every single one count.*

"Glad you could join us this fine night," one of the pilots' voices said over the radio.

"Thanks for having us," Leon responded, "What's the plan here?"

"We have been scoping it out for a while up here," a female voice with a Chinese accent said, entering the conversation over the radio. "Figure the best course of action is to target the thinnest section of the limbs and attempt to sever a couple completely off. When you are in place, we will begin with its front left leg and then move on to the front right. We don't know how fast the creature is capable of moving when agitated, so you need a good lead on it before we start."

"Let me know when you feel like you are in optimal range, Kaito," Leon said as he sped the armadillo up to get ahead of the giant's path.

"I am always in range," Kaito laughed. *Wow, that was dumb,* he thought, second guessing his lame attempt to make a joke. "But really, I *should* be good," he confirmed, squinting in the viewfinder as he drifted his aim up and down the goliath. "A hell of a lot bigger in person, huh?" *With four legs and two arms, it is almost like an enormous stone centaur. With its tusks and plant life growth all over its body, the mountain is a stranger, distant from any mythical beings ever conceived by man.*

"We should be good," Leon said into the radio.

"Alright, open 'em up," the male pilot said as he and the other began volleying an array of weaponry at the goliath from above.

Kaito started to launch the explosives through the air and towards the giant. The first one fell significantly short and, after recalculating the lob of the massive shells, he fired again-- successfully hitting above the foot. Every shot climbed higher until effectively pelting the same location that the hellcats struck, the weak-most part of the giant's leg.

Upset with the attack, the beast raised its front legs up in the air and let out a loud, deep cry that sounded like tall metal structures colliding into one another. With the creature's pitch backwards, every shot Kaito took missed, exploding on a different section of the giant's body. The creature then slammed its feet into the ground with enough force to toss the armadillo up into the air.

"Holy shit," Leon grunted from up front as they landed back on the ground.

Kaito realigned his shots to hit the designated area. One after another, he blew away chunks of rock from the giant, which was now chasing after them.

Every stomp of his feet shook the ground so violently, it sent a shockwave pulsing through the ground and the armadillo would raise briefly up into the air, allowing the safety gap between them and the giant to close rapidly.

Kaito, beginning to panic, squeezed the trigger faster until empty, hollow clicks suggested his magazine was empty. He pushed the mag release button and the empty steel dropped to the floor with a loud bang. He reached into a crate and pulled out a full mag. This time, with ease thanks to the strength granted by a fear-induced adrenaline rush, he slammed the mag into place with a click and continued firing.

Just as soon as he had attached it, his trigger pulls resulted in empty clicks. He had already burned through another forty rounds. Kaito released another empty mag and dipped into a crate for another full one.

"He is closing in fast," the vehicle's AI, Amy, called out.

With one of the stompings of its feet, the vehicle again kicked up into the air. This time Kaito went along with it. When the armadillo descended, he smashed his head up into the roof and fell to the floor with blood running down the front of his face.

The magazine that he was holding fell with him and was now half empty. With loose explosive shells rolling around on the floor, Kaito flicked the blood from his eyes away with his wrist, then went back for another full mag. With all his strength, he heaved it up and into place before taking a seat back at the controls of the weapon.

"He is too close. The railgun cannot aim vertically up to hit the target area," Kaito screamed.

"Keep firing," Leon barked. "Hit it anywhere to get him off of us!"

Kaito's next squeeze of the trigger blasted the giant in the hand as it reached down and swung at the vehicle. Kaito's drone, Libra, who was attached to the outside of the armadillo, exerted a barrier field, which absorbed most of the blow from the beast. But nothing could prevent the force from tossing the vehicle up and out, like a child throwing a tantrum and flinging his little toy car. The armadillo flew for miles until spinning and rolling to a smoky, dusty stop.

Libra burnt out and exploded after absorbing every impact except the last few rolls. Indicators of system failure, flashing lights and sensor sounds, filled the interior of the vehicle along with smoke detectors from fire that had erupted from the vehicle's engines. Due to the death of Libra, all shielding power was gone--not that she would have much impact on the fire and the damage exerted throughout the inside of the vehicle where Kaito now lay, passed out, and covered in blood.

***

Jason watched as the armadillo sailed off through the sky and he felt his stomach drop knowing the crew within it was flying off to meet with a reaper to arrange the details of their deaths.

"Launching nova missile to detach limb one in seven seconds," he said over the radio to Lanfen, trying to stay focused. "Ceasefire on my mark, four, three, two, one."

The sounds of chaos halted as they stopped firing all of their weapons. Only a single silent missile drifted from Jason's hellcat and worked its way into the open wound on the giant's leg. The timed explosion soon erupted from the crater after reaching its target depth and, with a radiant light, the leg was severed clean off.

"On to the next one. Reinforce firepower on my target area."

Jason swiftly and accurately adjusted the wings and weaponry to properly take aim at the giant's other front leg before unleashing a barrage of firepower. All weapons set to overdrive triggered alarms and lights within the cockpit: warning of imminent systems failure due to abundant stress on the vessel's power core.

"Jason, relax. You are going to blow a reactor," Lanfen warned, detecting the inevitable.

Bits and pieces of the giant's exoskeleton were being vaporized into dust. Pebbles poured from wounds like blood gushing from laceration of skin and, reluctantly, Lanfen joined in on the added volley of firepower.

"Lanfen, arm a laser-guided missile and set it for penetration on the opening," Jason called over the radio. "We have to compensate for losing our ground support."

"Ready, fully armed and set to deploy."

"Ceasefire and deploy in three, two, one."

Again, silence as a single missile traveled through the air and penetrated the giant's open wound. The damage was significant, but the two of them had not dished out nearly enough to detach the leg.

Now limping, the giant swung its arms through the air trying to swat off its attackers, but with ease the two hellcats drifted in and out of harm, while re-engaging with their target area.

"Prime your final two missiles Lanfen."

"Fully armed."

"Three, Two, One."

The two missiles made their way to the target zone but were intercepted mid-flight by the colossus, who swatted at them with the palm of his hand. They exploded on impact and sent severed stone fingers falling from the sky until they slammed into the ground. Once more the giant let out a cry of pain. Rocks poured from its wrist, which was now split wide-open. The hand looked as though it had been fed through a blender and retrieved only still partially intact.

"Damnit," Jason screamed as he shifted his wings and thrusters to dip down close to the giant's target leg, "Distract him!"

"How?" Lanfen shot back.

"I don't know. Get up in its face. Hit 'em in the eyes."

Now as close to point blank as he could be, Jason hailed a storm of lasers into the open wound, before pumping out a half a dozen anti-grav grenades and taking flight out. Slowly, the explosives ate away at what was left of the ligament that attached the mangled limb to the body.

Burn marks stretched across the giant's face as Lanfen continued firing into its eyes. As its leg finally gave away, it tipped forward, smashing into the ground and taking her hellcat with it in a sizeable explosion.

"No!" Jason screamed, "No! No! No!"

His friend and partner was instantly vaporized in the collision. She was killed executing an order he had given her in order to protect himself.

***

Leon reached through an endless sea of black smoke, searching for the bright red release hatch designated for an emergency hydraulic blowout of the armadillo's door. Finding it, he punched it with all of his strength and the door blew out, taking with it a heavy mass of the smoldering air.

Choking and coughing on the thick smoke that still lingered in the vehicle, Leon crawled over to Kaito, who wasn't moving. Grabbing hold of his comatose friend, he began dragging him out.

His heart felt like it was beating in slow motion. The will to survive was, at core, the fundamental utmost basic of man's primitive instincts. Amidst times of chaos, the human body is capable of switching into automatic mode, executing the command of a million years of genetic code.

Once outside, Leon tried to get to his feet to carry his companion away from the armadillo, which was on fire with a stockpile of explosives still inside. But in climbing up, he immediately fell back down. He discovered he had been wounded from a large piece of metal lodged deep within his leg.

Clenching Kaito by the vest with his sore and blackened fingertips, he continued crawling, dragging himself and his comrade as he grunted and screamed in agony, leaving a thick trail of blood behind him.

Booms in the distance suggested the hellcat pilots were still combating the giant, but Leon had no time to look. He continued clawing and scraping at the ground, trying to reach safety behind a cluster of large, tan rocks.

Blasts began sounding off in the armadillo and Leon pushed himself to slither forward faster as the piece of metal stuck in his leg dug deeper, sapping and draining him of more energy and blood.

Now leaning against the safety of the boulders, Leon listened to the vehicle emit crackles and roars as the explosives erupted behind him. He peered back as bits of the armadillo's thick protective shell were blown out with such a force that they could slice a man clean in half. Faster the barrage of thunder cried out until the armadillo took off like a rocket and tumbled out of sight.

Panting, Leon looked down and was afraid to remove the clothing and inspect the damage to his leg. He knew the wound must be bad from the intense amount of blood that oozed forth.

Glancing down at Kaito, who was covered in black soot, eyes closed, and motionless, his only thought was, *he may very well be dead.* He wanted to check if his friend was breathing or had a pulse, but figured it best not to. Extinguishing the illusion of hope that he held of his comrade's well-being by confirming him to be dead was something he just would not do.

"Just made it out of there, huh, pal?" Leon said out loud with no response from his stagnant ally. "Yeah, you are right about that one," he added with a laugh. "Yeah, no don't worry about me. I will be alright. Just gonna rest my eyes for a minute, then I will handle it," he finished softly, closing his eyes. "Alright *fine!* Stop fucking bitching about it! I will address the wound," he moaned with a face and beard covered in black. "You are a whiny little shit sometimes. You know that, Kaito?"

Looking down at his leg, he ripped back his pants and assessed the damage. The metal went deep and spurts of blood squeezed out from around the jagged edges at a pulsating rhythm. *As soon as I remove this thing, I am going to lose the rest of my blood,* he thought, looking around for an idea. Bits and pieces of the armadillo were scattered about, some still on fire. He clambered over to a chunk that was still radiant and red; wires on the underside were still aflame but the metal surface was cooling quickly.

So with no time to spare, he screamed a mighty soul-shattering roar like a bear lusting for a kill before he devours his target. The sound of his screams did little to distract the agony he felt as he pulled at the shrapnel that was lodged inside of him. It began to give way and started to slide out, taking with it chunks of meat and flesh from his leg. As soon as it was all of the way out and cast aside, blood began pouring forth from the open wound like an undammed river.

He continued to howl in misery, now from the pain of cooking his flesh alive as he pressed his leg up against the hot ingot. It was a different feeling--a different pain altogether. As grotesque as the stench of burning skin was, it was nothing comparable to the sizzling torment of cauterizing his own wound.

With the injury sealed off, he tried to remove the hot metal plate from his leg, which was now stuck and fused as one with the burnt skin. Spent of all his energy, he somehow mustered enough force to rip the glued-on sheet away, shrieking and gasping for air. Not wanting to know exactly how much skin was attached to the metal, he didn't bother to look at any of the gore before him. He just fell backwards under the early dawn sky and closed his eyes with a trembling, tear-filled sigh.

***

The beast hung its head in what looked to be an emotional expression of sadness. Perhaps it understood it was going to die and felt hopeless in knowing that one of the most tiny and insignificant of species to have ever crossed its path had successfully disabled its front legs and would ultimately be the curator of its demise. The alien intruder known as man had arrived to deliver death. The goliath had not placed the order, but this one was on the house.

Jason felt nothing as he hovered over the beast. He watched it slip away in agony as dawn approached. A new day was inbound. This fresh morning did not bring with it the hopes and aspirations of life, however. This daybreak would only serve to illuminate the truth that death was the only path of fate before the behemoth of stone.

Sporadic fires spread fast among the giant's backside, consuming all the living plant life that grew and thrived in the safety of the once mobile plateau. Even those not afflicted by the flame began to wither and fall to the ground, as if abandoning ship.

The giant stretched its neck and let out a loud, drawn-out moan that sounded of whales crying in the ocean. This was precisely the moment Jason was waiting for as he was quick to thrust forward and unload every last anti-gravity bomb he had aboard down into the giant's now open mouth.

Flinching in dismay, the goliath panicked and tried to upheave the twisting and turning that took place within its own throat. What was occurring was something the beast had never seen nor imagined. Its insides were literally being vaporized into nothingness and with this, Jason let forth a minute smirk of success.

"Sorry, not sorry," he whispered.

Looking around for any sign of the armadillo, Jason spotted a flame roaring off in the distance that leaked a thick, black plume of smoke into the sky. Forward he soared to check for survivors and leave the giant alone to die a torturous death.

"Armadillo, do you copy?" he said into his radio, "Anyone alive? I am en route."

He brought his hellcat down to the bare molten shell of the armadillo. What was left of the vehicle was nothing more than bits and pieces of warped steel wreckage.

"No one is alive in there," he mumbled with a sigh before elevating back up and out to drift through the lonely pre-dawn sky--his only solace of solitude. He made way for the highest mountain in a range--roughly a hundred miles to the east-- to watch the incoming sunrise.

***

The hour had approached to begin the work day, and everyone in block sixty-five calmly got ready, trying to ignore the fact that the two guards assigned watch through the night were still passed out, covered in their own sick.

"Oh, hey," Lucas said as he climbed out of bed and got dressed. "How long have you been awake?"

Ness didn't notice the words that Lucas formed. He was stuck in his own head, terrified that his younger brother would not be capable of the workload ahead of him. His mind raced for a solution to defend Lucas from the long, harsh, brutal day to come, but there simply was no such option available in any given route.

Lucas was to rejoin the workforce after being given time off to rest and heal after being trampled in a frenzied stampede of frightened victims during the day one massacre. Today would be his first day at work on the planet to be called home.

The inhabitants of block sixty-five shuffled into a line and made way for the doors of New Horizon. Once outside, Ness was surprised to see that the crews who had worked through the night had accomplished so much. The base framework for three future buildings were in place and were a staggering ten stories in height. A complex, multi-tier monorail system was being built around the city blocks, and a team of engineers was constructing the transport trains that would navigate the rails in the coming days.

"Alright guys, today we have a new site to dig out," the block's fat manager said with a look of exhaustion that carried over from the day prior.

The shepherd led his flock to a tapered-off zone of dirt where three guards pointed and laughed at two others, who wrestled about in the dirt.

"Let's get to it, people," the manager sighed.

"So, we are just going to dig all day?" Lucas asked his older brother.

"Probably so," Ness said as he heaved a pickaxe into the dirt to soften the soil.

"Well, that's easy," he said, driving his shovel into the ground.

Yea, you think that now, Ness thought. *Just you wait for us to be eight hours in and not even at the halfway mark.* The ground began to rattle, and Ness looked over to the warp gate, which began to howl to life once more as it worked its magic to pull in another carrier. *How many is that now?* Ness wondered, *Three?*

The boys and their respective block of companions worked the dry morning away, mostly quiet as to not upset the guards. They removed the dirt from the zone soon to be the location of another small skyscraper.

A few hours into their work day, a brute of a man, a soldier, jumped into the pit they had dug out and scanned through the cluster of workers. In full stride, he approached straight towards Ness and stopped but a foot away. His armor color was orange, similar to the soldier Ness had seen the night before that silently passed by with a drone and rifle. He looked over to Lucas and then back to Ness.

"You," the brutish man said as he pointed down to the two boys, "Come with me."

Oh my God, he knows about the rifle! They must have found it! Ness thought as the realization of what was happening before him came to fruition.

"Wait no, I can explain everything," Ness spurted out, ready to spill the beans of the murderous man Roger and his eyepatch.

"Not you," the man growled. "The smaller one, you," he

said, pointing to Lucas.

"What? No, wait!" Ness cried as he grabbed his brother's shoulder.

Losing him would be even worse than getting caught with the rifle, he thought.

"He is just catching his breath for a minute. He will get back to work," Ness pleaded.

"Come on now, I don't have all goddamn day!" the soldier barked.

"He is supposed to stay with me! That was the deal when we signed onto this project. We are not to be separated!"

"We need someone small enough in size to fit into a section of the warp gate that requires maintenance," the man said with firm clarification.

"I will come with him, I-"

"I only need one boy," he snarled, cutting him off.

"But I am his legal guardian. He-"

"It will only take a couple of hours kid, relax," he said, again cutting Ness off midway through his sentence.

"It's okay. I will be back in a little bit," Lucas said, drenched in sweat as he turned his head and forced a pathetic smile back to his concerned older brother. "I could use the break away from this pit of stink anyway."

Chapter 11
Where No One Knows Your Name

Tyler felt foolish for being so worried about navigating out of New Horizon. Aries had led him out with ease and now, with dawn approaching, the two crossed through the city's construction sites. Sparks fell to the ground from above where crews welded steel together. An industrial skyline was beginning to rise and blend in with the high desert mountains off in the distance. It was all starting to come together, and here he was, leaving, perhaps never to return.

"What happens after we save Scorpio? We can't come back here, can we?" he asked his drone upon realizing any welcoming party in their return would be holding handcuffs and a noose.

"I will figure something out, Tyler."

"Yeah, I am sure," he said rolling his eyes.

How crazy to be adhering to the will of a robot, Tyler thought. *It is supposed to be the other way around--robots executing the commands of man. Are artificial intelligence drones advanced enough to have desires and aspirations of their own? Who programmed free will, and how? Or were the bots so far gone that they are now capable of freeing themselves from software boundaries and restrictions? A true form of life in the flesh of a metallic chassis and circuitry. If this were true, is man a god for having engineered such life?* The conscious debate within himself over what he did not and likely never would understand scared Tyler out of his wits. He tried to shift his thinking towards a different topic. "Where are we going?" he called out.

"The only known entrance to the hive. We will try to navigate deeper once we gain entry and ping Scorpio for a more specific location."

"But shouldn't it be collapsed from the bomb?"

"Yes. The missile navigated successfully through the tunnels and made its way into the heart of the city. However, when I mapped out the caverns, I discovered many smaller tunnels that likely lead deeper via alternative routes."

As they walked, civilization began to fade away. The wind was refreshing, bringing a crisp, cool, pre-morning air that smelled simply marvelous and abstract compared to the scents back in the industrial world brought into Flare by the carriers and their populous.

The sky slowly began turning pink as the sun was starting its rise. Its shine on the red rocks of the distant mountains composed a symphony allure like nothing Tyler had ever seen. "I am not sure what is more beautiful, the sun rise here or the clear midnight sky," Tyler said in awe over the greatness before him.

"Certainly a wondrous planet before us," Aries added.

Down below the lower edge of the mountain range, where the rocks trickled off to expose a faraway sky, Tyler could make out dark clouds that sparked a silent red lightning. It was too far to tell for sure, but he assumed the lightning was accompanied by the odd balls of fire that spewed down from such storms. "Haven't seen one of those in a while," Tyler said in reference to the storm off in the distance as he looked at Aries. "Will it cross our path?"

"Their trajectory seems unpredictable, but given the gap between us and it, I would say that we should make it to our destination well before it becomes a problem."

Looking ahead at all the detail painted about the landscape, Tyler noticed what looked to be a pack of dogs roaming in the desert. "Do you see that?" he asked her.

"See what?" she questioned, turning to look in the same direction as his gaze.

"You don't see those," he paused, thinking of what exactly to call them as he made out more of the detail in their figure, "Four-legged, purple creatures out there? There are three of them."

"I am not sure what you are talking about, Tyler."

How could she not see? he wondered. *Her optics are light years more advanced than inferior human eyes.* Though now at a much slower pace, the two of them continued walking. Tyler squinted to gather more detail on what exactly the creatures were: veiny, furless, purple dogs. None of them had faces: no ears to hear, no nose to smell, and no eyes to see. Just blank, empty faces. Standing still, they turned their heads in the direction that Tyler and Aries walked, as if somehow observing them.

"I think they are watching us," he said, beginning to feel creeped out.

"Tyler, when is the last time you have ingested water?"

She was implying that he was hallucinating the creations in his head. Purple, four-legged, faceless dogs wandering about in the foreign desert definitely sounded a little crazy.

"I don't know. I am really thirsty though. I don't have stimpacks, either," he said in a panic. He began feeling overwhelmingly dizzy and lightheaded as he started to perspire through his clothes.

"It is okay, Tyler. Try to remain calm. I will figure something out."

His heart rate began to elevate. Not because of the realization that he had no rations for their journey, but rather in fear of the dogs; for they began walking towards him at a steady, eerie pace. He was overwhelmed with a sense of imminent harm: a threat caused by the creepy presence of the devious, yet blank creatures. He pitched forward feeling more and more woozy. Holding himself up with his palms against his knee caps, he vomited into the dirt, before losing his balance and falling down onto the dusty ground, unconscious.

***

"Vice Admiral Fox," said the humanoid bot, Linus, as he entered the bridge of the ship where she was reviewing data across her command table.

"What, Linus?" she mumbled, maintaining eye contact with the intricate display of colors and numbers sprawled out before her.

"Tyler Flynn has escaped."

This quickly caught her attention and drew her gaze from the data before her over to Linus. The bot approached and handed her a tablet with a video from a security camera.

Her eyes boiled with anger as she watched the feed of Tyler and Aries walking down a hallway and making their way out of New Horizon without the slightest bit of effort. They passed soldiers who barely even made eye contact. "When was this?" she hissed.

"Directly after you left."

"Where are they now?"

"They made it out of New Horizon and exited the city. We are unsure of which direction they went as the bot, Aries, scrambled video footage once they were outside."

In a fit of rage, she screamed like a barbarian echoing a furious war cry before battle, then slammed the glass tablet into the ground, shattering and distorting the display. The zoomed image of Tyler looking directly up at the camera overhead became stuck in a loop. "I should have just killed him myself right then and there. Now I have another problem to deal with," she said, shaking her head at the broken glass.

"What are you going to do?" Aisha asked.

Fox pressed her temples inward with the tips of her index fingers and closed her eyes, letting out a long, drawn-out sigh.

"First, I am going to kill the person that gave Tyler Flynn a bloody weapon. Then, I am going to hunt down this worm and his robot. I will peel the layers of skin from his body in little sections while he is alive, and then hang him with the bot's inner circuitry!"

"We know who gave Tyler the weapon: a guard from block ninety-one was found dead with his neck broken this morning, and his rifle was missing," Linus explained.

Aisha looked to the ground. How foolish she was to glimpse up at Aries in that hallway when they were leaving and think anything other than the scenario where the robot saves its master. She felt partly to blame for not holding better intuition, however far-fetched and unlikely it would have seemed at the time.

"Get out, Linus," Fox said flatly.

The human-like robot nodded in acknowledgement and left the two alone on the bridge of the ship.

The glass wall began to flicker to life with color and sound, indicating a live video feed call was pending.

"Answer," Fox said firmly.

President Walker appeared on the display with a look that suggested that he too was not pleased.

"Sir," Fox said as she straightened her back and focused on him.

"I hear things are not going so well down there, Natalia," he said with disappointment.

"A slight hiccup in security, but things are progressing ahead as scheduled," she defended.

"Yes, well, I believe the deal was for you to be granted a period of time to establish the city and implant a sense of trust in government," he said, keeping his eyes perfectly still.

The vice admiral had nothing to say, and what could she? Aisha wanted to step in and defend her, but knew that doing so would be like signing up for a public crucifixion.

"If you cannot maintain order, I will replace you with someone who can. It may have only been five soldiers on a dig site, and one night guard aboard your ship that got killed, and one terrorist extremist in your retention you allowed to get loose… petty in the grand scheme of things around here, but the events of Tyler Flynn will have a rippling effect on the citizens of Flare. You do follow, right, Natalia?"

She nodded in comprehension, "I will send out teams to track him down and bring him back for a public execution."

How did the president already know about Tyler and his escape when the vice admiral had only just learned about his escape a few minutes ago? Aisha pondered. *Was someone reporting information to him before bringing it to Fox? They must.*

"Don't waste the resources now. You do not even know which direction he has gone off to," he said with a sigh. "Let him run off and die in the desert. With no food or water, he will perish by nightfall. Focus on getting the city built, satellite coverage up, and unifying the people on the ground. When the sats are up, if he is still alive, they will find him and we can hit him with an air strike."

"Yes sir," she said with a nod.

The president took a deep breath. "I like you, Natalia, and I think you are capable of leading the charge on Flare, but you are facing a real invisible threat here."

"I know, Sir, and thank you."

The open communication feed ended and the vice admiral let out a sigh of relief whilst turning to face Aisha and prop herself up by leaning against the table.

"What was he talking about with invisible threat?" Aisha asked.

A glass tablet beside her began flashing, delaying her response to Aisha's question. Fox picked it up to read the message awaiting her eyes.

"Well," Fox said, pausing to think for a moment as she finished reading the message. "There are three types of people allowed access to Project Salvation. Members of military, members of the civilian workforce, and the rich, elite, political leaders."

"What deems someone rich in a society without money?" Aisha questioned.

"Money exists; you just can't see it. While most military personnel are signed up for a life of service, the workforce population has to work X amount of years to pay off the free ride across space. X is determined by multiple factors, such as type of workload, performance, what they contributed prior to lift off, etc. What nobody knows is that in most cases, the debt you owe exceeds the amount of years you will live. So the exact figure of money you must work off is blurred behind a complex algorithm of smoke and mirrors," she paused to take a deep breath, "And then there are the rich. It is basically a class put in place by the elite back on earth that would ensure they would not have to fall into the other categories of work. They paid for their entry and gave themselves their titles of political leadership. They most often refer to themselves as CU, Citizens United."

"So, the president is just a self-purchased politician?"

"No, he is military. In the fear and chaos leading up to this point, a leader was chosen based on strengths and ideas. So, in that regard, we were lucky."

"So, who exactly are we talking about? Who is Citizens United?"

"It seems as though I have an unannounced meeting with them in less than an hour," she said, placing the tablet back on the table. "So, you shall see firsthand shortly. Just remember why you are here. Stay on your toes, Aisha Sayegh."

"What is this, some conspiracy? We are all supposed to be on the same team here."

"Conspiracy? No, my dear. This is politics."

***

Kio-Kai slept in a chamber, submerged in lifeblood along with hundreds of other survivors from the bombing of Val-Muel. Millions died in the city--now turned ruined wasteland-- but the rest of the hive was mostly untouched. Tunnels collapsed that networked deeper underground for miles, but in doing so, they sealed off and saved most of the hive from any backdraft blast. No active queen was hurt in the bombing, all nestled away safely, many miles deeper into the ground; and so in enduring times of hardship, the Vai-Zik would again press on with their undying legacy.

The queens had instructed their clans to retreat deeper into the hive and stay dormant while they assessed the damage and determined what the best course of action to take might be. Aside from those telepathic instructions received, Kio-Kai's time spent asleep as he regenerated his broken body left him trapped in his own mind. The sorrow that he felt for his dead friends was an endless pit that one hundred stone giants could not fill.

Today, telepathic commands were given via the queens calling for some of the greatest of clans to convene in the assembly halls of Sta-Bel, a major city nearby. So Kio-Kai awoke, poked through the thin layer of mucus that encased him in the lifeblood, and fell to the floor--wet and sticky. He squirmed to his feet as if born again and stretched his wings in an attempt to dry and free them of the goo that dripped heavily from them.

He felt weak and yet anew. His limbs, which were once broken, were now healed. His bones ached, but were again whole and solid. His antennae had grown back atop his head and hung down to his sides where they rightfully belonged. His skin abrasions were alleviated-- healed closed during the time he spent regenerating in the lifeblood. A little more time in the chamber wouldn't have hurt by any means, top out on healing of his body and soul, but for the most part, he felt revived, made full again, and ready to carry through battle to avenge his dead friends and family.

"How are you feeling?" asked a young twitcher drone that inspected him from head to toe with his big, efficient eyes.

"I have never felt better," Kio-Kai responded as he rolled his stiff neck in circles until loose. Looking around the chamber, Kio-Kai could see some of the other survivors from the ravaged city. Still suspended in their cocoons, not many were as lucky as he to have survived the tragedy. Even fewer were healed enough to escape their mending prisons as soon as he. Grateful to be alive, but knowing that the attack on the city was a moment in history he would never forget, he stretched his wings and took flight towards the city of Sta-Bel.

***

"Vice Admiral, the council is here to see you," Linus announced.

For the first time in the past forty-five minutes of awkward silence, Fox lifted her head from the table she sat before. She had not spoken a word to Aisha or anyone else for that matter. She simply waited for this moment. Giving a nod, she stood, stretched, and assumed a professional, straight-postured stance.

Three men and two women entered the room wearing long, thick, gold and black silk robes. Below the cuff line, on their right arms, they each sported what look to be oversized, shiny metallic wrist watches with curved displays that wrapped around their arms like a bracelet. They shuffled in line and took a seat at the other end of the table.

No smiling, hellos, or eye contact. Just entering, walking to their chairs, and parking their old, decrepit asses in a seat, Aisha thought.

"Counselor Lewis, Guajardo, Axstrasa, Ivanok, and Scott." Linus said walking behind each member of the group, stopping to introduce each by surname. Just as soon as he had concluded his introduction of the lot of them, Aisha had forgotten their names.

How does the vice admiral keep track of all this? she thought.

"Good to see you, Miles, it has been a while," the vice admiral said with a smile.

Even Aisha knew that such a smile was forced and fake, and she was quick to pick up on Miles being the leader of the posse, as he was the first to speak.

"Vice Admiral Natalia Fox, the council is very displeased with your leadership as of late and deems to find you accountable for a list of unjust, immoral actions, on top of multiple violations of the laws set in place via the Project Salvation terms. Not only have you violated these terms on multiple fronts, but *you* above all others should have a very good understanding of these laws as you personally took an oath to uphold them."

"Wow, getting right to it, huh?" Fox spat.

"This is a serious matter, Miss Natalia, for you to take it lightly would be to add another charge against you," Miles fired back, his eyes burning through her.

"I think the president would speak in a positive manner on my behalf. I would like to request time to find a suitable lawyer and gather a defensive strategy for myself against these charges, as well as reach out to the president for his input on any matter of injustice."

"Denied. The days of lawyers and strategies of lies within trials has been long since abolished. When accused of a crime, it is best to swing down the hammer of righteousness swiftly and justly. Something you failed to do in the case of Tyler Flynn."

Wow, that was incredibly low, Aisha thought. *Is that what this is about?*

"Is it true that you were the last person to see Tyler Flynn in his cell before his escape?" one of the two women on the council pressed. Her face was old and full of wrinkles like a dried-out grape.

"This is true. Though it is currently to the best of our knowledge that his escape was carried out with the help of his artificial intelligence drone," Fox defended.

"You see, what irks me is that you made no attempt in searching for the escaped terrorist. Turning the other cheek is quite suspicious in itself with this case," the second councilwoman added.

The president told her not to, Aisha thought. *Tell them,* she screamed in her own head.

"Given we do not know which way he went, I determined it unnecessary to waste resources hunting down a man who will die by sundown without proper rations. Also, I did not want to upset the workforce by flaunting the idea that a radical escaped imprisonment."

"What of the species extinction executed via your command?" one of the old men chimed in, turning the direction of the prosecution to another forefront.

It was then that Aisha realized that they were ganging up on her. Hitting her from all sides with legal jumbo to benefit whatever cause they held at stake.

"All acts of engagement protocol were followed in the extermination of the locust hive. They initiated an attack and we countered in a swift manner that-"

"No, Vice Admiral, the other one," Miles snapped, cutting her off mid-sentence.

"I am afraid I do not follow," Fox played.

"Do you deny sending your nephew on a secretive mission early before dawn this morning to eliminate a nomadic alien entity?" the man pressed.

Natalia stayed silent. She could self-incriminate herself or deny the accusation, but it was clear that this council had knowledge of the mission to dismantle the stone giant.

"This is true," she finally said, breaking the awkward silence in the room.

"To what grounds were the acts of engagement protocols followed there, Natalia?" one of the women interjected.

Fox stayed silent. It was discernible that talking was no longer going to help her through the situation.

"What say you, Natalia Fox?" one of the old men scoffed.

"Do you wish to forfeit this trial we have brought to you?" Miles suggested. "It may well be wise to do so, sparing you from the rest of the charges we have against you."

Still, Fox said nothing. She just maintained eye contact with the floor, as if peacefully reading from some imaginary novel embedded into the steel.

"So be it," he continued. "Due to your previous list of honors, you are given two options. Option one, we strip you of all titles, achievements, and rank, then-- and only then-- may you be allowed to conform into the civilian workforce program. Or," he paused, "Option two, you keep hold of your military achievements and ties and are euthanized with dignity intact. It really is a question of how much you value your own life and if you wish to end it within the institution you have dedicated your life to, or continue it in the civilian-based caste."

How the hell are those options? Aisha thought. *This is insane.*

***

Ness worked through the morning, which had now dissipated, submitting to an afternoon swelter in the desert. He peered over his shoulder every ten minutes or so to look and see if his brother had returned from being pulled away to help with some foreign task up at the warp gate. Every second that passed, another pebble of guilt was added into the pit of his stomach.

I should have told that big, ugly brute no, or I should of went with him, he argued within his mind. *It will only take a few hours,* he reminded himself of the words the man spoke to him. But many hours passed by, and while Ness continued to sweat and perform his own job in the heat, his brother did not return as promised.

"Break time," a man bellowed from down the line and Ness, on edge, anticipating the call for some time, was the first to drop his tools into the dirt and take off, pushing through crowds of workers until he could climb his way out of the pit and head towards the warp gate.

He walked around work zones, careful to not enter them and risk being confused for a worker that should be assigned there. It took him much longer to reach the gate than anticipated, and he knew that his break had been long since over when he actually managed to reach it. He just prayed that no one would notice; no one would come looking and drag him away, at least not until he got eyes on his brother, who had been gone for far too long.

A single warden in his thirties with a rifle slung across his chest stood guarding the single entrance to the fenced-in warp gate. "The hell you doing, kid?" the guard called out to Ness.

"I am looking for someone."

"Looking for someone? Shouldn't you be to work? Who the hell told you to come over here and look for someone?"

"My pit boss did," he lied. "A kid got pulled over this way to help with something, and I am supposed to bring him back."

"Well, there are no kids here, 'cept you."

"Please, I just need to go in and retrieve him. My boss will whip me if I do not return with him," Ness desperately begged.

"What did I say, kid? No one is in there! Only entrance is through me. A team of engineers entered a few hours ago to pull in a carrier, and every single one left after the job was complete. Besides, the warp gate is in a state of cooldown. Anyone foolish enough to go near it now would be dead within minutes."

He is not here, Ness realized, spinning around to look out across the vast desertscape. *Oh, my God! He is not here!*

Chapter 12
Thought Crimes

Now in the great assembly halls within the city of Sta-Bel, with no seats left to take, thousands gathered to learn the next course of action decided by their leaders. Kio-Kai squeezed into an opening on a crowded stairwell to see the stage and listen to the speech.

A queen Kio-Kai did not recognize walked across the stage. She had evolved from a grinder; gone from processing bodies into lifeblood to nurturing, laying eggs, and birthing life from self.

"Today, hundreds of queens convened on the issue of the humans that dwell above us," the queen began as she hissed off into the crowd. "The suspicion has been confirmed, that the humans were indeed responsible for the destruction of our once great city Val-Muel. Determining our best course of action was not an easy thing to do. Deciding whether or not to send lives off to war is never a choice any queen wants to make. But after much debate, we have concluded to sound the drums of war."

The crowd erupted into cheers. They were hungry, but not for food: for blood. Kio-Kai felt it himself, the desire to not only fight the humans, but to rip out their throats. Even if he should fall on the fields of battle, he wished to be remembered for killing thousands in the name of his fallen friends, for not even a thousand human lives could pay the debt of death in claiming one of his comrades.

"Now to speak on behalf of the queens who have made this decision, I introduce you to one of our finest warriors. From the clan of Kai, an elder at heart, this hunter will be the general that leads the assault on the humans," she paused to allow the hunter she spoke of time to come forth, "Qaz-Kai."

Lai-Kai's father, Kio realized.

Because queens do not require a male to lay their eggs, a father within the Vai-Zik was an elder to his children; a teacher in the ways of survival and duty.

"The Via-Zik empire," Qaz-Kai began, his voice deep with authority, "has seen and overcome countless times of hardship. We have faced a bounty of foes and eliminated copious threats. We have defended our lands and spread our empire against all odds. We have conquered everything from rock giants to anolems, and even hydra worms. The humans are weak compared to the strength of the mighty rock giants that still roam our planet. We will overcome, we will prevail, and our way of life will continue. The Vai-Zik together will not fall at the hands of the squishy, weak race of man." The horde grew in admiration, but Qaz-Kai was quick to continue his message. "They are vile little creatures, greedy to take and possess land they do not own. But their tragic invasion may serve as a blessing. While they are no doubt a hostile species, they are simpleminded and quite easy to defeat. Once dead, their bodies are full of nutrients that we can harvest and stockpile in the form of the lifeblood that fuels us all.

We have decided to send a battalion of eighty thousand to the surface in the assault. The assault that will begin in a few hours."

"Eighty thousand? If we send eight hundred thousand, we could end them all, every last one by nightfall," a grinder hissed beside Kio-Kai.

He is right. While a crew of eighty thousand could likely handle them, sending eight hundred thousand would certainly guarantee their demise in a quick and easy fashion.

"Qaz-Kai is wise in battle," a hunter before the disgruntled grinder proclaimed. "Have faith in our leaders. War is chaos, and you don't want to be stuffed shoulder to shoulder in a fight.

"In addition," Qaz-Kai bellowed, "The anolem champion, Brutalius, lived through the collapse of Val-Muel. The best arena fighter we have ever seen will be joining us for the strike against the humans."

Brutalius stepped forth and once again the crowd burst into praise. Brutalius was not a native to the Vai-Zik empire, but all adored him. He was their champion and considered to be as much a part of their family as any hunter, twitcher, or grinder. He did not speak the language of the Vai-Zik, Kio-Kai assumed, but he certainly understood it. Standing upright, he towered over Qaz-Kai and the grinder queen beside him. He was indeed an instrument of war crafted by God and gifted to them all.

"I know that many of you are eager to volunteer for this fight, certainly, more are interested than we actually need. Queens will initiate a draft and select soldiers to join us in the assault. There shall be two groups consisting of forty thousand fighters. I will lead one of them underground to infiltrate the human strongholds, while Brutalius will lead the other into a direct frontal assault.

Our desire is for the humans to be drawn forward to engage Brutalius's battalion. This will grant my army the ability to sneak into one of the hatcheries that spawn the humans and wreak havoc from within, crippling any chance they may have of gathering reinforcements."

The elder hunter's speech was stocked full of youth backed by copious amounts of vitality, ambition, and pride. Brutalius and himself backed away while the queen moved forward. Together, the three shared in a moment of praise and recognition for their resolution in deciding how to best handle the situation with the invaders from above.

***

Vice Admiral Natalia Fox stood before the council of Citizens United facing the ultimate choice of life as a civilian or death as an honored and respected member of the military.

Aisha couldn't believe this was happening, and felt a responsibility to prevent her commander from facing this extreme criticism. By definition, protecting the life of her superior was her greatest priority, and yet she felt hopeless against the council that hid behind the technicalities of law. Political conflict felt personally violent, revealing the uneven distribution of power between levels of authority. In this battle, Aisha was a machine of war, feeling helpless against her opponents.

"I have made my decision, but also have a request for the council," Natalia stated swiftly, not wasting any time contemplating her options in the slightest. "I ask that my execution be carried out on the bridge of my beloved ship. Drifting off into the cold grasp of death while at the helm of my carrier is a fitting death for someone with my ranking and achievements. My assistant, Aisha Sayegh, will carry out the execution." Her statements were bold and full of authoritative demand as she was defining the details of her own death.

Aisha's eyes lit up as if she were being pierced through the belly with a blade. She did not want to have to commit an act of murder--and it would be murder, even if the vice admiral had chosen Aisha as her executioner. Although she felt a sense of pain in the truth of it all, the reality was that her commander would be the real casualty.

A civilian life, where all ties to the military are revoked, was as much a death sentence in the mind of a proud, loyal captain as facing death itself. Natalia was one of the lead architects of Project Salvation, and she had no desire to brand her legacy as a smear in human history.

"Your personal bodyguard, re-assigned to the task of carrying out your execution sentence. A poetic man may find interest in such theatrics. I will grant you your wish," the lead council member said with a twisted smile, as if amused. "You will have thirty minutes to make arrangements with your executioner as to what must be done with your effects in your passing. Any messages you may have for family members or what to do with your personal belongings needs to be addressed. This council may be dismissed into the next room until your capital punishment is carried out and you are confirmed deceased."

The council silently stood up and exited the room to sit and wait for confirmation of death in the next.

There was no appeal, no goodbye, no I am sorry, or good job on the progress of Project Salvation, Aisha thought of the cynically cold group of men and women as they left.

The clicks of Natalia's boots rhythmically echoed across the metallic floor at a slow pace as she took her time in admiring the magnificent ship that she had commanded over for so many years.

New Horizon was her home-- an extension of herself that she had put every last ounce of her soul within. She ran her fingers along its walls in silence and awe with a faint smile, as if being aboard her again for the very first time.

Aisha had no idea how to proceed, and did not understand how the admiral's decisions justified the consequence of death. Fox stopped in her pacing, took a seat on top of her command table, and began.

"A few years ago, Dr. Evelyn Gray was experimenting with overriding the human brain with the artificial intelligence software developed for Project Salvation. The software was uploaded into nanobots and then converted into a liquid-based serum to inject in the brain. It would work like a virus to overtake its host and be in complete control of the subject's intellect. The trials seemed successful, but the human brain would burn itself out trying to eradicate the foreign virus. The body would literally overheat, turning the brain into mush trying to fight off the virus. In time, another strain was tweaked to allow the human body to accept the foreign substance. However, when the virus spread and overtook the brain, it killed the human host and claimed the body as its own. The original idea was to have all the information supplied by limitless intelligence embedded into the human body. Unfortunately, human minds are fragile and unable to share its limited space with a superior being. It will ultimately submit to the greater power. This weakness proved inferior and the virus was able to eliminate the human soul.

Dr. Grey felt as though a host with the will and intelligence to peacefully coexist inside their mind with a foreign intelligence might serve as the only true way to reach a successful trial. She locked herself in her lab and performed the neural injection upon herself. For a few minutes, she successfully tapped into the software overtaking her body and established communication. But when revealing the sense of joy, the human emotion was a trigger for the AI to kill her. A few of her colleagues broke into the lab and injected her with an antidote that killed off the virus. She lived through the experience to tell the tale. Shortly after the incident, the project was shut down and the doctor was stripped of her ranks within the UIGN.

She drifted off into the sunset and continued her work secretly in the private sector where, through corporate backdoors, Citizens United picked her up and funded her to ultimately perfect a simpler version of the serum. This version started out slow and progressed in linking the two entities in a safe speed. This served to not overwhelm the human, and together the software and its host could co-exist for many years within one vessel.

I have no jurisdiction over Citizens United. They are the political entity that keeps the military in check, and the military handles the civilian workforce."

"Who keeps the hierarchy in check?" Aisha questioned, trying to follow in with the history lesson.

"It was the only way to kick start Project Salvation," Fox said, completely ignoring the question, as if implying there was no answer.

"Well, why would CU want to convert all of life into supercomputers?" Aisha questioned, indulging down a different path of curiosity.

"Did you see their wrist watches?"

"Yeah," *How could I not?* she thought. *Every single one of them were sporting the watches like some estranged occultist fashion statement.*

"Those watches can do a many of things. First and foremost, they are linked into their nervous system via a CPU chip that rests in the base of their spine. The single most frightening thing those watches do is allow the user total control over the software serum developed by Dr. Evelyn Gray."

"Why are you telling me all of this?"

"Too many people that are part of this project are naive of how things truly work. We only have ourselves to blame, really. Dumbing down society for so many years, we created the perfect little sheep: obedient, blissfully ignorant, and content in every way. Due to the scale and importance of Project Salvation, humanity needs a team of people aware of the true nature of things to carry on the torch through the darkness of night."

The following silence between the two of them reminded Aisha that she was tasked with killing the vice admiral. An uneasiness overcame her as she tried to reignite any form of conversation. "What of family members and personal effects?" she pressed.

"Bah, I have neither," Fox said coldly, as if not fazed by the lack of friends or companions acquired through her life's journey.

"What about Jason? Isn't he your nephew?"

"Yes, cocky little bastard will be fine," she let out with a sigh before rolling her shoulders and cracking her stiff joints loose. "The president will reassign a replacement to take charge of Project Salvation. My execution is nothing more than Citizens United sending a message to him that the next fool he sends better play by their rules. I have strongly opposed their injection theory. I fear that in my death, there will not be many that stand against their notion for a false sense of security, and in time, Proposition Zero will be passed."

"Proposition Zero?" Aisha questioned, wide-eyed.

"The bill allows for the injection of the military and civilians with a restricted version of the serum that would not have unlimited access to the AI's database of knowledge. If you were a doctor, you would be granted access to anything in that category of intellect. A cook may have access to an unlimited array of recipes and ways in which he may conjure as such. A pilot would be a master of his craft alongside all his fellow pilots. The AI living alongside the host would secretly monitor and report thought activity to anyone wearing the watch. Anyone with the full dose, control watch, and authority could wirelessly project thoughts into the heads of the lesser subjects."

"That is insane," Aisha paused to try and reflect on what she was just told. "No one would agree to artificial intelligence controlling their mind."

"Most of the human populace are sheep to the flock. If presented in a desirable way, the bill will pass." Fox said in a condescending manner to convey a truth she held to a standard as high as the law.

"We would never have the resources to fulfill the proposal. We mustered everything we had just to arrive here."

"The developmental phase is behind us. The nanobots carrying the software can self-replicate, making the process of mass production cheap and easy to achieve."

"How could that ever be presented as desirable?" Aisha said with doubt.

"People can be convinced. If I didn't present the facts and instead told you of all the different possibilities in which life as we know it could be improved-- that we have developed a means that could detect crime before it happened, we could fix the broken mind, and not only eradicate the existence of atrocities caused by man, but truly unify all beings under one banner, a flag representing peace and prosperity? In those scenarios, wouldn't you take the injection?"

This is crazy, Aisha thought.

"Natalia, I can get you out of here. I can-"

"I thought you to be smarter than that, Miss Sayegh," Fox interrupted, as if angered at the thought. "Let us forget you even conceptualized suggesting an escape plan. I have served my country well in life and no one can choose when and how to die. Passing on the bridge of my ship is an honor, and I could never in a million years think of a more fitting way to leave this world. Though I admit, I would have liked to live long enough to see our new city built, but that's okay, no need to be greedy."

"But I can't do it," Aisha wailed tearfully.

"I have been sentenced to death and you have been given an order, Miss Sayegh. Now please do me the favor of carrying out my last wishes so that I may die at the hands of a friend; perhaps the only one I have ever had."

She brushed lint from her uniform and adjusted her collar before standing straight with perfect posture and interlocking her hands behind her back. Her final moments were spent looking across the bridge of her ship, which had escorted her safely across galaxies and into the heart of their new home on Flare. Her ship was the lead carrier in the fleet designed for species self-preservation. The gears were in motion, and some of the most difficult of times in human history had been conquered. Vice Admiral Natalia Fox was at the helm in overcoming countless obstacles and solving a myriad amount of those challenges.

Aisha grasped her blade firmly and took a deep breath. The more force she put into her swing, the cleaner the kill would be. Suppressing her emotions, she focused on the task at hand. She raised the blade, taking aim and positioning it directly behind Fox's neck before pulling it back and swinging it horizontally with as much strength as she could muster.

Natalia's head was severed clean off and Aisha couldn't bear to look down at the body that thumped to the floor in a pool of thick blood.

Turning with tears in her eyes, Aisha wiped the blood from her blade onto her shirt, like a badge of honor for her service, then she sat in a seat at the head of the table while Natalia's decapitated body bled out on the bridge of her ship, New Horizon.

***

You have been chosen, young hunter, to join the forces that march off to battle. Bring honor and pride to our clan as you become an instrument of war. Make your way to the outskirts of the city with all of the others chosen to enlist, and assemble with your peers, Kio-Kai's queen whispered into his consciousness.

Though the odds were not in favor of him being chosen for this draft, he had suspicion that he would make the cut. He obliged to the demands of his queen and made way towards the city of Sta-Bel's main highway, where the draftees were rendezvousing to ship off to battle.

He searched through the crowds for Qaz-Kai, who was at the front of the lines assigning captains to squads for better control of the troops in the thick of the fight to come. In spotting him, he fluttered ahead and landed beside him.

"Qaz-Kai," he called out in admiration as he approached.

Qaz-Kai turned and squinted at first to recognize the hunter who called him by name.

"Kio-Kai?" he called out with a laugh. "It has been far too long since I last saw your face," he added in putting his hands on the much younger hunter's shoulders. "You have grown so much."

"Of all the clans to choose from, a general being selected from the clan of Kai is quite the honor. I could not think of anyone I would rather follow into battle," Kio-Kai said, praising his elder.

"Thank you. Your words are kind. Now stand behind them in giving me your all in the heart of battle and we might just stand a fighting chance."

"Your plan is audacious; I will give you that. It sounds to be promising in avenging our fallen brothers and sisters," Kio-Kai added, before shifting the conversation into a sad direction to convey his respects for his fallen companion. "I am sorry for your loss in Lai-Kai. She was my friend and a wonderful huntress. A true example of what it is we should all strive to be."

"Aye, that she was, and I hold hope that perhaps she may still be."

Kio-Kai wrinkled his face in confusion.

"Her wounds were greatly severe, and while her chance of survival is minimal to say the least, she is currently still technically alive, submerged in a rehabilitation cocoon."

When I was recovering within lady Kai's spawning pools, Lai-Kai was only a cocoon or two away, he thought. *I was in such a hurry to leave for the announcement, I did not even notice her there.*

The ground began to gently rumble and Kio-Kai looked over to see Brutalius approaching the troops. He was closer to the anolem than ever before and couldn't help but feel uneasy about his strength. At any given minute, he could pull apart their limbs with ease and smash their bodies into pieces. He towered over all of them with his body of sharp and jagged stone. Being this close, Kio-Kai could see that the veins of the anolem had a red-like glow to them that radiated through his thick, grey skin. Perhaps the rumors of being born within volcanos were true.

"Looks like we are nearly ready on my end. The queens have made their selections and the remaining forces are assembling now," Qaz-Kai informed the anolem.

The two had already gone over their strategies of war long before the public announcement to inform the hive of the decision for battle. Brutalius was to lead forty thousand above ground to engage one assault, while Qaz-Kai worked through the underground network with his forty thousand for the flank.

"Good luck, my friend. We will see you on the battlefield," Qaz-Kai said to golem.

"*Akanta sumanta butal fanokous*," the living, breathing rock chuckled out loud in his indigenous dialect before turning to his legion of four thousand and shouting a phrase in the Vai-Zik native tongue. "Today, may I die a thousand deaths for my queen so that my hive may live to serve a thousand lifetimes!" His war cry was in a broken accent, but no one seemed to care. The fact that he had taken the time to learn the ancient phrase that not many Vai-Zik clans even knew today by heart was an inspirational moment in history.

Kio-Kai felt the very basin of his spine tingle as Brutalius's troops erupted into war cries and cheers alongside

Qaz-Kai's battalion and the millions of other Vai-Zik that had come to see the armies off to battle.

He began flexing the bone-like blades from his forearms; outwards and inwards, again and again in repetition. This was it. The moment of vengeance was upon them.

***

Tyler roused-- sweating profusely and gasping for air-- to see Aries but inches away from his face. Startled by seeing the bot so close, he flinched back and she ascended above him, discarding an empty stimpack.

"Where did you get that?" he gasped, still choking for air.

"I went back and collected a satchel of them," she explained.

Looking about his surroundings, Tyler noticed that they were in the cave. As he slept they had arrived, but how exactly they got there he was unsure.

"No one stopped you?" he questioned.

"No, no one stopped me."

"You just walked in, took a satchel of stimpacks, and then left."

"I cannot walk, but yes, in terms of human vocabulary, I did just that."

Jeez, Tyler thought. *I would have been shot dead for trying to enter the city.*

"Well, how did we get here?" he pressed, his mind feeling misty and confused.

"I levitated you."

"Ah, right. Well, thanks," he said, scratching his scruffy face and climbing to his feet. "It was quite literally like sleeping on a cloud."

"Shall we continue?"

"Yeah, sure."

The two of them walked down the cave for a few minutes as Tyler shook himself back into full consciousness. In looking up, he noticed that the enormous bats that once lingered in the cavern were now nowhere to be found. He figured the blast from the bomb must have scared them out from their home.

"Did you dream, Tyler?" Aries asked, as she lead the way.

"Uhm, well, I don't know."

"I dream sometimes," she added.

"You dream?"

"Yes, when engaged in standby mode, my mind still races in thought, though all my other functions are dramatically slowed down to conserve as much power as possible. Sometimes, like humans, I cannot recollect my dreams, as my memory banks hold very little storage in standby mode."

That makes sense, Tyler thought.

"What do you dream about?" he asked.

"Of home, and friends, and sometimes even whales. I am very fond of whales. Usually though, my dreams are very abstract in their layout, making it tough to draw logical conclusions from them."

That is fascinating, Tyler thought. *How is that even possible?*

"This should be it," she said, stopping to investigate an opening off to the side of their path.

Plain as day, a hole in the side of the rock lead down into unknown territories: it was large enough for a man to walk through if he ducked his head just a bit.

"How did we not see that the first time we were here?" he questioned with a grin.

"Because you three were not looking for it."

Tyler kneeled down and looked in the opening. A few yards in, it shrunk in size and would become too small for him to walk through but large enough for him to crawl comfortably.

She drifted in ahead. Slinging his rifle behind his back, he hunched down and followed her through.

The channel was lit up by neon flora of green and blue: beautiful little plants that swayed back and forth despite the lack of a breeze or draft to give them a push. Reaching out to touch one with his glove, the little blossom reacted by illuminating brighter, so much so that the exterior became transparent, and Tyler could see the thousands of cells within that made up life for the spectacular flower.

With a smile on his face, he looked up to Aries, who stared at him and the plant, as if right alongside of him, she too was observing the magnificent piece of life they had stumbled across.

After sharing in a moment of awe, the two worked their way through the tunnel, which declined deeper underground. Every few feet, the air became cooler by a degree or two.

The shaft began to resonate as pebbles fell from above. The two of them advanced quickly towards a point that opened up into a chamber large enough to stand in. Looking back, rocks continued to vibrate and the floor gave way, revealing a much larger tunnel that ran horizontally below.

"Holy shit, we were crawling across a bridge," Tyler gasped.

The hole in the shaft revealed the source of upheaval tremors below. It was a large golem made of red and brown stone. Behind him were thousands of the insect-like creatures: locust and larva alike.

"My God," Tyler said in awe. His eyes were as wide as a deer standing in front of a car's high beams the moment before impact. "Where do you think they are all going?"

"I do not know," Aries admitted.

"They look to be marching," he whispered. He then paused as the realization swept over him like an upsurge of high velocity water. "They are going to attack the city."

Aries said nothing. The two peeked over the ledge above as the legion of locusts and maggots followed the golem.

"We need to warn them," Tyler cried.

"We would never make it back before them," she pointed out.

"Well, do something," he screamed. "Send them a transmission, a warning, anything!" After his brief uproar, he looked back down to see if any off the bugs had heard him, but luckily they were oblivious to the man and his robot that dwelled but thirty feet above.

"Our depth underground and the radiation from the bombing is interfering with my long distance com systems," she explained. "I could try and overload my core to get the message out, but I do not know if it will work. Also, doing so would definitely both physically fry you and literally alert them of our presence at the same time," she added.

"Can you levitate us back over the gap?" he questioned, looking back across the large void in the tunnel that carried them safely over top the path below. "We could try to make it back to the surface in time to get the message out.

"I can only levitate you the distance I can glide, and that opening is fourteen feet wide with a thirty-seven-foot drop below," she pointed out.

Frustrated, Tyler pounded a fist down on the cold stone floor. Blood quickly began to trickle down his fingers and through his glove as he pulled his hand back and twitched his lip in anger. Helplessly, he watched the battalion below march forward with aspirations he could only assume were to kill off his friends as he continued to save hers.

Turning away from the horde of insects below, Tyler stood to his feet to inspect the opening that hid himself and Aries. Lit up by more of the colorful glowing flora, another tunnel could be seen about three yards away that descended further underground. Due to the height of the tunnel, he and Aries would be able to walk down instead of crawl.

"You said the radiation from the bombing is interfering with your com systems?"

"Yes," the bot said, blinking ahead.

"Well, what is stopping the radiation from poisoning me?"

"Nineteen years ago, the decorum treaty was signed. This made radiation as a result from a blast considered to be a war crime along the lines of chemical warfare."

War crimes, what a ridiculous concept, Tyler thought. *Throughout the history of man, since the very beginning when one held a club and another fixed a rock to better bash in the skull of his brother, there has always been a vile struggle to one up your opponent to ensure they are eradicated before you. The turn of the twentieth century, countries began calling foul on one another for dirty tricks and plays, as if there is a right and wrong in warfare. It's all genocide at the end of the day.*

"Before the treaty was signed into law," she said, continuing with her history lesson, "Popular weapons left over from the twenty first century would subject blast survivors to radioactive fallout. This had various life shattering effects on all organic creation. Reactions differed based on how close you were to the center of the blast. After the signing, all weapons of mass destruction had to be redesigned so that fallout radiation levels could be within an acceptable level."

"Nineteen years ago," Tyler considered out loud. "That was the end era of the onyx wars, and the resistance at the time was known to have had a stockpile of old-school nukes."

"That is correct, Tyler."

"The decorum treaty was put into fruition to place a mark on the backs of the resistance, another tally in justifying them as the evil side. Political warfare at its finest. But what about you?"

"The damage to electronics via fallout radiation is not protected under the decorum treaty, for we are not considered to be living organisms."

The awkward silence that followed her statement was cut short when the tunnel they walked along opened up into a large room. The size of a warehouse, the room held nothing but bare stone and darkness. Small pockets of the illuminant blossom were found in well-placed corners of the large room, which allowed for a bit of visibility. Requiring a bit more light, Tyler flipped on his flashlight. He quickly spotted what looked to be human beings off in the distance. "Are those people?" Tyler choked as he squinted to make out the blanched-white humanoids ahead.

Tyler led the way in curiosity as the two crossed through the massive room towards the people, but the closer they got, the more Tyler realized that the beings he thought to be human were not such a familiar species. They looked like men and women but had ears, noses, and faces that were far pointier in their shape. Their bodies were naked and pale. So pale that there was almost a transparentness about them. Their veins could be seen clearly through their skin.

They looked over to Tyler and Aries. Tyler froze, gazing within one of the being's eyes, which consisted of pure black. There was no sclera, no iris, only a pupil-- permanently dilated and broad, it embodied the eye as a whole.

After a minute of Tyler's frightened stiffness, the creatures simply reengaged in their conversation--not caring for the man with the rifle who had come from the surface accompanied by a drone.

Reaching to disengage his flashlight in a frightened, clumsy fashion, he snapped off the switch, forcing the light to be stuck in the 'off' position. No longer would he be granted the luxury of having his own portable light source in their journey below the surface of the planet. "I... um, do not know which way to go, Aries," Tyler said, admitting he no longer wanted to take the lead--let alone hold any desire to further approach the creatures.

***

Ness did not return to work in fear of repercussions against his abandonment. While he wanted nothing more than to find where his brother had been taken away to, the hopes of getting any answers were evaporating quickly under the hot sun radiating heat down onto planet Flare. Instead, knowing the soldier that had abducted him had wandered off in this direction, he stayed put, figuring this to be the best location to wait for the man in the orange and white armor.

While waiting, he conversed with the guard who stood at the entrance of the warp gate. Being alone for some time, the man didn't seem to mind the company, though frequently he suggested Ness likely had someplace to be.

"What kind of military member wears white and orange armor?" Ness questioned the guard.

"Orange and white, huh? Well, that would be for spec ops guys. Never seen one myself, but they were the first men to land on this planet. The warp gate was constructed by design using the engines of their ships."

What would a spec ops guy want with Lucas, and where could he have taken him? Ness contemplated, looking off into the desert.

"What ch'ya think of them clouds, kid?" the man asked, gazing up to the darkness that crept its way over nearby range of mountains. Red lightning and fire dropped from the sky, pelting the sierra with a barrage of loud and violent hatred.

"You think it is coming this way?" Ness said with concern.

"I don't know, but if it does, I guess we will see how well these energy shields hold up."

Energy shields, Ness thought, *I never really could understand how exactly they worked. They seem like something out of some sci-fi novel.*

Suddenly, movement below caught his attention, sapping his train of thought. It looked to be a muscular man that was made entirely of stone. He was running in towards the city and the workers who constructed it. The closer he got, the better

Ness could make out the figure to be at a height well over three times that of a man.

Behind him charged a swarm of the insects that had attacked the first day Ness was out on the planet's surface. They rushed forward at such a speed, Ness wasn't sure anyone in the city had even seen them come until it was too late.

"Woah, what the fuck?" the guard that stood at the gate with Ness blurted out in shock as he too noticed there was a full-blown onslaught unfolding before their very eyes.

The golem wasted no time gripping workers and slamming them into one another, breaking the bones in their bodies with ease before dropping them to the ground to move on to his next set of victims.

Witnessing a man fall to the ground, still alive but with no bone structure intact was a horrifying sight to see, but still Ness kept his eyes glued to the scene that played out below.

The locust-like insects leaped and fluttered over one another, sticking their blades into the faces of the unsuspecting civilians while the maggot-like creatures wormed through the crowds, spewing acid onto clusters of bunched-up, frightened people. Screams and gunfire were the only sounds Ness and the guard could hear as they stood and watched the one-sided battle spread like a plague across the land below.

The creature of stone pounded fleeing civilians into the ground like a man bothered with the annoyances of a fly buzzing loudly. Only these flies were not so agile in their retreat, and in no time the golem left puddles of mush as he battered away, single handedly clobbering and killing one after another with ease.

A group of soldiers began focusing their fire on the stone golem but, coming to its defense, a swarm of the insects flew through the air, landing on the array of soldiers, dismantling them into heaps of shredded kevlar and flesh.

Ness couldn't believe it. He wanted to flee, but nowhere would be safe from the invasion.

Chapter 13
Count Bodies Like Sheep

Qaz-Kai came to a halt as the highway broke off into close to a hundred smaller channels that twisted their way upwards towards the surface. Three of them had torches aflame laid out by their entrances.

"Our scouts appraised the tunnels about an hour ago. Only three are still intact and suitable for our attack. Would like more, but this should do so long as we keep quiet," he announced without looking back to address his officers directly. "Split 'em up neatly. We need all of our grinders in the front so that when we reach the surface, we can get straight to burning our way into one of the hatcheries. It should only take us a few minutes to reach the surface and by now, Brutalius and his troops should already be engaged on the front lines."

Kio-Kai wasn't sure if it was luck or by the will of some greater power that the humans--of all places to land on the planet-- chose the outskirts of an entrapment field. These fields were basically a cluster of tunnels that led to the surface in a location designed for ambushing and hunting prey. Almost all of the Vai-Zik's entrapment fields were abandoned and collapsed due to neglect. There simply was not much use for them when most of the planet was starved for life from the overfishing of prey.

It was never like the Vai-Zik to overstretch their reach in acquiring more than they needed, but when the overlords came along, the queens shifted their thinking along with the will of the hive.

It was also never like the Vai-Zik to engage in all-out war. Where they fit in the food chain called for killing of those below and sometimes even those above, but to organize a small number as eighty thousand in the name of vengeance and self-preservation against an enemy that didn't kill them for food, but rather sought to eradicate their very existence like some undesirable pest was a new concept entirely to the hive.

They sounded their drums with the intention of playing by the rules of the humans, seeking to kill and destroy every last one until none lived to walk the surface of Flare.

Qaz-Kai was first to enter one of the channels. Forty thousand, split evenly into the three canals. They began their final push up towards the surface where they would reclaim their planet from these vile foreign invaders.

***

Following Aries into a hallway that twisted down lower underground, Tyler found himself entering a room where three of the bleached skin humanoids-- girls-- danced together nakedly in a corner lit by candlelight. Their bodies were thin and frail, yet somehow sexually appealing. One girl in particular swung her hips provocatively and ran her left hand down her small but curvy frame as her right hand caressed her inner thigh. She made eye contact with Tyler and his spine went cold. Her black eyes seemed to pierce through his being and wrench his gut into liquid. He slowly came to a standstill, simply floating out of his body and into hers. In that moment she was everything he had ever desired. Lusting to hold her, grasp and kiss her neck, he shook his head and disengaged eye contact.

What the hell am I doing?

He slowly began pressing on and couldn't get the desire he felt for the girl from his head. He felt her eyes burning into the back of his head, and he wanted nothing more than to turn around and once more look upon her.

Turning the corner that led into the next room, his affectionate infatuation with the girl perished quickly when he saw two holes dug into the red rock floor. These holes shaped out couches where two creepy men--one thin with greasy, slicked-back hair and the other short with a potbelly--lay sprawled, gazing up towards two naked young men dancing with each other. The two young men looked uncomfortable, but their movements and thrusts were accurate and precise, as if they had been partaking in amusing the eerie gentlemen on the ground for quite some time.

The shorter, fatter one took a sip from a chalice of red goo and smiled, for his entertainment was a pleasure of unmeasurable feats. His teeth were jagged with a sort of rusty appearance. He raised his long, decrepit hand, pointing to the young boys and ushering them towards himself. They climbed down into the hole with the man and lay on top of him just as Tyler turned the corner out of sight.

The fuck is this shit? Why do these people... these creatures pay no mind to me? Only Aisha and her drone are equipped for stealth, so clearly these things can see me, Tyler thought to himself.

Up ahead was a twisting corridor that did not grant much light to see what lay beyond. Aries silently drifted down before Tyler. She knew the routine. He closed his eyes and opened them anew through hers. He could see perfectly into the dark thanks to her night vision. He gave her a nod to signal he was ready to continue on as he adjusted his mind to walking behind his new eyes. Like a zombie with his eyes white, rolled into the back of his head, the experience of seeing through a drone was one he never fully got used to. It was a trip to say the least.

He followed the drone, twisting and turning from one tight passage into the next. Each one seemed to be stranger and more fluctuant in its layout than the last. Buried into the wall of this passage were bodies, well preserved and detailed. Most had permanent facial expressions of horror and pain. Tyler reached over to touch the face of a girl. Her nose had begun to rot out from her face, but her cheeks were still soft.

"This is insane," he mumbled.

His eyes moved on while his body stayed behind, examining the dead within the wall. Quickly, he again faced himself forward and caught up to his set of floating eyes.

Canals of what looked to be blood, slowly flowing like pipes carrying water, led the two through an opening out into a fairly large room much greater in size than the first one they had found. Various fires lit up the area via torches, candles, and scattered piles of seemingly random flame.

Tyler's eyes rolled down and his vision was again his own as Aries drifted back up and into her position.

Screaming could be heard off in the distance and this broke Tyler into a jog to investigate.

***

Thousands of grinders spewed acid onto the outer shell of a carrier. The burning sound of melting steel being eaten away by the liquid secreted from the glands within their mouths and beneath their tongues was loud. But the sound was vastly outweighed by the screams of the humans preoccupied with the immediate conflict they faced in their front lines.

A line of hunters guarded the grinders as they continued crafting holes into the ship for them to enter through.

Fleeing from the battle, a human came blitzing around the corner as he huffed and puffed in fear for his life. Before he had a chance to comprehend what it was that he had stumbled upon, Kio-Kai, fluttering forward, rammed one of the blades that stuck out from his arms clean through the man's face. Both he and the man fell into the dirt and Kio-Kai stood up, withdrawing his blade from the caved-in skull. He looked around to see if any of the other humans had noticed the kill, but they had not. They were too busy still fighting in the front lines against Brutalius and his contingents, who were already engaged in their full-blown assault.

"We are almost in," Qaz-Kai announced. "Ready the dwellers," he added in reference to the troops that stayed hidden underground.

Kio-Kai ran over to the three large holes with two other commanders to relay the message to all that awaited a chance to come to the surface.

The grinders continued spewing acid onto the walls until there were holes burnt into the vessel large enough for the Vai-Zik forces to squeeze through. Qaz-Kai looked back to Kio-Kai and gave a nod before charging inside himself.

Half of Qaz-Kai's battalion stayed outside and engaged in flanking the frontlines of combat while a stampede of Vai-Zik, hunters and grinders alike, surged from the ground and made their way into the vessel behind their heroic leader, who was not afraid to be the first to enter into the unknown.

Once inside, they burned and cut their way through thin walls to find rooms packed full of humans by the thousands. Caught off guard, they were easy kills; perhaps the easiest of prey Kio-Kai had ever hunted in his entire life. They screamed and ran, but had nowhere to flee for safety. Most, if not all of the humans, were unarmed. None of them fought back and soon, room after room was filled with blood and corpses.

"Why do they not fight back?" a grinder yelled after spewing acid into a horrified crowd, who fell to the ground as their skin bubbled away.

"It is a hatchery. Perhaps these are nothing more than children and workers," another grinder suggested.

"Kio-Kai, Nast-Kai, Drak-Zo, and Mala-Nan, with me," Qaz-Kai called out to Kio-Kai, a grinder, and two other hunters.

The five of them veered off down a hallway that steered them in the opposite direction of the spreading chaos brought in with their invasion. They passed many doors and chambers, but they did not stop to enter.

A human exited one of the rooms and began to flee down the hallway. One of the hunters leapt up and fluttered over to the frightened man, landing on his fat back and crushing his bones as he forced him to the floor. The hunter thrust his blades into the man's back again and again until the body went from flailing about in terror to stopped limp in death.

"What are we doing?" Kio-Kai asked as they passed more of the chambers that they should have been entering and clearing.

Qaz Kai was looking up to hieroglyphic-like letters that were stamped above the doorways to each area they passed by. The rooms had been marked, possibly to better organize whatever the humans did natively within.

"Here," Qaz-Kai said, stopping at a door and pointing at the symbols above as if he knew their meaning.

The grinder that accompanied them stepped forward and began burning away at the door until its frame liquefied and dripped to the floor, exposing a room of frightened children.

Entering, Qaz-Kai quickly caught one of the unnerved boys. Gripping him by the arm, he inspected him for a moment before puncturing his blade with precision through the elbow, whilst pulling on the wrist to separate it from the boy who flailed about in horror.

Slowly, the wrist and forearm detached, exposing strings of tissue, muscle, veins, and blood. All the while, the boy screamed in agony for having his arm plucked away from his body. Qaz-Kai slid a piece of jewelry down the segregated arm and looked it over.

"Harvest them of their bracelets and be careful not to damage them," he commanded. "We need every single one we can find."

Kio-Kai watched as the two other hunters sprung forward and detached the arms harboring the bracelets, just as Qaz-Kai had shown them.

"Drak-Zo, come here," Qaz-Kai said, summoning the grinder forward. "I am sorry, my brother," he muttered before gutting him from the belly up and cleaning him of his insides.

The grinder squealed in pain and confusion at being betrayed until his head was removed. Qaz-Kai flipped over the now calm, empty torso and continued with the fillet.

"Get their bracelets, Kio-Kai," he barked, catching the young hunter staring at him with a look of disgust.

Turning towards the cluster of humans who were now crying and cowering together in a corner, Kio-Kai saw half of them on the floor, still alive and weeping with their arms ripped off.

He approached one. It was a young boy with an ugly face who was wearing strange clothing. Poking him through the face with his blade, Kio-Kai made haste in killing the child before severing off his arm and harvesting the jewelry.

"Throw them in here," Qaz-Kai command as he flipped the grinder's belly inside out to use as a large sack for safely carrying the contraband.

After they obliged, he buttoned the pouch together using bits of broken bone and then slung it over his back before turning to exit the room.

"What use does the Vai-Zik have of these?"

"Kio-Kai, as much as I would like to tell you that our mission today was carried out in the name of vengeance, that simply would be untrue. We are here to collect as many of these as possible."

"But why?"

"Because when a queen gives her command, Kio-Kai, we oblige. That is who we are: an extension of her. Only through her do our lives serve purpose and have meaning. We do not question her demands."

The sounds of screams and murder could be heard just outside the door. The Vai-Zik militia had spilled over into the hallway, where they were going from room to room, clearing out all life.

Exiting out into the chaos, Kio-Kai spotted a group of humans setting up what he could only assume were large, powerful ranged weaponry at the opposing end of the corridor. A storm of firepower quickly came billowing down the hall, and hundreds of Vai-Zik began to drop to the ground as they were pelted and ripped apart by the immense weaponry.

Retreating off into another hall, the horde was confronted with another squad of humans, who began raining the projectiles down upon them. Hundreds of hunters heroically tried to fly forward through the storm, but that proved foolish as they were all but disintegrated within seconds. This was the most effective counter attack the humans had mustered yet. Close combat was an advantage served in favor of the Vai-Zik, but the positioning of the human's weaponry against the congested horde of Vai-Zik troops in the halls was proving fast a victory for the humans. Now panicking, the Vai-Zik began to retreat, and in the chaos, Kio-Kai spun around to see he had lost sight of Qaz-Kai.

***

White lights strobed a glimmering shine throughout New Horizon. Aisha lifted her head off the table she sat at and shook herself into full consciousness. She was unsure of how long she had been staring blankly down at the decapitated body of Natalia Fox. The lights above pulsed brighter and faster to alert everyone aboard the ship of a higher sense of urgency and danger.

Aisha reached for Natalia's glass tablet to investigate the cause for alarm. Alerts, streaming codes, and warnings flashed across the screen. Aisha swiped her fingers across one of the incoming messages. The display switched over to a live camera feed that overlooked the city in creation, Liberty. Below the skyline, there appeared to be conflict. With her attention grasped via the video before her, she leaned forward and zoomed in on the footage. Her eyes bulged as she witnessed the insects that had attacked days prior running through the city, slaughtering civilians and military members alike. Behind their wake was a trail of dead bodies by the hundreds of thousands.

Aisha felt sick in realizing every single human being on the surface of Flare faced immediate extinction. Jumping to her feet, she took off out of the room and made way to the ground floor of New Horizon to exit, fight, and defend anyone still alive out there against the onslaught.

Making it to the ground floor, she approached one of the exits, guarded by an artificial intelligence soldier wearing all grey. "Step aside," she commanded the human-like robot.

"New Horizon is in a state of lockdown. No one enters and no one leaves," he said in a threatening tone.

The sound of bangs and scrapes echoed in from the large metal door that the drone stood before. The walls were too thick to listen and determine the cause of the pinging with certainty, but Aisha assumed it could only be the sound of people trying to gain access to find shelter and safety, only to be denied and cut apart as they pounded against the locked door.

"People are dying out there," she screeched.

"New Horizon currently harbors twenty-six members of Citizens United. The safety of these individuals are of the highest priority."

"The lives of twenty-six government officials are worth more than the millions being slaughtered out there?" flared the girl, whose eyes now began to burn in anger.

"Miss Sayegh, please step aside or I will be forced to place you under arrest for obstruction and endangering the welfare of unarmed peaceful government personal. Those charges would equate to a five-year prison sentence, minimum."

I thought robots were supposed to be intelligent, Aisha thought. *This is insane.*

Backing away, Aisha engaged her stealth cloak. She had heard enough from this puppet and intended to decommission the robot so that she might freely exit the ship.

"My vision exceeds the standard spectrum of light human beings are restricted in seeing. I have the ability to see in thermal heat signatures, Miss Sayegh. This is your final warning," he advised as two more AI guards stepped into view in his defense.

Disengaging her cloak, Aisha huffed off to the elevator shaft that would return her to the bridge, where she could think of another way to get help out to the people enduring a full scale holocaust.

Entering the server room, a dozen or more military members plugged away at their computers, trying to regain control of the situation outside from the safety of their seats.

"Alpha niner fiver squad, meet up with the counterinsurgency forming four degrees east of your location," a man yelled into a microphone before moving onto screaming various obscenities and slamming his headset against the wall.

The squad he was trying to get repositioned was butchered as he spoke to them. As his headset fell to the ground beside Aisha, she could hear the screams of the men and women through the earpiece on the floor.

"They have breached one of the carriers!" a woman screamed.

"Which one?" a random voice questioned in panic.

"Heart and Soul, the carrier furthest in the back."

"They flanked us? Smart bunch of roaches," said a man, commander of the units at work in the room.

Scanning the room, Aisha found Linus standing off in a corner with his arms behind his back, awaiting a command. "Linus!" She called, "Come with me."

The two entered the bridge of the ship and, paying no mind to Fox's body still lying decapitated on the ground, Aisha picked up the deceased commander's tablet and handed it to the AI drone.

"Get a message out for me to Jason, the hellcat pilot that left this morning."

***

Tyler reached the source of the screams to find a young girl. She was one of the pale humanoid aliens native to Flare's underworld. Naked, kicking and screaming, she was struggling to fight off a man who was on top of her. He was overpowering her with ease. After slamming her face into the ground, he drove his long, sharp fingernails into her eyes. Her body began twitching as blood dripped out of her face.

"Vaktin-Nolous," the man uttered with a deep, cynical chuckle.

Withdrawing his nails from her face, he sat upright and gathered himself. Slightly winded from fighting her, he ran his fingers down her chest and towards her pregnant-looking belly. He rolled his thumbs on her abdomen as if gently massaging it, but then abruptly plunged his fingers deep into her stomach as violently as he had done her face. Struggling to retrieve his hands back out this time, he was holding something. It was a child, alive and flailing about in his blood-soaked hands.

His black eyes lit up with a sort of joy as his pale, ugly face filled with a grin from ear to ear. The umbilical cord connecting the squirming child to the dead, lifeless mother on the ground just a few feet away was as shocking as ever a sight to see. Before Tyler could fully process what it was he was witnessing, the man squished the child's skull in like an empty bottle and ripped away its head like a piece of unwanted bread. He asserted his lips around the dead child's neck and began sucking the fluid out.

The room lit up with gunfire. Tyler had seen enough. *Fuck this planet, fuck these people, no... fuck these demons!*

The lasers from his rifle ate right through the demon-like man. His soft skin burned away and he dropped the carcass of his last supper. He then began to laugh as he fell to his knees. He was not afraid of death. It was just another pleasurable experience for him in his long list of sickening self-indulgences.

As if receiving the massage of a lifetime, the creature closed his eyes and let out a moan of gratification. Tyler wanted the act of killing him to be satisfying, but this pale monster had robbed him of that satisfaction. Now on the ground, he coiled around, disguising his pain for bliss. He rolled over and looked into Tyler's eyes with a smile, his final act before embracing death.

Tyler looked to the child, or what was left of it. Having been sucked of its insides through its neck, it looked like a dried-out peach, withered of all life. Painfully, Tyler shifted his eyes over to look at the mother. Her mouth was wide open and her face was covered with the blood from her empty, open eye sockets. The display on the ground before him was the most befouled thing he had ever experienced in his entire life. Never in a million years could he have imagined such an atrocity and yet here he was, standing above this scene of senseless carnage.

"Let us continue," Aries suggested.

"Yeah," he agreed, locked into a blank stare with the empty eye sockets of the pasty-skinned, dead woman on the ground. "Let's."

***

Jason sat beside his hellcat atop the peak of the highest mountain in a range of hundreds. He had landed to watch the sunrise and stayed to sulk the day away. He was arguing with himself in an attempt to justify the loss of his fellow pilot, Lanfen, and the ground squad in the armadillo that accompanied him in the takedown of the four-legged stone giant in the early morning.

Deep down, he knew he was to blame for their deaths. He was in charge of the assault and had done a poor job in balancing their safety with the success of the mission. He had tipped the scales in his favor to defeat the goliath beast while placing the lives of his comrades directly into the face of danger. Eliminating the giant was a success, but the victory was paid at the price of death. Their lives were not his to offer in payment, and yet he had done so anyway.

An alarm began sounding in the cockpit of his aircraft, signaling an incoming transmission. Jason climbed up off the rocky soil beneath his feet and clambered his way into the ship to listen to the message.

He punched a button before him. A video feed played a message that was sent from the girl with the metallic arm.

"Terminator girl?" Jason questioned, making out the familiar face.

"Jason," she yelped as the video statically cracked in and out of clarity. "You and your copilot need to get back here asap. Your aunt is dead and the locusts are attacking the city. They are slaughtering everyone."

He wasted no time in slapping the lock to his cockpit shut and firing up the hellcat's engines.

***

Tyler and Aries continued deeper underground. They crossed over a rickety wooden bridge that extended overtop a stagnant river of red. Now on the other side, their only path forward was a thin piece of land that stretched around a large lake of crimson.

The sound of high-pitched laughter echoed from the other side of the blood lagoon and Tyler took cover behind a large cluster of rocks. He peeked out from behind the safety of the stone to see what it was that had passed by. A group of tiny creatures hopped around the pool, dancing and singing. They were small no doubt, if standing beside Tyler, they would only reach his hips at full posture. They had large mouths that were jam packed full of teeth, strange, horizontal, oval-shaped heads with a huge set of ears similar to that of a bat's, and straggly arms that hung down to their feet like an ape's. The tips of their fingers were blade-like and their heads had a set of thick horns that stuck out like a ram's, though each of the creature's horns varied in its particular twisting shape.

"Imps?" Tyler muttered under his breath, disturbed to find such a creature existed.

They laughed and played, but their means of play-- Tyler quickly noticed-- was actually a means of murder. They were stabbing one of their own. The runt of the litter squealed in pain while the rest chased him down. Catching it, they stabbed it with their sharp claws repeatedly and then set it loose only to chase after it again. Singing, laughing, and stabbing in full repetition.

Tyler came forth when the imps were out of sight and continued off into the next room, where Aries believed Scorpio resided. Once inside, the room proved to be the largest yet: a vast underground canyon with enormous trees and cacti that grew from a rocky ravine below.

One of the largest of trees was thick with many branches that stretched from the ground and twisted at least fifty feet up into the rock ceiling above. Hanging from its limbs were the bodies of a couple dozen of the pale-skinned, human-like beings. Naked and bound by the hands, some were still alive, though barely. Their eyes drooped in sadness and their bodies were skinny down to the bone with rib cages that looked as though they were about to poke through the frail skin at any given moment.

One of the imps below walked over to a woman hanging up in the tree. It stabbed at her foot with one of its needle-like claws and held a chalice of bone up to catch the stream of blood that followed. When his cup was full, he picked up a smoldering rock from a pile of embers and fire. The sound of the stone sizzling in his hand suggested the notion to be painful, but he did not seem to mind. He sealed off the girl's wound as if turning off the spigot to running water, then left to drink in his spoils.

The girl simply stared off into nothingness throughout the ordeal. Pain and sorrow was all she knew now and, while the event made Tyler cringe, it was obvious that she was used to this torture. She had lost all hope and was dead inside. Her body now was nothing more than an empty, soulless vessel.

"I think we took a wrong turn," Aries informed.

"Yea, cool," Tyler said in relief, gazing down into the valley, where hundreds of small holes lit with fire homed clusters of the imps within the valley. The sound of them laughing echoed through the canyon, raising the hairs on the back of his neck. Getting out of this gully was as satisfying a suggestion as any.

Turning around, the two backtracked to the room with the pools of blood and entered through a cavity with skulls draped across the border. *Not the kind of room you want to enter*, Tyler thought as he wearily walked inside the dimly lit area. Through the shadows he spotted the glimmer of Scorpio's metal chastise. "He is here!" Tyler announced, running over to the disabled bot.

"Let me take a look," Aries said, floating over.

Tyler stepped aside and allowed her the chance to attend to her fallen friend. He was scraped up pretty good, but fully intact from the looks of it.

"Cover your eyes, Tyler," Aries warned before emitting an enormous spark. A pulse so bright that, even with his eyes clenched shut, Tyler felt as though he had been temporarily blinded.

Blinking his eyesight back into functionality, he could hear Scorpio's systems coming back online as the drone flickered to life.

"Aries and Tyler," he said in awe. "You journeyed into the pits of hell to save me."

"You may very well be correct there, old friend," Aries said, looking down at the floor below.

Tyler peaked over the ledge to see thousands of candles lighting the room below them. In the center was a pentagram painted in red. Each corner of the star had the severed limbs of a young boy staked into the ground: his arms, legs, and head.

A few minutes passed as Tyler was paralyzed in a memorization of total shock and awe. Five humanoid-like beings entered the room, forcing Tyler to react. He dipped low behind some large rocks and watched the five humanoids wearing black robes. They carried skull chalices bearing their beverage of choice: blood. Taking a seat at each corner of the star, they sipped their drinks and kneeled in their designated corner to begin the bizarre ritual.

A sixth individual, this one wearing a stretched-out leather mask made of another man's skin, entered into the candlelit room from where he lingered in the shadows. He walked around the circle, breaking off chunks of a sharp purple cacti and handed the portions off to the five participants. He gave each of the creatures a kiss on the forehead. He then consumed what was left of the final piece, which was much larger than the rest of the other portions that he had handed out.

He too drank from his own chalice before kneeling in the center of the pentagram atop a pile of the boy's organs.

The central leader then began chanting in a foreign language that was harsh and coarse in tone. He ripped away his hood and lowered his mask of flesh, revealing a grotesque face with many open wounds. As he chanted louder and louder, his peers began to join in the hectic screams of chaos.

"*Akudimatre Lakistivera Nahamadikinous, Akudimatre Lakistivera Nahamadikinous,*" they collectively repeated over and over, each time louder than the one before until one by one they fell back and hit the dirt, seemingly unconscious. They were not dead-- minute twitches and convulsions confirmed this to be true-- but they also were not professedly there. After each follower in their respective corner fell back into their trance, the leader in the center rose to his feet, now screaming violently. Echoes of madness sliced through the room and Tyler felt as though he were being physically sapped of all of his energy in listening.

"*Akudimatre Lakistivera Nahamadikinous!*" the leader screamed before falling back onto the dirt. Aside from occasional twitching, he too was mostly unconscious now. They were in some type of trance or hallucination.

"What the hell is going on, Aries?" Tyler asked, terrified in witnessing the horrific ritual.

"They are astral projecting their souls into another dimension. Essentially one that is within our own, but so physically far away that sidestepping reality with a celestial portal is an instant means of transportation," Scorpio answered.

Tyler stood silent, trying to understand in his own head what exactly that meant before asking for it all in layman's terms. *They are projecting themselves into another universe via walking through dimensions? That is perhaps the craziest thing I have ever heard!*

"Is it so hard to believe?" Aries asked, reading Tyler's thoughts. "Do we not do something similar with you in working through me via wireless telepathy?"

She was right, but this ritual lacked any technological grounds to be similar to what humans had achieved, and yet it was well beyond the bounds of reality that human beings lived within. It was both simplistic and complex at the same time, and something Tyler was not only terrified of but interested in understanding.

"Where have they gone?" he asked.

"There exists a race of celestial beings who live in pure nirvana. A high state of transcendence and freedom. They wish to visit them," Scorpio continued.

"Like Buddhist?"

"Essentially. If you must relate them to something comprehensible in human history, you may substantially relate them to the ancient human religion of Buddhism. Though they hold no link-- past or presently-- to humanity from what I can tell. They are in a sinless, desireless state of existence. At least this is what I have gathered from listening to and translating the conversations of the creatures that dwell in these lands."

"Why are they visiting them?"

"I am unsure. All I know is that while these demons have been projecting themselves across the universe for eons, they could not achieve communication with the Shik'ar without the sacrifice of a pure and innocent being who also lived presently within this dimension as a virgin. There was some form of temporal barrier that prevented them from accessing the holy race and the virgin sacrifice was the key."

"So the pieces of flesh and limbs found in the pentagram, they belonged to a human sacrifice?"

"They abducted many humans from the assault using the Vai-Zik, the race of bugs you fought the day I myself was captured, but the assault provided no such virgin. So they sent out Abram, who collected a specimen worthy of the sacrificial ritual."

"Abram is alive?" Tyler questioned, wrinkling his face, trying to piece it all together.

It all felt like too much to take in. This was pure madness descending upon the reality of man. Tyler quickly began to feel sick to his stomach in anxiety and hurled over, holding himself upright by the knees as he vomited into the dirt.

"What if we stopped them?" Tyler suggested, wiping sick away from around his lips and struggling to again catch his breath. He felt slightly better after heaving out some of his insides. "What if we *killed* them while they were gone, out of their bodies?"

"I do not know," Scorpio admitted. "I am no expert on their means of astral projection, but as for killing these beings, I believe they hold the power to resurrect each other, as well as reincarnate themselves within an empty vessel."

"That's," Tyler clamored then paused, unsure of what exactly to say, "Terrifying."

"No, for them, this way of life and existence is the norm," Scorpio added.

"How do you know this, if you were unconscious?"

"I was aware of my surroundings and fully functional to a degree. Just sapped of my power core. I was in a motionless state, stuck in power saving mode while my emergency energy reservoir slowly ticked the remaining seconds of my life away. My time was spent listening to their conversations and evaluating their language. I believe I have their entire vocabulary mapped out, or at least close to."

Tyler cautiously made his way down to the pentagram. The face of the boy who was sacrificed looked to be very young, perhaps in his early teens.

How sad, he thought. *I bet they tore him to pieces while he was still alive.*

Moving onto the beings who had left their bodies vacant for the time being, Tyler felt horrified in looking at their appearances up close. As if the entrails of a human sacrifice sprawled across the ground were somehow a walk in the park in comparison. Tyler felt it difficult to maintain a gaze upon them for too long.

How can one feel excruciating pain in the literal sense from simply looking at something?

Tyler then removed his belt of grenades and began stripping the string from it. Tying the threads together in layers to strengthen them into one solid cord, he then attached the string to each of his five grenades' release pins. He positioned them so that a good pull to the left would release all five pins, then he jammed one of each of the explosives into the mouths of every outlying member of the ritual.

"Tyler, what you are doing is useless. All you will do is upset them, and then they will seek another human sacrifice to restart their ritual. That is to say if killing off their bodies actually interrupted what it is that they are even doing," Scorpio warned.

Ignoring the bot, Tyler climbed up behind the rock they all initially hid behind, took cover, and yanked on the line. Connected by the improvised cord, the pins silently drifted through the air towards him and fell to the ground, clinking against one another.

"You might wanna get down," he said, covering his head with his arms as he kneeled behind the wall of stone.

Chapter 14
The Wings of Icarus

Jason slowed down his hellcat as he approached the row of carriers behind the city under construction, Liberty.

Darkness began its creep over the land as a storm made its way through the outskirts of the city. Nature cared not for imaginary borders. These were but lines drawn in the sand by man. Nor did she take interest in the ongoing conflict against the two species pit against each other in war below. She had a song to sing and had arrived to sing it as thick, red lightning violently struck down upon Flare.

The intense breaks and crackles in the air forced Jason's heart to skip a beat. He could pilot through just about any circumstance or scenario, but weaving about a storm such as this was suicide in and of itself.

Jagged lumps of stone aflame followed suit in freefall from the sky. They almost had a gentle appearance as they slowly fell, until making impact when they would all but disintegrate anything foolish enough to be standing below.

A cluster of construction mechs sat idle seconds before being rained down upon from the fires above. Quickly the metal vehicles were nothing more than scattered bits of broken ingot aflame in the dirt.

Pylons, constructed with the purpose of defense against the dangerous storms, were in place. But only a handful of the units erected their energy shielding that absorbed the balls of fire. Most of the structures were unmanned in the chaos against the insects below, and the only shields online were the ones linked into automated computer systems.

The insects pushed their attack up against the carriers as the raging firestorm lingered in behind them. The storm pressed into the city, destroying structures and works zones with ease. It laid claim over the sea of dead bodies that were littered everywhere in puddles and pools of blood.

Jason spotted a couple hundred people pounding against different entrances of the front-most carrier, New Horizon. Her doors were sealed shut, leaving what was left of the survivors outside to face the onslaught. These men and women climbed atop of piles of dead bodies, trying to escape from the bugs that hunted them with success. Jason shifted his aircraft's wings into a position to allow himself to swoop down close to the ground. Halting his speed to be nothing more than a light drift, he began casting his weapons against a large crowd of insects, and quickly the hordes were being fractured into separate piles of broken remains.

Jason spotted a large, stone-like creature fighting alongside the roaches that captured and smeared fleeing humans against the ground with such ease that it was as if he were finger painting using the corpses as oils to his canvas.

Placing aim at the golem, who paid him no mind, Jason released a volley of firepower into the target. A plume of dust and smoke shot up into the air, and while clearing, Jason could make out the silhouette of the creature as it climbed to its feet, still alive.

Now with its gaze upon Jason and his ship, the insects came to the defense of the stone golem, attempting to leap towards him. Jason reacted quickly to punch the aircraft's weapons systems into a state of overdrive and again he released an assault, this one much more powerful in its potency. When the smoke cleared, the creature of stone and the couple dozen insects that defended him were gone, vaporized into powder and dust.

Most of the insects were scattering and retreating as the fierce storm crept in closer, devouring everything left before it. The bugs that stayed in the fight looked to Jason for killing what was likely their commander, and well over a hundred took flight up towards the man in his aircraft.

Pulling back, Jason sniped countless from the sky, but there were too many approaching from separate angles, and very quickly he found himself flying blind as his hellcat was encased by insects, who pounded and scratched at the hull of the ship.

The added weight compiling against him put the hellcat into a spin. He lost all control as he helplessly watched the insects smash their faces against the glass, hissing and screaming at him with desires to disassemble the very fabric of his being. The sounds of more pelting against the craft as they accumulated on top was like that of raindrops being cast down from a hurricane.

The ship pitched backwards, and soon the interior went completely dark as Jason watched faint trickles of light creep through clumps of bugs encasing the ship in their attack. The light hit his face in a strobe-like fashion, which suggested the speed in which the aircraft twisted about through the air.

Closing his eyes, he began to silently pray. Apologizing to a higher power he never really believed in for the deaths of his comrades in his negligence. For living a life where acquiring and maintaining a legitimate friend was not something he had ever achieved. For never showing affection or building any sort of valuable relationship with another, and never relaying compassion for anyone other than himself. He had lived a life of self-narcissism, and as the orbs of rock and fire began tearing through the insects that entrapped him, so too did they split open his ship, tearing through his body like a sharp knife through soft butter.

***

Hordes of Vai-Zik spilled through the holes they burned into the ship to gain entrance. Only this time, instead of entering with ease to face a healthy collection of unarmed sacks of meat and bone, they now exited the vessel to face a crowd of the humans armed and ready to fight.

Funneling through the holes, the Vai-Zik poured directly into the line of gunfire. Bodies accumulated high and in little to no time, the exits were fully blocked with the dead. A group of hunters dug through the piles of their dead brothers and sisters that clogged the way out. Even when one could manage to squeeze through, the sound of gunfire would suggest that they made it no further, and only served to add another tally to the pile of dead.

They were completely trapped on the inside, and teams began to split off in panic to find another way out.

"No!" Kio-Kai shouted, "Wait!"

But nothing could calm the frenzied swarm that dispersed in all directions.

"Grinders! To the wall. Burn through!" A young officer ordered of his unit.

They quickly obliged. At a panicked rate, they spewed acid onto the wall faster and faster until sunlight began to poke its way into the ship. The hope of escape was short lived when the humans tossed their explosives in through the freshly cut windows.

A blast sent Kio-Kai to the ground. With his ears ringing, he struggled to regain his footing by trying to stand upright once more. The couple dozen units that were trying to break through the wall were now nothing but puddles of liquid on the floor. The humans were now firing their weapons in through the cracks and Kio-Kai backed out from the room of death.

One of the projectiles struck him through the belly. His heart was racing all too fast to allow his mind to stop and evaluate the wound. *How fast the tides of battle have turned,* he thought, watching his comrades drop at a radical rate. There was no escape. They were trapped on all fronts. Those that retreated into the hallways were gunned down and those that stayed shared the same gruesome fate.

A hunter missing the lower half of his torso crawled up against the wall, trying to claw his way out, helplessly getting nowhere as he bled out and slumped back down to the ground-- embracing death's cold advance on his existence.

This was never even a battle we were supposed to win, Kio-Kai cynically reflected. *It was merely a distraction so that we might score something for the hand that feeds.*

It was then, in this moment that Kio-Kai realized the overlords were using the Vai-Zik to carry out their own will. This conflict was not a form of vengeance, it was perpetual war-- a means of keeping tensions high and order in place. United against a common foe, the Vai-Zik would have no time to reflect on their masters, who worked queens like puppets via invisible strings.

Two more projectiles sliced with ease through his right leg, forcing him to pitch forward and lose his balance, falling to his knees. As he struggled to stand, another projectile entered in through his belly, just inches away from the first. He wanted to fall back down and cry himself into the sleep of death. Perhaps in closing his eyes before meeting with the agent assigned his passage into the afterlife, he might see his loved ones one last time.

Just as all hope seemed lost and his death an imminent fate to be shared with the countless already ahead of him on the journey laying lifeless on the ground, screams could be heard that were not of the Vai-Zik forces. It was the humans who attacked from outside of the vessel, keeping the Vai-Zik trapped within. Something was killing them and scaring them off.

The steady sound of rain began its heavy thumping against the structure's exterior and Kio-Kai was quick to distinguish the sound of rain from that of fire.

Inching towards one of the holes, he could see the humans scattering as most were engulfed by the spheres of rock and fire that pelted the ground from the heavens.

Squeezing through one of the holes, he looked up to the sky, which was dark as night in the afternoon of day as fire and lightning blasted away at everything in eyesight. The world around him was engulfed in flame as he crawled towards one of the pits his army had arrived through.

Rolling forward, he fell into the tunnel, hitting bits of rock in his free fall down before thudding to the cold ground and crawling forward into the safety of the cavern.

***

"What are you still doing in here, girl?" a cold voice said, cutting through the room as Aisha sat glued to the feeds before her of the chaos in the outside world.

Twitching in surprise, she jolted around to face the intruder. Her eyes were greeted with the menacing stare that belonged to a councilman whose name she did not remember. It was the leader of the group in the trial against Natalia. He was followed into the room by a little over a dozen other members of Citizens United.

"Get out," he barked at her, his eyes piercing through her very soul. "And you, robot," he said, turning to Linus. "Get that corpse out of here," he instructed, pointing over to Natalia's decapitated body still on the cold floor.

Jumping out of the seat, Aisha made for the door, but in approaching the exit she stopped to turn and face the collection of elitists. They were finding seats around the table and bickering amongst each other, not paying Aisha any mind.

Linus had to wait for them to get out of his way before he could retrieve Natalia's body. Two women even trampled the lifeless corpse, caking the heels of their shoes in blood so that they might quickly find a seat around the table.

Aisha engaged her stealth cloak and slowly observed the room from left to right. No one noticed, and quietly she worked towards a corner of the room where she could lay low to listen in on the convention about to take place.

The lead councilman turned too late to catch her. Assuming she had left, he followed Linus to the door, watching him drag Natalia's corpse out. After the hydraulic door sealed behind the drone, the man punched in an override code, which locked the exit from within.

"Everyone sit down and be quiet," he yelled to the other council members, who were still clucking about like a brood of hens.

"What of the fire?" a younger man squealed. "It's raining down onto the ship!"

"This thing was made to withstand warping across the galaxy. A few fire pebbles are not going to penetrate her hull," another man mocked with a laugh.

Taking the commander's seat at the head of the table, the lead councilman rolled his neck, beaming his gaze down before himself to type commands into the table's computer software.

Aisha's heart began to ache as a result of the power drain cast upon her by keeping her stealth cloak engaged. Rubbing her chest, she looked for something to take cover behind so that she might disengage it. Spotting a computer data tower in the far corner of the room, she scurried over and knelt behind the piece of machinery before returning herself to a state of one hundred percent visibility.

Sticking her face above the tower she hid behind, she watched as the large glass panel at the front of the room materialized into the hologram of President Walker sitting beside a bottle of scotch with a full glass in his hand.

"Well, if it isn't the courageous leader of Citizens United, Miles Ivanok," the president groaned upon seeing the leader of the council before him. "Tell me, Miles, do you ring me to plead for help in dealing with the mess you find yourself in?" he questioned as he swirled his glass and took a drink.

"No, no, President Walker," Miles laughed out with a sick smile. "The fight outside is actually coming to a close. Seems as though the environment of our newfound home was gracious enough to cleanse us of the wicked that came knocking at our door."

"Well, Miles, it should go without saying that I have suspended travel to Flare," he said, throwing back what was left in his glass down his throat before continuing, "No more carriers will be warped in until the city provides a reputable level of security. As you executed the best woman for the job, I do not foresee Flare being a viable option for our future any time soon."

"We are going through with proposition zero," Miles announced, not caring of the words spoken by the president. "The skills and abilities that the workforce will gain should offset for the lack in numbers in the general populous. When we are ready to bring new citizens into our planet, you will not stop us simply because you do not wish to come. You know damned well that when we fire up the warp gate and lock it on to your ship, there is little you can do to stop the draw through time and space towards us."

President Walker clenched his jaw, seething in anger. It was clear that between the two men, this was a game of chess, and Miles had just declared check.

Aisha could see all of the members seated around the room wearing the watches that Natalia had told her about before. They wirelessly connected to one another and gave them the ability to access an immense amount of data right at their fingertips. The technology also gifted them with maintaining their freedom of thought from any form of higher authority. If proposition zero went through, all of life would be injected with the serum that granted Citizens United total control. The will of humanity could be bent and shaped to execute the desires of a hundred elitists.

"You are using the invasion as a means to ram this bill through," he flared. "I will not allow it!"

"With all due respect, Mr. President, you are light years away, and I do believe that this new society will collectively agree you are no longer fit to be the man for the job," Miles chuckled. "I would like to think a fitting leader for the future of humanity would be one of charisma and intelligence. Possibly a blonde with blue eyes and good thick, broad shoulders," he added, referring to himself.

"Miles! You know what will happen if you do that," the president hollered, his upper lip twitching.

"Say, Walker. Is that William Lawson's you have there? A damn fine scotch. Always was your favorite, wasn't it?"

The president's lips began to tremble violently as his face went stiff and his veins began to raise out of his skin. He dropped his glass, and the shattering sound it made in hitting the floor was quickly followed by snorting. Walker's throat was closing up on him. His attempt to gasp for air resulted in him obtaining none and it looked as though all of the muscles, joints, and limbs in his body were undergoing some paralysis-like spell.

"I heard that you had barrels of the stuff brought aboard your carrier before leaving Earth," Miles taunted. "Say, you don't look so good, Walker. Are you alright?" he added, raising his eyebrows and putting a finger to his lip. "What is it, boy? Did little Timmy fall down the well? Did someone taint your drink, Walker? Oh jeez, I would call for help but you are just so doggone far away, ya know?" He smiled as he watched the president grip his chest in pain, unable to breathe. "Oh, the irony of being poisoned by an already poisonous beverage."

The president's face began to drip sweat as it turned beet-red in color. Wheezing for air, he mouthed a phrase Aisha could not quite make out before he fell to the floor.

Turning to face the members around the table, Miles left Walker up on the display to die in front of them all.

"Looks like the president just signed off on proposition zero. On top of that, he appointed me the new commander and chief. What a guy, huh?" He laughed. "Axstrasa, get the fleet on the line. Let them know proposition zero is passed and to begin injecting the populace on their end.

Lewis, I want you to collect all the survivors on Flare into the carrier directly behind New Horizon. I believe it is called Rising Sun? Anyway the carrier has an assembly auditorium that should be large enough for everyone.

We will begin injections immediately, folks. After which we will get straight to work in building a *proper* defense around our new city so that we may warp in more carriers. The darkest of days are behinds us, my friends. The winds of our future have shifted in our favor, and tomorrow holds hope and prosperity that the citizens of man will truly unite once and for all."

***

Peering up over the rock that shielded him and his two drones from the blast of the grenades, Tyler glimpsed down to the mess of ravaged bodies from the strange ritual he had interrupted. If these demons could resurrect one another as Scorpio had suggested, they would have a tough time picking up and sorting out the fragmented pieces of their friends. That was if Scorpio's assumption was even correct, or if their souls had anywhere to return to given the destruction of their bodies.

"What happens now?" Tyler asked the two bots with his eyes fixated on the mesh of limbs and insides stretched below.

"It will take me a minute to ping and map out an exit for us," Scorpio said.

"No, not with us," Tyler paused to look over to the bot. "With them," he corrected.

"I do not know, Tyler. What I know of these beings, I gained in analyzing their dialects and learning their vocabulary. I would not suggest staying down here to wait and find out, though. These individuals are very violent in nature with one another. Judging by the way they dissected that young man they had captured, I can only imagine what they will do to you for having disrupted their sacramental ceremony."

Nodding his head, Tyler turned back to look at the scene of gore, "Yeah, ok. Let's get out of here."

***

Ness poked his head out from under the steel beam he had been hiding under for the better part of the afternoon. The one-sided massacre had come to an end and the storm of lightning and fire was passing through to the west. Being up by the warp gate, Ness had a clear view of the slaughter down in the city. It was like nothing he had ever seen or anything he could have ever imagined. To witness countless lives lost to a slaughter, then any survivors be eaten by fire from above was the stuff of nightmares.

Climbing to his feet, he scanned the horizon for any movement, but there was only black smoke from fires still burning and stagnant death embodying the sea of mass genocide.

Bodies that were piled high against New Horizon began to shift and fall. Someone had opened the doors from within and was pushing the piles of corpses out of the way so that they might reach the outside.

There are survivors, he thought with a slight glimpse of hope as he began making way towards the carrier.

Ness froze when he noticed the man who had abducted his brother was also on the city's outskirts, but three to four hundred feet away. The man was accompanied by two awkwardly pale men who wore only thin shreds of a linen-like cloth. Most of their bodies were naked and exposed to the hot late afternoon sun.

Being on the edge of the city himself and knowing that the men must have approached from the east, Ness was unsure as to where exactly they had come from.

Crouching low, he observed as the two men that accompanied the larger soldier scavenged dead soldiers of their weapons and armor. When fully armed and fit from head to toe, they set off towards New Horizon, whose doorways were almost fully clear of corpses and debris.

Cautiously, Ness followed the three through the ruins of the city towards the entrance of the carrier, where a couple thousand survivors were *exiting* the ship that had served as a safe haven amidst the chaos outside.

Trying not to step on any of the millions of bodies that littered the ground, Ness tiptoed on ahead. Hearing a crunch below his feet, he stopped to see that he had stepped on the lower half of a detached jaw, its teeth scattered about, littering the ground. Wanting to vomit in disgust, he continued forward until approaching a point where a decision had to be made.

His only path ahead was up over a long stretch of dismantled corpses. He could go around the mess, but that would cost him twenty-five, thirty minutes minimal. He would risk losing sight of the three men.

Feeling a sense of urgency to catch up to the man who had abducted his brother, he closed his eyes and crawled overtop the dead. He begged and pleaded with himself to try and ignore the sounds of squishing and popping beneath his hands and feet as he crawled. Each step forward, his fingers seemed to sink further into the mush of the fallen, and he did not get far before fully caking his uniform in the blood of the bodies below.

Coming down off the freeway of corpses, Ness slipped on a pile of insides and fell forward yelping. Some of the entrails belonging to the unidentifiable individual had gotten into his mouth. Quickly, he began to cry and struggle to regain his footing as he vomited onto the corpse he had fallen into.

Looking ahead, the men hadn't noticed his cry, and he was close behind them so, with tears in his eyes, he made haste forward.

"Where are you going?" grunted the brutish man to the crowd of nomads who were leaving New Horizon.

"All survivors are to head over to the convention hall within Rising Sun," said a soldier to the brute, "that means you three as well."

"Na, not us," the large man said, pointing to his wristwatch. The other two paler men also wore the data watches that signified they were members of the rich elitist group that was above all law.

But they are soldiers, Ness thought, *soldiers don't sit in that position of power.*

The three armed men entered the carrier past the crowd leaving the ship, and Ness quickly followed behind.

"Hey! Kid!" yelled a voice from behind that stopped Ness dead in his tracks. "The hell you doing?"

Turning to face the guard, he felt his face turn red, as he couldn't think of a viable excuse for needing to enter the ship and follow the three men.

"Yea...I just need to get to my block to retrieve my unconscious father. He has been in a coma for several days. If I don't retrieve him, he will not make it there," Ness lied.

The soldier looked him up and down.

He will never buy that! Where did I even come up with that? My unconscious father?

Ness's uniform was covered in blood from the bodies he had scaled to get here. This forced the soldier to lower his eyes in sympathy, then he gave the boy a nod of approval.

"Hurry up, kid. This is a mandatory meeting for all."

With his heart racing, Ness dashed through the doors of New Horizon and made way down the main hallway of the ground floor until reaching his block. He ran over to his bunk and climbed to the top where he had stashed the rifle from the day prior. The weapon was stuffed behind a heap of clothes. Ness retrieved the rifle from his cubby and began to inspect it.

Fairly standard stuff, he thought as he looked it over.

Even though he had never pulled the trigger of a firearm before, this one seemed pretty straightforward. It was a cartridge-less firearm, so that meant no bullets needed to be loaded. It fired energy drawn forth from its power core.

Just disengage the safety and pull the trigger.

Ness climbed down from his bunk and scurried for the door. He poked his head out of the room, but the man that had abducted his brother was gone and out of eyesight.

Trying to get his eyes fixated once more on the brute, Ness began a light jog down the dimly lit corridor.

The echoes of conversation approached from behind and Ness clumsily took cover behind a cluster of crates, knocking a handful of them over as he waited to see who it was that approached.

"Pick up the pace, ladies." a voice echoed from down the hallway.

It was a unit of men and women. They were strolling towards him with weapons.

Realizing they would see him, he tried to cram himself further into the pyramid of crates. This dislodged one stacked above and sent it tumbling down to the ground, cracking on impact, right in front of the path of the crew that approached.

They stopped to investigate and Ness tightly squeezed his eyes shut.

You are so stupid, he thought. *They probably would have just kept walking had you not panicked, you fool. Does keeping your eyes shut help any? No, you ass… it does not.*

Ness slowly opened his eyes to see the barrel of a rifle was pointed directly atop of his forehead. The wielder of the weapon was the man with the scarred, bearded face and eyepatch that Ness had seen the night before. He was accompanied by a squad of civilians, half of which were also armed.

After a moment of looking Ness over with his one good eye, the man seemed to have realized where he recognized the young boy from. The rifle he was holding was the one he had given to him after strangling and breaking the neck of his guard friend. Lowering his weapon and scrunching his lips, he turned to his companions.

"Come on. Let's go," he said softly.

The group continued ahead. They turned a corner and were quickly out of sight. Ness took a deep breath and slumped down to sulk in his cowardice for a moment before getting back up, tripping over more of the crates in the process. He picked up his rifle and walked down the hall, again searching for the large man that had taken Lucas away. Only now, Ness was not so confident in his ability to confront the man when he found him, but he knew he must.

Passing a collection of empty blocks and rooms, Ness was quickly losing hope that he would find them in the massive carrier. The stillness about the ship, with all the populous evacuated to the convention, made for an eerie sight. It made the sound of gunfire all the more identifiable, and while his heart skipped a beat in hearing it, he promptly sought out the source of the sound. This led him just outside of a set of glass doors that led to a medical bay.

Peeking through the transparent entrance, he could see the man of white and orange armor who had taken Lucas. He was sitting on a table, watching as the two men that accompanied him tore open halcyon corpses. Halcyon corpses were dead bodies preserved and frozen for scientific purposes. The two skinny, pale men were digging into the bodies of the dead and ripping out organs for some sick and twisted means of self-indulgence.

"Alright, that's enough," The brutish man groaned, hopping off of the table as the other two pulled the intestines of a dead man on the ground from a hole in his belly like string from a shirt.

Terrified, Ness withdrew from looking at the blood-soaked scene and pressed himself against the wall out in the hallway. He was quickly losing control of the rhythm of his breathing and felt dizzy. Across the hall, there was an open block. He dove across and slumped down to the ground, feeling as though he were having a heart attack.

The three men exited the medical bay and Ness thought his stomach was going to rupture out of his backside. He was more scared in that moment than he had ever been before in his life.

***

Aisha stayed hidden on the bridge of New Horizon until she was certain that all of the members of Citizens United had left to execute their beloved proposition zero.

In a matter of hours, all of what was left of humanity, both on Flare and floating about in space awaiting their turn to warp in, would be shaped to the will of a hundred men and women. These individuals had taken their seat of power by means of a long game of politics and cruelty. One that Aisha herself could not quite fully grasp in these confusing, dark times of chaotic survival.

Climbing out from her hiding spot, she scurried to the door and peered out of the room. The server room directly outside was also now empty. All of the workers in the data room had left for the assembly to be injected and molded into the future that Citizens United had designed.

She lifted the keypad and inputted the lock sequence she had observed Miles punch in earlier. The automated door sealed, then gave off a *click* that confirmed it was locked, and Aisha slid over to the commander's seat. She quickly pulled up the computer HUD that was embedded within the table. Her fingers punched in 'Rising Sun camera feed' and hit enter. A long list of options appeared before her and she scrolled down until she found a section labeled 'convention hall cameras' and double tapped her fingers to gain access to the video.

Multiple camera feeds appeared on the table, each with different angles within the auditorium. Tapping one video would enlarge it over the others, but she kept all of them at a reasonable size so that she might drift her attention between them all equally.

People slowly began trickling into the convention halls and onto the stage. Men and women wearing white lab coats set up dividers for twenty to thirty dedicated injection stations.

Aisha watched for thirty minutes as the people packed into the enormous room aboard Rising Sun. When it looked as if there were no more left to arrive, Miles took the stage.

"Ladies and gentlemen," he began. "You do not need me to tell you that today has been one of the single greatest tragedies mankind has ever seen. You do not need me to tell you how we lost more lives today than any other single day in human history. You also don't need me to tell you excuses as to how we plan on picking up the pieces of our shattered existence.

"No, you need a solution. An idea: one rich, pure, and full of life. A solution that you can place your heart upon with one hundred percent certainty and ease. You need comfort in knowing this idea isn't just right amidst much wrong, but something pure and whole.

"We have had a team of scientists working on this project for many years, and today every last one of you will gain access to it. We wanted to get this out to the public sooner, but politics sometimes prevent progression. I will not point fingers or play the political role. No, today we unveil that which will make us complete again. Today we bring you the *solution*.

"Humanity has always been fortunate enough to have a deep interest in figuring out just how exactly things work. How a clock ticks, how the sun sets, how neurons transmit data within the mind. Well, folks, today we know the answer to all three of those questions. We know the answer to almost all of life's major questions for that matter and, in knowing so much, we have developed a serum that-- when injected-- will fill in the gaps of the human brain. This will allow us all to be faster, smarter, healthier, and stronger amidst these difficult times. This is not some late night limp dick pill that falsely promises to deliver on quelching your deepest insecurities and costs twenty-nine ninety-nine. This is the cure to humanity's *future*. We have it completed and available for all. If someone had the cure to that which handicaps everyone, he would be sick to charge a cost for that cure.

"So we will begin injections, right here, right now, and free for all. By nightfall, we will be complete, united as one and stronger than ever before!"

There was very minimal applause throughout the crowd. Everyone in the room had lost someone that day and listening to a glorified sales pitch of some estranged cure-all drug was something no one seemed to really understand or care for.

The video was capable of zooming in, both visually and audibly. If the picture was made bigger from a target area, so too would the sound from that area be targeted and increased to a higher decibel. People were talking within the crowd and Aisha zoomed in on a random group of civilians.

"I don't want to be injected with this. I do not even know what *this* is," a frightened woman whispered to those around her.

"No doubt, these are scary times," Miles added, as if anticipating that some might be skeptical within the crowd. "The fear of a needle being passed to you from a stranger is a legitimate cause for concern. But we are no strangers here. We are all on the same side in our struggle for survival. Now, we are not done tallying the dead as of yet, but early projections are that we have lost over eighty percent of our populous today. The harsh truth is that what is left of our fragmented species is simply not enough to build and secure a city. And the remaining carriers that are out in space, awaiting their turn to be warped in and help will not be arriving until we can establish a *safe* and secure haven for all. The president has signed off on this proposition and extensive testing has been done to ensure its safety. Those in the carriers still out in space are undergoing injections as we speak.

"This serum will provide the ability to access data wirelessly within your own mind. If your job is that of a welder, you will have access to anything and everything that fits in that category of knowledge, and accessing that pool will be instant down to fractions of a millisecond. This will allow for what is left of our population the crutch it needs to continue forward."

Aisha scanned over the crowd with the cameras, where she found some people had begun to panic.

"Access denied," said the automated voice outside the door to the bridge where Aisha sat watching the video feed.

Feeling her heart drop in realizing someone was trying to enter, she leaped to her feet and raced towards the door.

Peeking through a small glass peephole, she saw a group of men and women had taken control of the server room just outside. One of those men were trying to gain access to the ship's bridge, but was having trouble with the access code.

"Access granted," the automated door chimed.

Aisha engaged her stealth cloak as the door lifted. A man with an eyepatch and a rifle slung around his back entered the bridge and tossed a keycard off to the side that hit her right on the nose.

"Worthless piece of shit," he groaned in regards to the discarded key.

He had not noticed that his throw only went a few feet and stopped mid-air before falling to the ground. He was oblivious to her being present.

No way is this guy military, Aisha thought as she looked the man up and down. *He is too rugged to belong to any formal authority*. His hair was brown and messy. An unkempt beard did little to disguise his scarred face.

"Well, look at that, the feed is already up," he said as if he had caught a break, approaching the command table. "Varis, what ch'ya got out there for headcount?"

"Looks like every member of CU that is still alive and on Flare is present at the conference, either onstage or in back," yelled a much younger voice from the next room over.

"If they detect us in their systems, they will dispatch someone in a hurry," a female voice chimed in. "I would say that the time to act is now. I am uploading their GPS signals to you guys so that you can track 'em down and end this quickly."

Peeking around the corner, Aisha laid eyes on the woman. She was wearing a headset and her statement was directed towards whoever was listening on the other end.

"They are beginning injections," said the man with the eyepatch. "Seal all the doors to the convention hall. It's go time," he commanded as he repositioned the cameras in the table to watch over pre-determined specific angles.

"Execution is a go," called the women with the headset.

Aisha disengaged her cloak and approached the man seated at the table. He was so focused on the feed in front of himself that he had no idea she was directly behind him, watching.

Gunfire coupled with screams could be heard over the video feed from the convention hall. The individuals this group was commanding were assassins who were killing off the members of Citizens United. It was a coup, an organized resistance against those in power.

Aisha took a seat beside the man with an eyepatch. He jumped up from the table and pulled his rifle around front, pointing it towards her.

"I am not here to stop you," she said, comforting the man.

He looked over his shoulder, then lowered his frenzied eyebrows and alleviated his tense posture before giving her a nod and gluing his eye back onto the video feed.

The people locked inside were frantic, running wild in craze amidst the gunfire as the assassins streamed through the hordes of panic-stricken civilians and targeted anyone wearing a wristwatch.

There was no court hearing, no jail sentence, no fair trial or any sort of questioning as to who was in the right and who was in the wrong. The price one paid for being caught with a wristwatch was public execution. This was a cleansing of society and these individuals had decided that the best course of action was one hundred percent compliance.

Military personnel began firing back upon the assassins in an attempt to calm the squall, but this made matters worse, as now unarmed civilians were being struck in the crossfire.

"They are shooting back," yelled one of the members from the next room over.

"We knew they would," said the man with the eyepatch softly. "There are always innocent casualties in war," he finished, his one good eye sinking as he watched the video.

Aisha observed the assassins now target members of the military to defend themselves before jumping onto the stage after any remaining members of CU.

Aisha heard the faint sound of gunfire just outside the data room. Those in the next room had heard it too, but the man with the eyepatch must have thought the sound had come from the screen before him as he did not turn to see the door open.

Three men stood with rifles pointed into the data room. They burst a cluster of shots that traveled down into the bridge of the ship, where it struck the man with the eyepatch in the head.

He was smiling as he watched the video feed before him with a sense of satisfaction for his planned coup unfolding with success. Whatever thought he had in that moment was his last as his head quickly expanded and exploded.

Bits of brain and bone splattered onto Aisha. Flinching, she jumped to her feet and raised her metallic arm to her face to shield her eyes from the oncoming gunfire. She dropped to the ground and engaged her stealth cloak, while simultaneously rolling forward. Entering the data center room, she took cover behind a tower of circuitry as the half a dozen men and women in the room underwent the assault.

Chapter 15
Pardon Me

The men and women working in the data center let out rally cries as they grabbed their weapons and began to fire back at the three intruders. Unfortunately, only four of them were armed. The other seven or eight were not. The defenseless ones made an attempt to stow away their lives, hiding behind pillars and underneath tables. Doing so was futile as the men that had entered with intentions to kill sprayed around the room, striking and killing anything and everything that moved.

Aisha crawled around to the other side of the computer tower and began making her way up towards one of the three attackers, who advanced inward. They were too focused on their slaughter to stop and wonder as to why one of their first targets had fallen to the floor and vanished.

The three men, now split up to hunt down everyone in the room, made easy targets for Aisha to take down. She stood to her feet and turned the corner behind the man closest her. He advanced towards his victims and away from her slowly. Every foot step clacking against the floor was in sync with his own gunfire. He stopped only to marinate in a moment of pleasure in butchering his victims like innocent, squealing little pigs. He was the giver of gifts who offered pain, suffering, and cruelty. Neatly wrapped in a box with a bow, he distributed the present of death without discrimination to all before him.

Aisha made it up to him and sprang forward, gripping the back of his collar with her artificial arm. Quickly she worked her fingers in place and jerked her wrist, snapping his fragile neck with a clean, quiet break before dropping his lifeless body to the floor with a thud.

Shrieks and screams echoed from all around and Aisha's chest began to ache. Her stealth tech was draining her of too much energy so, disengaging her cloak, she withdrew her sword and cautiously crept around the next corner.

The second shooter was about fifteen feet away and was kicking over work stations to check for anyone who might be hidden underneath. Aisha lurked forward as swiftly and quietly as possible. She jumped ahead faster with every desk he flipped and every shot he took as to conceal the sound of her own footsteps, until she was directly behind him. He froze, as if sensing her essence lingering about and, whilst he was quick to spin around and face her, she was faster. Slicing diagonally through his useless armor, his soft flesh effortlessly split apart. She had severed his head and right arm from his torso in one easy swing of her blade. His two halves fell to the floor and spouted blood in all directions like a broken hose.

Now covered in the man's blood, she was granted a somewhat satisfying feeling. There was no time to wipe it away now, she figured. She was on the hunt and her primal instincts told her that the third and final target was aware that his comrades were now dead.

The room was silent, only the soft, sniffling sound of a lone survivor-- a girl hidden away beneath a desk-- could be heard. Aisha froze to listen for the third killer, but the girl's sniffling and crying grew louder and louder in the silence until gun fire punctured down through the desk into where she was hidden. The girl squeaked in shock of being hit and immediately began screaming the final seconds of her life away. The sound of her dying screams were painful to listen to.

With her eyes bulged, Aisha remained frozen still. The shots had come from around the corner directly ahead of her. That is where the final assailant was standing-- only a foot or two away. He was stuck in a stalemate. Just as aware of her as she was of him, the final killer contemplated if he himself wanted to turn the corner and inspect the cause of his comrade's demise. To ultimately face the hero that had the courage to face the three monsters.

Quietly, Aisha raised her sword into the air, as if holding a bat preparing to be swung at the pitch of ball in a crucial inning of the world series. But this was no game; this was life and death.

Blood dripped from her face. Each bead that free-fell from her chin to the floor sounded like heavy raindrops crashing into a calm, quiet lake. Her heart beat heavy; so heavy that one could only wonder if a man so close as he could hear it bursting from her chest from where he stood. Still she waited. Waited for the son of a bitch to turn around the corner and look her in the eyes for all but a fraction of a second before she severed his head cleanly from atop his neck. She waited to claim another life with her precious blade. But he did not come.

"I am a fool, having not realized sooner that it was you, Aisha," a familiar voice said coldly from around the corner. "You look different with your hair shortened."

Abram? You're alive? But how? And what the hell are you doing? she thought, confused for a moment.

"Look at the man below your feet, Aisha. Look him in the eyes. Do you recognize him?"

Without moving her head, she rolled her eyes downward to inspect the dead man at her feet. His decapitated head was similar to that of a human's, but he was not human. Much paler and with a more pointed shape to the ears, nose, and face than that of the average man, he was something alien to what she could comprehend. His pupils were enhanced and she soon noticed that they were not just dilated, but the blackness embodied the entirety of his eyes. There was not a shred of pallidity within his ghoulishly dark eyes.

"You shouldn't," he cynically continued. "He is not of Earth. But so easy it is to scavenge the dead of their weapons and armor. To outfit ourselves in their disguises. Everyone is so desperate for a sense of security, they allowed us to walk right through the doors with weapons in our fists and lust in our hearts."

"He bled like a man, Abram! Much like you bleed," she finally said before backing away and slipping through a corner to the other side of the electronic towers in an attempt to deceive and catch Abram off guard.

A canister rattled down the hall and began spewing gas into the air as it rolled to a stop just below Aisha's feet. Another followed, bouncing down past her.

"I had the feeling that these would come in handy. Didn't occur to me that it would be to flush out a stealthy," he laughed.

The gas quickly entered through Aisha's eyes, nose, and throat. She forced back all urges to cough and vomit as her face burned in irritation. Sniffling back seemed to only make matters worse in inhaling larger fractions of the tear gas.

"An outdated form of crowd control, but easy to construct and efficient against civilians. You should have seen how many of these things the military had stockpiled on this carrier alone. It was like they were prepping for an uprising," he said, again injecting a cynical cackle into his rant.

***

Shakily, Ness exited the block he had hidden within. The dorm had safely stowed him away from the three crazy men who had passed by and were now long since out of sight. He had blown his opportunity to kill the man in orange and white armor.

A trail of blood led down the hall. The specs were laid out like the markings of a treasure map. Plain as day, the route in which the men had gone was lit up for Ness to follow. He had been given a second chance and he pointed his rifle ahead as to not waste this opportunity he was granted.

The path led him to the entrance of an elevator, which he stepped inside. *What floor have they gone to?* he thought in a frenzy as he looked down at all the choices.

One button in particular, labeled 'deck', had a bloody thumbprint stamped onto it. Ness wiped the blood with his index finger and pressed it against the tip of his own thumb. *Still wet and sticky,* he concluded as he pressed in the button. It was the only viable hunch to go on.

The elevator ascended to the top floor and as it did, Ness forced himself to realize the truth: that the time to become a man had come. No longer would he stow away like a scared little boy. He had to confront this demon.

Ness's sense of confidence was restored just as the elevator reached the top floor and opened. Gunfire echoed from down the hallway ahead. The hair on the back of Ness' neck raised as he flinched. The sound of the weapons ahead confirmed he had made it to the correct floor.

He wanted to be afraid, to turn around and cower in fear, but the desire to murder this brute of a man outweighed the uncertainties that dwelt in his gut. He had to confront the man that had abducted his brother. He needed to look him in the eyes as he took his life away and claimed it as his own on behalf of his younger sibling who was, by now, surely dead.

This man had taken away the only thing of purity and value Ness had on this vile, chaotic planet, so distant from his native world. It was his own flesh and blood; the little boy Ness was to protect in their distant travels across the galaxy. The mission given to him by his beloved mother, who was stuck back on Earth to face her own tragic fate. He had failed himself, he had failed his brother, and he had failed her. Now he sought to avenge. Bringing his brother back was a chance as slim to none. The least he could do now was cast down vengeance for his family. So ahead he pressed with his rifle leading the way.

***

Abram's boots clicked against the cold floor as he strolled down one of the pathways, searching for Aisha, who was lodged in an opening, fighting back the tear gas that felt as though it was burning into her very brain.

"Why do you hide, Girl?" he said in mocking anger. "It's not as if you could escape. *Where* would you even go, back to Earth?"

Trying to open her eyes, she quickly realized she was blind from the gas burning away at her vision. Snot dripped from her face as she got on her hands and knees and began crawling her way towards the entrance of the room. Aisha clumsily banged up against a desk and a glass tablet fell to the ground with a loud crack. She knew that Abram was now honed in directly to her position and was en route.

Catching a faint glimpse of the brute's rifle extending around the corner, Aisha gripped her sword and jumped forward, swinging blindly. She had successfully sliced through the weapon.

Now unarmed, Abram turned the corner holding what was left of his broken rifle.

This was the first time Aisha could look upon him. Despite the burning sensation in her eyes, she could see that he was different. Something had unhinged him, inducing a blood frenzy. His eyes looked to her as if killing her was the single most important task before him.

With a maniacal grin, he heaved his broken weapon towards her and her face caught the entirety of the blow. Blood quickly gushed from her nose and mouth alongside the mucus and tears. She fell backwards, slamming into and tumbling over a desk.

Abram took the opportunity of her flinching and falling to leap forward with a bare arm attack.

With a burning and broken face illustrated in misery, Aisha got back up and swung her sword downward in a defensive manner to keep the beast at bay. Abram raised the palm of his hand up to stop the blade, but human flesh serves as no such shield for a blade like hers. Aisha drove it straight down the center of his hand, splitting his arm in half from his fingertips down to his elbow. Blood spilled in all directions and Abram began to laugh as he pushed up against the blade. He forced it to dig deeper through his elbow and up into his forearm while maintaining direct eye contact with Aisha.

What the hell has happened to him? He hasn't just lost it; he has gone full blown psychotic!

Aisha tried to withdraw her blade, which was lodged deep into Abram's arm, but it was stuck in the bone, encased by the thick muscle of his forearm. In her seconds of being defenseless, Abram backhanded her using his good hand with such force that she lifted off her feet and fell back into a stack of data towers, which quickly fell down upon her.

"Such a weak girl," he spat, ripping her blade from his arm, which was now literally split into two. Tendons and veins hung down from the open flesh with blood that sprayed like paint relentlessly across the floor.

Woozy and concussive, Aisha pushed through the computers and stumbled again to her feet as Abram slowly walked towards her. Just as he swung down at her with her own weapon, she rolled forward and engaged her stealth cloak.

"Again with this cat and mouse shit?" he laughed, lifting his surrealistic open wound to his face. He began sucking out a mouthful of blood before spraying it forward from his mouth in all directions.

The blood hitting Aisha outlined her invisible body. It was a clever move to expose her and served to once again make her fully visible to him. Now she was trapped directly between him and a wall.

Disengaging her stealth, she looked Abram in the eye as she panted for air. His face radiated with hatred.

"This is it," she said calmly with a mouthful of blood.

"Yes," he moaned, as if taking immense amounts of pleasure in killing her. "This is the end of everything you have ever known and anything you will ever know. When you close your eyes, they will not reopen. It will be life as you knew it prior to being born, only now, it will be in death," he taunted, lifting her blade and resting the tip against her rib cage, directly above the heart.

Just as he thrusted the blade forward, Aisha turned with the blow, causing the weapon to only cut across the surface of her skin as she sprung forward and lifted the hand that held her stolen weapon.

With tremendous effort, she stretched her artificial arm down his until making contact with his armpit. The jab involuntarily forced him to drop the blade as his shoulder dislocated and snapped.

She spun him around like a spider attacking its prey. For a brief second, he was her puppet to control. From his back side, she climbed up and perched atop his shoulders before raining down onto his head with her metal fist.

She entered into a state of bloodlust as she pounded away relentlessly. She kept swinging, not stopping for the cracks and grunts the ogre of a man let out. He slammed her against the wall like a bull trying to dismount an unwanted rider. She did not let up her grip or cease in her attack. There was no dismounting this girl riding a steer. Neither the pain of being thrown against the wall nor the sound of cracks emitted by her own ribs being fractured could stop her as she continued pulverizing his face.

They were now on the ground, and soon there was nothing left to his head, just the mush of what he once held inside.

She began to cry, realizing that she was tenderizing dead meat. Perhaps for anywhere upwards of ten minutes, she had been pulsating his dead, broken face. Her rampage had taken over and in doing so, her sense of time and self was lost.

With one final thrust into the mound of gore, she released his remains and rolled onto her back into a pile of the carnage as she succumbed to a well-deserved cry. Her arms were sore, her face was broken, her ribs were cracked, and her chest was cut open. She was covered from head to toe in the human remains of others, and still she forced herself to stand to her feet. Depleted both mentally and physically, she just needed to get out of New Horizon.

***

Approaching a locked hydraulic door, Ness kneeled down to one of the dead bodies on the floor. It was a man who was completely missing his face. His brains were splattered on the wall behind his corpse. Ness alleviated the deceased of its security card and slapped it against the door's keypad, which granted him immediate entry.

The room was *covered* in blood. A server room of sorts with bodies split open and scattered about the floor.

Ness poked his rifle into the room cautiously. On making his way thus far, he had seen a tremendous amount of gore, so much so that he now felt numb to it.

Tear gas canisters, though depleted, still exerted a faint trail of smoke, and the blood that caked the room still dripped from the walls like a thousand buckets of fresh paint. These were fresh kills exerted by his prey. So the man who had abducted his brother had to be near.

***

Leaving her blade behind, Aisha stumbled to the door. It clicked and began to open. Someone was entering the room from the outside, and she took cover against the wall just beside the door.

A rifle poked into the room and scanned about as the owner of the weapon was cautious in entering. Aisha could only see the weapon and the arms that wielded it. Aisha knew these people were still in pursuit of blood, as if it were some thirst that simply could not be quenched.

Her eyes still stung from the gas. Her body, sore and broken, was controlled by a shattered mind. She had simply had enough. Enough of the killing, enough of the blood, enough of the politics, enough of being hunted like a rabbit with a broken leg by wolves chasing and nipping at her feet for the sport of the kill.

Screaming out in frustration, she turned the corner, grasping at the barrel of the rifle with her natural arm, pushing it off in a safe direction and, with every inch of power that she could muster, she swung at the assailant with her bionic limb.

Before her brain could even begin to analyze who it was she was swinging at, the fist of her artificial arm was clean through the chest cavity of a teenage boy. She had disarmed him with ease and punctured straight through his sternum.

She tried to withdraw her hand from his now open chest, but it was stuck. Ripping it out with force brought what looked to be pieces of the boy's heart, blood vessels, and chunks of random tissue. He was quick to drop to the floor and die, but not before staring into her eyes with a look so horrified, Aisha felt as though the boy had burned through her very soul with his innocent gaze.

She fell to the floor with him in shock for what she had done.

"I am so sorry," she cried over the boy's now deaf ears. "I am so, so very sorry," she repeated as she broke into a severe cry.

The boy was gone, but that did not stop her from repeating the plea for forgiveness, again and again and again.

There was a time not long ago when she looked at the mission to Flare with excited, aspiring eyes, in high hopes for doing something of value with her life. To do something for the greater good. To look at life from outside of herself and to make those around her proud. To honor her heritage and upbringing with a life of exploration and adventure. But there was not a trail of hope to be found on this hostile planet, only death and sorrow.

The human race was naive to think that things would be any different on a planet so far from home. Like somehow running off through the stars would leave behind their evil past. Or the interstellar distance would somehow cleanse themselves of the sickness that plagued their demise from the start. Humanity had arrived and brought with them their wickedness. They were the evil that spread through the universe, deteriorating everything that they touched.

She felt as though she were the monster. No better than the bugs that came from the ground and claimed innocent lives, the politicians that enslaved the race of man, or Abram and his pointy, pale-faced friends, who slaughtered the fragmented survivors of Project Salvation.

She touched the boy's face, whose skin was soft like a baby. Though in his late teens, he still wasn't fully developed or anywhere close to being built like a man.

She closed his eyes, smearing the blood from her hands to his face, then she closed her own as they continued to stream tears.

***

"Lady Kai-Zul," Kio-Kai said, bowing in the presence of his queen.

His body was broken badly and maneuvering the tunnels and caverns to get back to his queen, who resided in her spawning pools, was as difficult a task as any.

He had faced certain death but hours ago. The sky, while known for her violence, had granted Kio-Kai a favor in life, saving him from the demise of being entrapped as a victim to the human's counter attack. He was not going to spit in the face of the sky who had given him a second chance, a gift in life, and he knew now that he had to rise to the task of saving the lives of those he called his family.

"We must leave here at once," he said in exhaustion. "The overlords are using our queens to spread their will across the lands."

Her eyes shifted to that of disgust. "My child, we cannot abandon the swarm in times of despair. We are a proud and noble family within the empire. Why would we throw that away on the notion of such a conspiracy?"

"It is true, my Queen. They have asserted themselves to power alongside all, including yourself, I fear. They whisper echoes of greed and madness into your consciousness. We must liberate ourselves from their maleficent grasp," Kio-Kai pleaded.

"What you speak of is treason, my Child," she hissed. "After all we have built and achieved, you wish to brand our family as traitors and rebels? Have you not learned what it is that becomes the fate of an outcast band of rebels?"

"Please, my Queen. I just want what is best for my family," Kio-Kai said.

"It is not up to you to determine what is best for anyone, little hunter. You are a sword that pokes through the night in exerting my will. Not the other way around."

"Please," he cried, beginning to tear up. "Please trust me."

"Leave me, my Child, and may we never speak of this ever again," she warned, turning her back to him to walk away.

He rose to his feet and approached her from behind with tears in his inkblot eyes that began to subtly flow down the front of his sharp face. "I am sorry," he sniffled.

Grabbing her by the head, he stuck her through the back of the neck with his blade. "If you will not see reason, I cannot leave you breathing. I cannot lead our clan to freedom with you alive, constantly spreading the will of our masters into our minds."

He turned her around, looked her in the eyes, and held her arms so to prevent her struggle to cover the hole in her neck that poured forth red. The ninety-seven seconds that it took for her to choke away her final breaths on her own blood felt like eons for Kio-Kai to sit and watch over. Even in such a violent death, she was beautiful. Truly one of the best queens to have ever served within the hive.

Kio-Kai immediately became overwhelmed with guilt and confusion as she faded away. His whole life, he had lived to serve the will of his queen but now, in her dying minutes, he began to feel relief. The nerves in his brain that linked him to her were quickly dissolving and breaking away and for a brief second, he had the suspicion that this is what she had wanted.

Maybe she knew that turning away from the overlords was never really an option for her, that her children freeing themselves of them by cutting out the pestilence rot linking them together through her was the only true way of breaking away. He wasn't sure if there was any truth in that suspicion, or if it was just something he had conceived in his own head to cope with murdering her. With her now dead, he would never really know.

Delicately folding her arms and placing her hands on top of one another and across her chest, he leaned forward to kiss her on the forehead before standing. Now with her blood on his lips, he looked down on the corpse of his once noble queen.

"What! What have you done?" a twitcher squeaked in entering the room to find his queen motionless and dead on the floor.

"I have freed our clan. You and I are now bound to no one," Kio-Kai said calmly as he continued to stare down at his lifeless queen on the ground.

"She was our mother!" the twitcher screamed as he dived to the floor to hold Lady Kai-Zul.

"It is true. She was once our mother, but she died long ago, long before I ever stuck her."

"You are crazy," the twitcher moaned with a cry, continuing to cradle his queen. He intensely wept, as if in doing so would somehow bring her back to life.

Kio-Kai turned to leave. It was clear that he could do nothing to ease the heartache of the twitcher drone. Losing his queen was a sadness the drone would have to cope with on his own.

He left the chamber, which lead back to the now late queen's spawning pools where he limped his way up and down a lane of rehabilitation tanks until stopping to burst one open.

Falling to the floor unconscious and covered in red goo was Lai-Kai. Her body was scraped up, but she was mostly healed from her fatal wounds; injuries from the bombing of Val-Muel that otherwise would have killed her.

Kio-Kai raised her from the ground and wiped away the sticky lifeblood from around her eyes and mouth as he cradled his still friend back to life.

"Kio-Kai?" she mumbled in regaining consciousness. "What? Where are we?"

She was confused and took her time in recuperating sensibility as she shook her head about. Looking around the spawning pools, she seemed to gain a better understanding of where it was that she resided.

"What has happened?" she stammered.

"You were injured in an assault on the city where we were having drinks a few days ago. Hell, I thought you were dead," Kio-Kai choked out with a smile. "But here you are, alive and well."

Hunters, twitchers, and grinders all belonging to what was left of the clan of Kai began to make their way towards Kio and Lai.

"What are they doing?" Lai-Kai questioned out loud.

"Kai-Zul is dead and it is time for our clan to leave the swarm," he answered, wasting no time in moving things along.

"Dead?" she repeated, squinting her ink-blot eyes in disbelief. "Well, what are we supposed to do, then?"

"You tell me, Lady Lai," he said, bowing down before her with his family, who soon joined in with the symbolic gesture.

Regaining her strength to stand, she looked to her sore body to see that an extended abdomen had ruptured from her backside while she was suspended in the lifeblood. She wiggled to life her extra sets of feet and toes that bore the weight of the large abdomen, then looked back to Kio-Kai in astonishment.

"This is not the end of our family's saga, Lai-Kai, this is only the conclusion to a very long, very dark chapter. Today we must preserve so that tomorrow we might embark on writing the first page of what is next for our once great family. We are now destined to serve as the pillars of foundation for a wondrous new clan, a new chapter in the Vai-Zik empire. The clan of Lai!"

In the hours that followed, twitcher drones dislodged lady Kai-Zul's eggs from the ground. In doing so, the veins that carried blood across the dirt made squishy, popping noises as they spewed the liquid off into the air.

A hundred and six twitcher drones, carrying ninety-four eggs, led by sixty-four hunters, tailed by forty-two grinders made way to the surface of Flare. Though other clans and queens of the Vai-Zik empire were still alive, *this* was all that was left of Kai-Zul's once powerful and noble family. They would have to go on to be the rock that shields a fresh and dynamic family with a progressive set of new ideas. One no longer bound by the will of the overlords or doing what was best for the Vai-Zik hive, but rather a clan returning to its roots in the vast and wondrous wilderness of their sacred planet, Flare.

***

Tyler, Aries, and Scorpio made their way into what was left of the city of Liberty.

Tyler was skeptical about returning, for fear he would be captured and executed. As soon as he saw the city in ruins, he was not even sure there was anyone left alive to confront him.

The warp gate looked to be fully intact. Its energy shields were on an automated system that appeared to have held up against the chaos, but the skyline of the city was mostly gone. Only a few beams from the frames of the buildings under construction still stood. It was sad to see all the hard work man had put into shaping their new world be reduced to nothingness in a single afternoon. Sporadic fires burned away at what was left, releasing thick black trails of smoke into the dusky sky.

As he got closer into the city, Tyler noticed the pools of blood that littered the ground. Upon closer examination, hundreds of thousands of discombobulated corpses, perhaps even millions, displayed a scene of mass genocide across the land. The ground was painted with the blood and gore of bodies no longer recognizable.

The doors to New Horizon were left open, but no people were around, inside or out. Only the dead would call the city of Liberty home now.

Tyler noticed movement coming from one of New Horizon's doors. He tightened his grip on his rifle as his eyes made out the figure. It was Aisha. She exited the ship and was limping out towards a hill that was free from fire and bodies.

Tyler sprinted on ahead to meet her. "Hey," he shouted, but she did not respond.

She reached the top of the hill and fell back against a large boulder. Still standing, she leaned against the stone with a blank look. It was as if the person she was on the inside had packed her bags and fled out of town, leaving behind only a broken shell of a body.

"Hey, Aisha!" Tyler called out again as he approached her.

She turned to look at him but did not smile or show even the slightest sense of joy in seeing him.

"Hey, you okay?" he asked.

Her hair and face was sticky and red. From head to toe, she was covered in the insides of the fallen.

"Listen, there is some seriously fucked up shit going on underground," he said with a sense of urgency.

"Tyler," Aisha said, sniffling and shaking her head. "There is some seriously fucked up shit happening aboveground," she let out, beginning to cry and falling into his arms.

For a minute, the two of them embraced. Tyler fixed his eyes onto the fire that fell to the west with the setting sun as he held his broken friend. The red balls pelted a string of mountains as the storm climbed up over the range.

Aries and Scorpio hovered silently, watching as day was turning again to night, and with it, the stars and nebulas in the sky were becoming increasingly more visible. So much was happening in the space above. Blue gases trailed off into cyan ones and purple clouds with billions of stars looked to cut their own little section out of the very fragments of time and space.

Aisha pulled away, leaving Tyler red with a fair amount of the blood that she wore. The tears that streamed down her face cleansed the blood beneath her eyes like rivers carving through stone after a thousand years of flowing freely.

"Hey, did you know that robots dream?" Tyler said, beaming his gaze above to the wondrous detail in the outstretches of space before them.

Thrown off guard by the random comment, Aisha looked to Tyler and furrowed her bloody brows.

"Yeah," he continued. "Aries says she dreams of all sorts of weird stuff. Said she liked whales."

Joining him in his gaze above, Aisha stared back off into the canvas of purple and blue. In silence, they admired the architectural brilliance of the galaxies directly overhead. "It is probably because they are the one species from Earth she can most relate to," Aisha said with a sniffle. "Whales have the largest brain of any other animal native to our home planet," she claimed.

"Yeah, that makes sense," he added.

"Yeah", she sniffled out with a faint chuckle as she ceased her cry for a brief moment. "Whales would have never traveled halfway across the galaxy to enslave each other and massacre all of life on their newfound home," she finished with her eyes glued to the interstellar collection of clouds that composed the most magnificent recital she had ever seen.

"I don't know. I mean, if they were physically capable of doing so, wouldn't they?" Tyler pressed.

"No, Tyler. They would not," she concluded.

www.ingramcontent.com/pod-product-compliance
Lightning Source LLC
Chambersburg PA
CBHW022150170626
46807CB00005B/2142